THE AU[THOR]

Herbert George Wells was born i[n] [...] [...] [...], the third son of an unsuccessful shopkeeper. At eighteen he left his job as a draper's apprentice and became a pupil teacher at Midhurst Grammar School, from where he won a scholarship to the Normal School of Science, South Kensington, and studied biology under T. H. Huxley. Although distracted by politics, writing and teaching, he obtained a B.Sc. in 1890 and then lectured for the University Tutorial College until the success of his short stories allowed him to become a full-time writer. Idealistic and impatient, he flung himself into contemporary issues – free love, Fabianism, progressive education, scientific theory, 'world government', human rights. His personal life was equally restless: after an early marriage to his cousin Isabel in 1890 ended in divorce, he married a pupil, Amy Catherine Robbins, in 1895, and was later involved with a series of remarkable women including Amber Reeves, Rebecca West, Elizabeth von Arnim and Moura Budberg. He died in London in 1946.

H. G. Wells wrote over a hundred books, achieving unparalleled international fame for a British writer. His work ranged from the famous scientific fantasies like *The Time Machine* (1895) and realistic comedies like *Kipps* (1905) to provocative topical novels such as *Marriage* (1912), *Mr Britling Sees It Through* (1916), *The Autocracy of Mr Parham* (1932) and controversial or encyclopedic works like *A Modern Utopia* (1905) or *The Outline of History* (1920). He describes his own life in the two-volume *Experiment in Autobiography* (1934) and *H. G. Wells in Love*, unpublished until 1984.

The Hogarth Press also publishes *Mr Britling Sees It Through*, *Christina Alberta's Father*, *Marriage*, *The Passionate Friends*, *The Wife of Sir Isaac Harman* and *In the Days of the Comet*, as well as Norman and Jeanne MacKenzie's biography *The Life of H. G. Wells*.

THE
DREAM

H. G. Wells

10ᵗʰ June 1991.

New Introduction by
Brian Aldiss

THE HOGARTH PRESS
LONDON

B 3RP

First p   athan Cape 1924
Hog   al Cape edition
Copyright the Executors of the Estate of H. G. Wells
New Introduction copyright © Brian Aldiss 1987

Printed in Great Britain by
Cox & Wyman Ltd
Reading, Berkshire

CONTENTS

INTRODUCTION

When Arnold Bennett received his copy of *The Dream* from H. G. Wells, he wrote to say how much he had enjoyed it. "My boy, this is a very good and a disturbing book, as to which I am enthusiastic."

The prodigious "boy", who was six months older than Bennett, made no recorded response. He was busy – busy with plans for himself and for the whole world. Never was there such a commotion on the planet as in the brain of Mr. H. G. Wells. Never again will there be such a prodigal talent so optimistic about improving the world in which he found himself. Who in these days would venture seriously to describe our Earth turned into a perfect and pleasant place within two thousand years?

Wells was active in his plans for the transformation. But before that happened, there was time for one more delightful oyster of a novel. And so *The Dream* appeared as a serial in *Nash's and Pall Mall* magazine between the months of October 1923 and May 1924, at which latter date it was published in book form. I rejoice that it should be reprinted now.

There are two good reasons why it has survived the years so well. First, it contains a lucid survey of English social life earlier this century. Secondly, it is an infectious and well-told story.

Like many novels of H. G. Wells's, *The Dream* has been considerably underestimated. This one is, and isn't, the life story of Henry Mortimer Smith and his family, from poor beginnings, to comparative success through two marriages, to Smith's unexpected death. It is full of truth and humour.

The Smith family lives rather precariously; Henry's father is a greengrocer, managing to support his family until Uncle

John Julip arrives to live with them. Then comes the break up of the family, but not until Henry's well-loved older sister, Fanny, leaves home to go off with a man. The scene then moves to London, where we witness Henry's slow success, his developing intellect, and his rediscovery of his sister.

Interesting as all this may have been to Wells's first readers like Arnold Bennett, it has gained importance as a social document over the years. Henry, like Wells himself, becomes part of the success of those magazine and newspaper barons, Newnes, Pearson, Harmsworth, and so on, for whom he works. One of Wells's major standbys, London, in all its enticing chaos, also gets a good airing. The Smiths are seen as figments of this great roaring disaster area.

In his autobiography, Wells says, "Exhaustive character study is an adult occupation, a philosophical occupation. So much of my life has been a prolonged and enlarged adolescence, an encounter with the world in general, that the observation of character began to play a leading part in it only in my later years." The characters in *The Dream* are lightly but surely sketched. Fanny is of a type Wells enjoyed portraying, the modern young lady, in this case a modern young lady who becomes isolated and lonely because she is the mistress of a wealthy and mysterious man of the world. Fanny is a delectable creation. In the energetic Henry we see how thoroughly Wells understood the adolescent mind, capable of making great progressive leaps from week to week. One masterly stroke is the way in which Henry, faced with a crisis involving his first wife, behaves in exactly the same dogmatic fashion which so vexed him in his mother.

The comedy is well attended to. The disgraceful occurrences at Henry's father's funeral lead his mother to cry, "I'll never be able to look back on this day with pleasure!" The death of the mother, however, is extremely moving, as once again Wells relives the death of his own mother, with whom he had such an intense and painful relationship – made more difficult, he felt, by the distortions of the social structure under which they had to live.

I have said that *The Dream* is and isn't the life story of Henry Mortimer Smith. It is as truthfully described as the life story of

Sarnac. The frame of the whole novel is set some two thousand years ahead of our day, on the hillsides above Domodossola, in northern Italy. The civilization of which we and Henry Mortimer Smith are part has long been swept away by war. (Future war and the threat of it are never far away in Wells's novels; this lends them a closeness to us missing in other novels of the twenties.)

Sarnac and his friends, holidaying among the hills, come across a ruined city. The city had been submerged by floods; it is now drained and accessible again, and Sarnac's friends investigate it. Ruins always hold intense interest for Wells, as do subterranean workings. Here they find wrecked trains packed in a tunnel, their carriages filled with the bodies of soldiers and refugees, victims of a war which overcame their civilisation. This wretched confused place serves as an emblem for the doomed city, London, in which the greater part of the novel's unfolding is staged.

Following their investigation of the city, Sarnac and friends take refuge from a storm in a guest-house in the hills. There, Sarnac falls asleep. He has been working too hard – "upon some very subtle chemical reactions of the nervous cells of the sympathetic system". In his sleep he dreams himself to be Henry Mortimer Smith; his life has merged with Smith's. The book consists of Sarnac's telling his dream to his friends. Their lively comments add to the spice of the story, as they marvel about the ghastly old times. "What's a hearthrug?" asks Firefly. Wells rarely made his didactic points so adroitly as here.

In essence, Sarnac escapes into what, for him, is a past fantasy world. For all his prodigality – with something like one hundred and twenty books spread over half a century – Wells was economical with his themes, and in the year following *The Dream* he wrote a novel which is its mirror-image, *Christina Alberta's Father*. In the latter, it is the small man, Mr Preemby, who imagines himself to be a great man from the past; no less, in fact, than King Sargon of ancient Sumeria. Again our civilization is contrasted with a happier one.

Wells, of course, is both Sarnac and Henry Mortimer Smith.

He also seems, like Preemby, to have identified strongly at this time with King Sargon, who is one of the early heroes in Wells's prodigious *The Outline of History* (published in 1920). Like Wells, Sargon emerged from humble beginnings. *The Outline of History* relates how Sargon, in the manner of Moses, was abandoned by his mother in a basket of reeds; the child was found and brought up as a gardener, from which modest position, by pleasing the goddess Ishtar, he became king.

When Wells wrote *The Dream*, his ten-year affair with Rebecca West was breaking up. He was in his mid-fifties. His divided life seemed to be falling apart. His biographers, Norman and Jeanne MacKenzie, in their book *The Life of H. G. Wells: The Time Traveller*, say of this period that "the shadow of mental illness lay across the four novels written between 1921 and 1924". It is hard to detect that shadow in *The Dream*; even its darker passages are delivered light-heartedly. Undoubtedly, though, Wells was at this period trying to take refuge in a mysticism rather insecurely based on evolutionary theory. He came to persuade himself for a while that the human race might evolve towards the perfection it was blindly seeking. He spoke of The Collective Mind, and of The Mind of the Race. In his *Experiment in Autobiography*, he admits that he can "believe in the great and growing being of the species, from which I rise, to which I return, and which, it may be, will ultimately even transcend the limitation of the species and grow into the conscious Being of all things".

This belief in a continuity of consciousness, a form of race memory, from early days, explains why Radiant, at the end of *The Dream*, can speak of having been a panther, and why Starlight can say, intensely, "Not a thing in the past, it may be, that has not left its memories about us. Some day we may learn to gather in that forgotten gossamer, we may learn to weave its strands together again, until the whole past is restored to us and life becomes one. Then perhaps the crystal sphere will break."

Perhaps the writing out of these fantasies brought Wells some relief. The mental illness of which the MacKenzies speak enters a year later in *Christina Alberta's Father*, where

Mr Preemby is shut in a mental institution because of his curious obsession. While The Mind of the Race is not the sanest idea going, it had some currency at the time, perhaps stimulated by Jung's theories of the collective unconscious, and was certainly no stranger than belief in UFOs or astrology. Our dreams, the promptings of which are still unresolved, lend credibility to the idea of a continued linkage with long-dead generations.

This is an unfamiliar Wells. It is by no means the materialistic Wells many people like to conjure up. Equally, this is rather an unfamiliar novel, with a sweeping freshness about it, full of pleasant detail but not cluttered by it. We can ignore the mysticism, which is not intrusive, and relish the portrait of Rebecca West as Fanny, and the struggle for existence in Matilda Good's shabby Pimlico boarding-house, with its inconvenient staircases ("There's no doubt this 'ouse will strengthen your legs, my dear"), or awful Uncle John Julip's rapid decline. And of course Wells is good here, as he generally is, on the various faulty relationships between lovers.

It does not hurt that, under the intriguing social surface, there are reminders – in the words of Starlight – that "We shall never conquer the mystery of what we are."

Brian Aldiss, Oxford 1987

Part 1

HOW HARRY MORTIMER SMITH WAS MADE

The Excursion

§ 1

SARNAC had worked almost continuously for the better part of a year upon some very subtle chemical reactions of the nervous cells of the sympathetic system. His first enquiries had led to the opening out of fresh and surprising possibilities, and these again had lured him on to still broader and more fascinating prospects. He worked perhaps too closely ; he found his hope and curiosity unimpaired, but there was less delicacy of touch in his manipulation, and he was thinking less quickly and accurately. He needed a holiday. He had come to the end of a chapter in his work and wished to brace himself for a new beginning. Sunray had long hoped to be away with him; she too was at a phase in her work when interruption was possible, and so the two went off together to wander among the lakes and mountains.

Their companionship was at a very delightful stage. Their close relationship and their friendship was of old standing, so that they were quite at their ease with one another, yet they were not too familiar to have lost the keen edge of their interest in each other's proceedings. Sunray was very much in love with Sarnac and glad, and Sarnac was always happy and pleasantly exalted when Sunray was near him. Sunray was the richer-hearted and cleverer lover. They talked of everything in the world but Sarnac's work, because that had to rest and grow fresh again. Of her own work Sunray talked abundantly. She

had been making stories and pictures of happiness
and sorrow in the past ages of the world, and she
was full of curious speculations about the ways in
which the ancestral mind has thought and felt.

They played with boats upon the great lake for
some days, they sailed and paddled and drew up
their canoe among the sweet-scented rushes of the
islands and bathed and swam. They went from one
guest-house to another upon the water and met
many interesting and refreshing people. In one
house an old man of ninety-eight was staying : he
was amusing his declining years by making statuettes
of the greatest beauty and humour ; it was wonderful
to see the clay take shape in his hands. Moreover,
he had a method of cooking the lake fish that was
very appetising, and he made a great dish of them
so that everyone who was dining in the place could
have some. And there was a musician who made
Sunray talk about the days gone by, and afterwards
he played music with his own hands on a clavier
to express the ancient feelings of men. He played
one piece that was, he explained, two thousand years
old ; it was by a man named Chopin, and it was
called the Revolutionary Etude. Sunray could not
have believed a piano capable of such passionate
resentment. After that he played grotesque and
angry battle music and crude marching tunes from
those half-forgotten times, and then he invented
wrathful and passionate music of his own.

Sunray sat under a golden lantern and listened
to the musician and watched his nimble hands, but
Sarnac was more deeply moved. He had not heard
very much music in his life, and this player seemed

to open shutters upon deep and dark and violent
things that had long been closed to mankind. Sarnac sat, cheek on hand, his elbow on the parapet
of the garden wall, looking across the steely blue
of the lake at the darkling night sky at the lower
end. The sky had been starry, but a monstrous
crescent of clouds like a hand that closes was now
gathering all the stars into its fist of darkness. Perhaps there would be rain to-morrow. The lanterns
hung still, except that ever and again a little shiver
of the air set them swaying. Now and then a great
white moth would come fluttering out of the night
and beat about among the lanterns for a time and pass
away. Presently it would return again or another
moth like it would come. Sometimes there would
be three or four of these transitory phantoms ; they
seemed to be the only insects abroad that night.

A faint ripple below drew his attention to the
light of a boat, a round yellow light like a glowing
orange, which came gliding close up to the terrace
wall out of the blue of the night. There was the
sound of a paddle being shipped and a diminishing
drip of water, but the people in the boat sat still
and listened until the musician had done altogether.
Then they came up the steps to the terrace and
asked the master of the guest-house for rooms for the
night. They had dined at a place farther up the lake.

Four people came by this boat. Two were brother
and sister, dark handsome people of southern origin,
and the others were fair women, one blue-eyed and
one with hazel eyes, who were clearly very much
attached to the brother and sister. They came
and talked about the music and then of a climbing

expedition they had promised themselves in the great mountains above the lakes. The brother and sister were named Radiant and Starlight, and their work in life, they explained, was to educate animals ; it was a business for which they had an almost instinctive skill. The two fair girls, Willow and Firefly, were electricians. During the last few days Sunray had been looking ever and again at the glittering snowfields and desiring them ; there was always a magic call for her in snowy mountains. She joined very eagerly in the mountain talk, and it was presently suggested that she and Sarnac should accompany these new acquaintances up to the peaks they had in mind. But before they went on to the mountains, she and Sarnac wanted to visit some ancient remains that had recently been excavated in a valley that came down to the lake from the east. The four new-comers were interested in what she told them about these ruins, and altered their own plans to go with her and Sarnac to see them. Then afterwards all six would go into the mountains.

§ 2

These ruins were rather more than two thousand years old.

There were the remains of a small old town, a railway-station of some importance, and a railway tunnel which came right through the mountains. The tunnel had collapsed, but the excavators had worked along it and found several wrecked trains in it which had evidently been packed with soldiers and refugees. The remains of these people, much

disturbed by rats and other vermin, lay about in
the trains and upon the railway tracks. The tunnel
had apparently been blocked by explosives and these
trainloads of people entombed. Afterwards the town
itself and all its inhabitants had been destroyed by
poison-gas, but what sort of poison-gas it was the
investigators had still to decide. It had had an
unusual pickling effect, so that many of the bodies
were not so much skeletons as mummies ; and there
were books, papers, papier mâché objects or the like
in a fair state of preservation in many of the houses.
Even cheap cotton goods were preserved, though
they had lost all their colour. For some time after
the great catastrophe this part of the world must
have remained practically uninhabited. A landslide
had presently blocked the lower valley and banked
back the valley waters so as to submerge the town
and cover it with a fine silt and seal up the tunnel
very completely. Now the barrier had been cut
through and the valley drained again, and all these
evidences of one of the characteristic disasters of
the last war period in man's history had been brought
back to the light once more.

The six holiday-makers found the visit to this
place a very vivid experience, almost too vivid for
their contentment. On Sarnac's tired mind it made
a particularly deep impression. The material collected from the town had been arranged in a long
museum gallery of steel and glass. There were
many almost complete bodies ; one invalid old
woman, embalmed by the gas, had been replaced
in the bed from which the waters had floated her,
and there was a shrivelled little baby put back again

in its cradle. The sheets and quilts were bleached
and browned, but it was quite easy to see what they
had once been like. The people had been taken
by surprise, it seemed, while the midday meal was
in preparation ; the tables must have been set in
many of the houses ; and now, after a score of centuries beneath mud and weeds and fishes, the anti-
quaries had disinterred and reassembled these old
machine-made cloths and plated implements upon
the tables. There were great stores of such pitiful
discoloured litter from the vanished life of the past.

The holiday-makers did not go far into the tunnel ;
the suggestion of things there were too horrible
for their mood, and Sarnac stumbled over a rail
and cut his hand upon the jagged edge of a broken
railway-carriage window. The wound pained him
later, and did not heal so quickly as it should have
done. It was as if some poison had got into it.
It kept him awake in the night.

For the rest of the day the talk was all of the
terrible days of the last wars in the world and the
dreadfulness of life in that age. It seemed to Firefly
and Starlight that existence must have been almost
unendurable, a tissue of hate, terror, want and
discomfort, from the cradle to the grave. But Radiant
argued that people then were perhaps no less happy
and no happier than himself ; that for everyone
in every age there was a normal state, and that any
exaltation of hope or sensation above that was happiness and any depression below it misery. It did
not matter where the normal came. " They went
to great intensities in both directions," he said.
There was more darkness in their lives and more

pain, but not more unhappiness. Sunray was inclined to agree with him.

But Willow objected to Radiant's psychology. She said that there could be permanently depressed states in an unhealthy body or in a life lived under restraint. There could be generally miserable creatures just as there could be generally happy creatures.

" Of course," interjected Sarnac, " given a standard outside themselves."

" But why did they make such wars ? " cried Firefly. " Why did they do such horrible things to one another ? They were people like ourselves."

" No better," said Radiant, " and no worse. So far as their natural quality went. It is not a hundred generations ago."

" Their skulls were as big and well shaped."

" Those poor creatures in the tunnel ! " said Sarnac. " Those poor wretches caught in the tunnel ! But everyone in that age must have felt caught in a tunnel."

After a time a storm overtook them and interrupted their conversation. They were going up over a low pass to a guest-house at the head of the lake, and it was near the crest of the pass that the storm burst. The lightning was tremendous and a pine-tree was struck not a hundred yards away. They cheered the sight. They were all exhilarated by the elemental clatter and uproar ; the rain was like a whip on their bare, strong bodies and the wind came in gusts that held them staggering and laughing, breathlessly unable to move forward. They had doubts and difficulties with the path ; for a time they lost touch with the blazes upon the trees and rocks. Followed a steady torrent of rain, through which they splashed and stumbled down the foaming rocky pathway to their resting-place. They arrived wet as from a swim and glowing ; but Sarnac, who had come behind the others with Sunray, was tired and cold. The master of this guest-house drew his shutters and made a great fire for them with pine-knots and pine-cones while he prepared a hot meal.

After a while they began to talk of the excavated town again and of the shrivelled bodies lying away there under the electric light of the still glass-walled museum, indifferent for evermore to the sunshine and thunderstorms of life without.

" Did they ever laugh as we do ? " asked Willow. " For sheer happiness of living ? "

Sarnac said very little. He sat close up to the fire, pitching pine-cones into it and watching them flare and crackle. Presently he got up, confessed himself tired, and went away to his bed.

§ 3

It rained hard all through the night and until nearly midday, and then the weather cleared. In the afternoon the little party pushed on up the valley towards the mountains they designed to climb, but they went at a leisurely pace, giving a day and a half to what was properly only one day's easy walking. The rain had refreshed everything in the upper valley and called out a great multitude of flowers.

The next day was golden and serene.

In the early afternoon they came to a plateau and meadows of asphodel, and there they sat down to eat the provisions they had brought with them. They were only two hours' climb from the mountain-house in which they were to pass the night, and there was no need to press on. Sarnac was lazy ; he confessed to a desire for sleep ; in the night he had been feverish and disturbed by dreams of men entombed in tunnels and killed by poison-gas. The others were amused that anyone should want to sleep in the daylight, but Sunray said she would watch over him. She found a place for him on the sward, and Sarnac laid down beside her and went to sleep with his cheek against her side as suddenly and trustfully as a child goes to sleep. She sat up —as a child's nurse might do—enjoining silence on the others by gestures.

" After this he will be well again," laughed Radiant, and he and Firefly stole off in one direction, while Willow and Starlight went off in another to climb a rocky headland near at hand, from which they thought they might get a very wide and perhaps a very beautiful view of the lakes below.

For some time Sarnac lay quite still in his sleep and then he began to twitch and stir. Sunray bent down attentively with her warm face close to his. He was quiet again for a time and then he moved and muttered, but she could not distinguish any words. Then he rolled away from her and threw his arms about and said, " I can't stand it. I can't endure it. Nothing can alter it now. You're un-clean and spoilt." She took him gently and drew him into a comfortable attitude again, just as a nurse might do. " Dear," he whispered, and in his sleep reached out for her hand. . . .

THE DREAM

When the others came back he had just awakened.

He was sitting up with a sleepy expression and Sunray was kneeling beside him with her hand on his shoulder. " Wake up ! " she said.

He looked at her as if he did not know her and then with puzzled eyes at Radiant. " Then there *is* another life ! " he said at last.

" Sarnac ! " cried Sunray, shaking him. " Don't you know me ? "

He passed a hand over his face. " Yes," he said slowly. " Your name is Sunray. I seem to remember. Sunray. . . . Not Hetty—— No. Though you are very like Hetty. Queer ! And mine—mine is Sarnac.

" Of course ! I am Sarnac." He laughed at Willow. " But I thought I was Harry Mortimer Smith," he said. " I did indeed. A moment ago I *was* Henry Mortimer Smith. . . . Henry Mortimer Smith."

He looked about him. " Mountains," he said, " sunshine, white narcissus. Of course, we walked up here this very morning. Sunray splashed me at a waterfall. . . . I remember it perfectly. . . . And yet I was in bed—shot. I was in bed. . . . A dream ? . . . Then I have had a dream, a whole lifetime, two thousand years ago ! "

" What do you mean ? " said Sunray.

" A lifetime—childhood, boyhood, manhood. And death. He killed me. Poor rat !—he killed me ! "

" A dream ? "

" A dream—but a very vivid dream. The reallest of dreams. If it *was* a dream. . . . I can answer all your questions now, Sunray. I have lived through a whole life in that old world. I know. . . .

"It is as though that life was still the real one and this only a dream. . . . I was in a bed. Five minutes ago I was in bed. I was dying. . . . The doctor said, 'He is going.' And I heard the rustle of my wife coming across the room . . ."

"Your *wife!*" cried Sunray.

"Yes—my wife—Milly."

Sunray looked at Willow with raised eyebrows and a helpless expression.

Sarnac stared at her, dreamily puzzled. "Milly," he repeated very faintly. "She was by the window."

For some moments no one spoke.

Radiant stood with his arm on Firefly's shoulder. "Tell us about it, Sarnac. Was it hard to die?"

"I seemed to sink down and down into quiet—and then I woke up here."

"Tell us now, while it is still so real to you."

"Have we not planned to reach the mountain-house before nightfall?" said Willow, glancing at the sun.

"There is a little guest-house here, within five minutes' walk of us," said Firefly.

Radiant sat down beside Sarnac. "Tell us your dream now. If it fades out presently or if it is uninteresting, we can go on; but if it is entertaining, we can hear it out and sleep down here to-night. It is a very pleasant place here, and there is a loveliness about those mauve-coloured crags across the gorge, a faint mistiness in their folds, that I could go on looking at for a week without impatience. Tell us your dream, Sarnac."

He shook his friend. "Wake up, Sarnac!"

Sarnac rubbed his eyes. "It is so queer a story. And there will be so much to explain."

THE DREAM

He took thought for a while.

" It will be a long story."

" Naturally, if it is a whole life."

" First let me get some cream and fruit from the guest-house for us all," said Firefly, " and then let Sarnac tell us his dream. Five minutes, Sarnac, and I will be back here."

" I will come with you," said Radiant, hurrying after her.

This that follows is the story Sarnac told.

The Beginning of the Dream

§ 1

"THIS dream of mine began," he said, "as all our lives begin, in fragments, in a number of disconnected impressions. I remember myself lying on a sofa, a sofa covered with a curious sort of hard, shiny material with a red and black pattern on it, and I was screaming, but I do not know why I screamed. I discovered my father standing in the doorway of the room looking at me. He looked very dreadful ; he was partially undressed in trousers and a flannel shirt and his fair hair was an unbrushed shock ; he was shaving and his chin was covered with lather. He was angry because I was screaming. I suppose I stopped screaming, but I am not sure. And I remember kneeling upon the same hard red and black sofa beside my mother and looking out of the window—the sofa used to stand with its back to the window-sill—at the rain falling on the roadway outside. The window-sill smelt faintly of paint ; soft bad paint that had blistered in the sun. It was a violent storm of rain and the road was an ill-made road of a yellowish sandy clay. It was covered with muddy water and the storming rainfall made a multitude of flashing bubbles, that drove along before the wind and burst and gave place to others.

" ' Look at 'em, dearie,' said my mother. ' Like sojers.'

" I think I was still very young when that happened, but I was not so young that I had not often seen soldiers with their helmets and bayonets marching by."

23

" That," said Radiant, " was some time before the Great War then, and the Social Collapse."

" Some time before," said Sarnac. He considered. " Twenty-one years before. This house in which I was born was less than two miles from the great military camp of the British at Lowcliff in England, and Lowcliff railway-station was only a few hundred yards away. ' Sojers ' were the most conspicuous objects in my world outside my home. They were more brightly coloured than other people. My mother used to wheel me out for air every day in a thing called a perambulator, and whenever there were soldiers to be seen she used to say, ' Oh! PRITTY sojers! '

" ' Sojers ' must have been one of my earliest words. I used to point my little wool-encased finger—for they wrapped up children tremendously in those days and I wore even gloves—and I would say : ' Sosher.'

" Let me try and describe to you what sort of home this was of mine and what manner of people my father and mother were. Such homes and houses and places have long since vanished from the world, not many relics of them have been kept, and though you have probably learnt most of the facts concerning them, I doubt if you can fully realise the feel and the reality of the things I found about me. The name of the place was Cherry Gardens ; it was about two miles from the sea at Sandbourne, one way lay the town of Cliffstone from which steamboats crossed the sea to France, and the other way lay Lowcliff and its rows and rows of ugly red brick barracks and its great drilling-plain, and behind us inland was a sort of plateau covered with raw new roads of loose pebbles—you cannot imagine such roads !—and vegetable gardens and houses new-built or building, and then a line of hills, not very high but steep and green and bare, the Downs. The Downs made a graceful skyline that bounded my world to the north as the sapphire line of the sea bounded it to the south, and they were almost the only purely beautiful things in that world. All the rest was touched and made painful by human confusion. When I was a very little boy I used to wonder what lay behind those Downs, but I never went up them to see until I was seven or eight years old."

" This was before the days of aeroplanes ? " asked Radiant.

" They came into the world when I was eleven or twelve. I saw the first that ever crossed the Channel between the mainland of Europe and England. That was considered a very wonderful thing indeed. ("It *was* a wonderful thing," said Sunray.) I went with a lot of other boys, and we edged through a crowd that stood and stared at the quaint old machine; it was like a big canvas grasshopper with outspread wings ; in a field—somewhere beyond Cliffstone. It was being guarded, and the people were kept away from it by stakes and a string.

" I find it hard to describe to you what sort of places Cherry Gardens and Cliffstone were like—even though we have just visited the ruins of Domodossola. Domodossola was a sprawling, aimless town enough, but these sprawled far more and looked with a far emptier aimlessness into the face of God. You see in the thirty or forty years before my birth there had been a period of comparative prosperity and productivity in human affairs. It was not of course in those days the result of any statesmanship or forethought ; it just happened,—as now and then in the course of a rain-torrent there comes a pool of level water between the rapids. But the money and credit system was working fairly well ; there was much trade and intercourse, no extensive pestilences, exceptionally helpful seasons, and few very widespread wars. As a result of this conspiracy of favourable conditions there was a perceptible rise in the standards of life of the common people, but for the most part it was discounted by a huge increase of population. As our school books say, ' In those days Man was his own Locust.' Later in my life I was to hear furtive whispers of a forbidden topic called Birth Control, but in the days of my childhood the whole population of the world, with very few exceptions, was in a state of complete and carefully protected ignorance about the elementary facts of human life and happiness. The surroundings of my childhood were dominated by an unforeseen and uncontrollable proliferation. Cheap proliferation was my scenery, my drama, my atmosphere."

" But they had teachers and priests and doctors and rulers to tell them better," said Willow.

" Not to tell them better," said Sarnac. " These guides and pilots of life were wonderful people. They abounded, and guided no one. So far from teaching men and women to control births or avoid diseases or work generously together, they rather prevented such teaching. This place called Cherry Gardens had mostly come into existence in the fifty years before my birth. It had grown from a minute hamlet into what we used to call an ' urban district.' In that old world in which there was neither freedom nor direction, the land was divided up into patches of all sorts and sizes and owned by people who did what they liked with it, subject to a few vexatious and unhelpful restrictions. And in Cherry Gardens, a sort of men called speculative builders bought pieces of land, often quite unsuitable land, and built houses for the swarming increase of population that had otherwise nowhere to go. There was no plan about this building. One speculative builder built here and another there, and each built as cheaply as possible and sold or let what he had built for as much as possible. Some of the houses they built in rows and some stood detached each with a little patch of private garden—garden they called it, though it was either a muddle or a waste—fenced in to keep people out."

"Why did they keep people out?"

"They liked to keep people out. It was a satisfaction for them. They were not secret gardens. People might look over the fence if they chose. And each house had its own kitchen where food was cooked—there was no public eating-place in Cherry Gardens—and each, its separate store of household gear. In most houses there was a man who went out to work and earn a living—they didn't so much live in those days as earn a living—and came home to eat and sleep, and there was a woman, his wife, who did all the services, food and cleaning and everything, and also she bore children, a lot of unpremeditated children—because she didn't know any better. She was too busy to look after them well, and many of them died. Most days she cooked a dinner. She cooked it. . . . It *was* cooking!"

27

Sarnac paused—his brows knit. " Cooking !
Well, well. That's over, anyhow," he said.

Radiant laughed cheerfully.

" Almost everyone suffered from indigestion.
The newspapers were full of advertisements of cures,"
said Sarnac, still darkly retrospective.

" I've never thought of that aspect of life in the
old world," said Sunray.

" It was—fundamental," said Sarnac. " It was
a world, in every way, out of health.

" Every morning, except on the Sunday, after
the man had gone off to his day's toil and the children had been got up and dressed and those who
were old enough sent off to school, the woman of
the house tidied up a bit and then came the question
of getting in food. For this private cooking of hers.
Every day except Sunday a number of men with
little pony carts or with barrows they pushed in
front of them, bearing meat and fish and vegetables
and fruit, all of it exposed to the weather and any
dirt that might be blowing about, came bawling along
the roads of Cherry Gardens, shouting the sort of
food they were selling. My memory goes back to
that red and black sofa by the front window and
I am a child once again. There was a particularly
splendid fish hawker. What a voice he had ! I
used to try to reproduce his splendid noises in my
piping childish cries : ' Mackroo-E-y'are Macroo !
Fine Macroo ! Thee a Sheen. Mac*roo* ! '

" The housewives would come out from their
domestic mysteries to buy or haggle and, as the
saying went, ' pass the time of day ' with their neighbours. But everything they wanted was not to be

got from the hawkers, and that was where my father came in. He kept a little shop. He was what was called a greengrocer; he sold fruits and vegetables, such poor fruits and vegetables as men had then learnt to grow—and also he sold coals and paraffin (which people burnt in their lamps) and chocolate and ginger-beer and other things that were necessary to the barbaric housekeeping of the time. He also sold cut-flowers and flowers in pots, and seeds and sticks and string and weed-killer for the little gardens. His shop stood in a row with a lot of other shops ; the row was like a row of the ordinary houses with the lower rooms taken out and replaced by the shop, and he ' made his living ' and ours by buying his goods as cheaply as he could and getting as much as he could for them. It was a very poor living because there were several other able-bodied men in Cherry Gardens who were also greengrocers, and if he took too much profit then his customers would go away and buy from these competitors and he would get no profit at all.

" I and my brother and sisters—for my mother had been unable to avoid having six babies and four of us were alive—lived by and in and round about this shop. In the summer we were chiefly out of doors or in the room above the shop ; but in the cold weather it cost too much trouble and money to have a fire in that room—all Cherry Gardens was heated by open coal fires—and we went down into a dark underground kitchen where my mother, poor dear ! cooked according to her lights."

" You were troglodytes ! " said Willow.

" Practically. We always ate in that downstairs room. In the summer we were sunburnt and ruddy, but in the winter, because of this—inhumation, we became white and rather thin. I had an elder brother who was monstrous in my childish memory ; he was twelve years older than I ; and I had two sisters, Fanny and Prudence. My elder brother Ernest went out to work, and then he went away to London and I saw very little of him until I too went to London. I was the youngest of the lot ; and when I was nine years old, my father, taking courage, turned my mother's perambulator into a little push-cart for delivering sacks of coals and suchlike goods.

" Fanny, my elder sister, was a very pretty girl, with a white face from which her brown hair went back in graceful, natural waves and curls, and she had very dark blue eyes. Prudence was also white but of a duller whiteness, and her eyes were grey. She would tease me and interfere with me, but Fanny was either negligent or gracefully kind to me and I adored her. I do not, strangely enough, remember my mother's appearance at all distinctly, though she was, of course, the dominant fact of my childish life. She was too familiar, I suppose, for the sort of attention that leaves a picture on the mind.

" I learnt to speak from my family and chiefly from my mother. None of us spoke well ; our common idioms were poor and bad, we mispronounced many words, and long words we avoided as something dangerous and pretentious. I had very few toys : a tin railway-engine I remember, some metal soldiers, and an insufficient supply of wooden building-bricks. There was no special place for me to play, and if I laid out my toys on the living-room table, a meal was sure to descend and sweep them away. I remem-

ber a great longing to play with the things in the
shop, and especially with the bundles of firewood
and some fire-kindlers that were most seductively
shaped like wheels, but my father discouraged such
ambitions. He did not like to have me about the
shop until I was old enough to help, and the indoor
part of most of my days was spent in the room above
it or in the underground room below it. After the
shop was closed it became a very cold, cavernous, dark
place to a little boy's imagination ; there were dreadful shadows in which terrible things might lurk, and
even holding fast to my mother's hand on my way
to bed, I was filled with fear to traverse it. It had
always a faint, unpleasant smell, a smell of decaying
vegetation varying with the particular fruit or vegetable that was most affected, and a constant element
of paraffin. But on Sundays when it was closed all
day the shop was different, no longer darkly threatening but very very still. I would be taken through
it on my way to church or Sunday school. (Yes—
I will tell you about church and Sunday school in a
minute.) When I saw my mother lying dead—she
died when I was close upon sixteen—I was instantly
reminded of the Sunday shop. . . .

"Such, my dear Sunray, was the home in which I
found myself. I seemed to have been there since my
beginning. It was the deepest dream I have ever
had. I had forgotten even you."

§ 2

"And how was this casually begotten infant prepared for the business of life ? " asked Radiant.
" Was he sent away to a Garden ? "

THE DREAM

" There were no Children's Gardens such as we know them, in that world," said Sarnac. "There was a place of assembly called an elementary school. Thither I was taken, twice daily, by my sister Prudence, after I was six years old.

" And here again I find it hard to convey to you what the reality was like. Our histories tell you of the beginning of general education in that distant time and of the bitter jealousy felt by the old priesthoods and privileged people for the new sort of teachers, but they give you no real picture of the ill-equipped and understaffed schoolhouses and of the gallant work of the underpaid and ill-trained men and women who did the first rough popular teaching. There was in particular a gaunt dark man with a cough who took the older boys, and a little freckled woman of thirty or so who fought with the lower children, and, I see now, they were holy saints. His name I forget, but the little woman was called Miss Merrick. They had to handle enormous classes, and they did most of their teaching by voice and gesture and chalk upon a blackboard. Their equipment was miserable. The only materials of which there was enough to go round were a stock of dirty reading-books, bibles, hymn-books, and a lot of slabs of slate in frames on which we wrote with slate pencils to economise paper. Drawing materials we had practically none ; most of us never learnt to draw. Yes. Lots of sane adults in that old world never learnt to draw even a box. There was nothing to count with in that school and no geometrical models. There were hardly any pictures except a shiny one of Queen Victoria and a sheet of ani-

mals, and there were very yellow wall-maps of
Europe and Asia twenty years out of date. We
learnt the elements of mathematics by recitation.
We used to stand in rows, chanting a wonderful
chant called our Tables :—

> " ' *Twi*-swun-two.
> *Twi*-stewer four.
> *Twi*-sfree'r six.
> *Twi*-sfour'rate.'

" We used to sing—in unison—religious hymns
for the most part. The school had a second-hand
piano to guide our howlings. There had been a
great fuss in Cliffstone and Cherry Gardens when
this piano was bought. They called it a luxury,
and pampering the working classes."

" Pampering the working-classes!" Firefly repeated.
" I suppose it's all right. But I'm rather at sea."

" I can't explain everything," said Sarnac. " The
fact remains that England grudged its own children
the shabbiest education, and so for the matter of
fact did every other country. They saw things
differently in those days. They were still in the
competitive cave. America, which was a much
richer country than England, as wealth went then,
had if possible meaner and shabbier schools for
her common people. . . . My dear ! it *was* so.
I'm telling you a story, not explaining the universe.
. . . And naturally, in spite of the strenuous efforts
of such valiant souls as Miss Merrick, we children
learnt little and we learnt it very badly. Most
of my memories of school are memories of boredom.
We sat on wooden forms at long, worn, wooden desks,

33

rows and rows of us—I can see again all the little
heads in front of me—and far away was Miss Merrick
with a pointer trying to interest us in the Rivers
of England :—

"Ty. Wear. Teasumber."

"Is that what they used to call swearing ? " asked
Willow.

"No. Only Jogriphy. And History was :—

"Wi-yum the Conqueror. Tessisstysiss.
Wi-yum Ruefiss. Ten eighty-seven."

"What did it mean ? "

"To us children ? Very much what it means
to you—gibberish. The hours, those interminable
hours of childhood in school ! How they dragged !
Did I say I lived a life in my dream ? In school
I lived eternities. Naturally we sought such amuse-
ment as was possible. One thing was to give your
next-door neighbour a pinch or a punch and say,
'Pass it on.' And we played furtive games with
marbles. It is rather amusing to recall that I learnt
to count, to add and subtract and so forth, by playing
marbles in despite of discipline."

"But was that the best your Miss Merrick and
your saint with the cough could do ? " asked Radiant.

"Oh ! *they* couldn't help themselves. They were
in a machine, and there were periodic Inspectors and
examinations to see that they kept in it."

"But," said Sunray, "that Incantation about
'Wi-yum the Conqueror' and the rest of it. It
meant something ? At the back of it, lost to sight
perhaps, there was some rational or semi-rational
idea ? "

" Perhaps," reflected Sarnac. " But I never detected it."

" They called it history," said Firefly helpfully.

" They did," Sarnac admitted. " Yes, I think they were trying to interest the children of the land in the doings of the Kings and Queens of England, probably as dull a string of monarchs as the world has ever seen. If they rose to interest at times it was through a certain violence ; there was one delightful Henry VIII with such a craving for love and such a tender conscience about the sanctity of marriage that he always murdered one wife before he took another. And there was one Alfred who burnt some cakes—I never knew why. In some way it embarrassed the Danes, his enemies."

" But was that all the history they taught you ? " cried Sunray.

" Queen Elizabeth of England wore a ruff and James the First of England and Scotland kissed his men favourites."

" But history ! "

Sarnac laughed. " It *is* odd. I see that—now that I am awake again. But indeed that was all they taught us."

" Did they tell you nothing of the beginnings of life and the ends of life, of its endless delights and possibilities ? "

Sarnac shook his head.

" Not at school," said Starlight, who evidently knew her books ; " they did that at church. Sarnac forgets the churches. It was, you must remember, an age of intense religious activity. There were places of worship everywhere. One whole day in every seven was given up to the Destinies of Man and the study of God's Purpose. The worker ceased from his toil. From end to end of the land the air was full of the sound of church bells and of congregations singing. Wasn't there a certain beauty in that, Sarnac ? "

Sarnac reflected and smiled. " It wasn't quite like that," he said. " Our histories, in that matter, need a little revision."

" But one sees the churches and chapels in the old photographs and cinema pictures. And we still have many of their cathedrals. And some of those are quite beautiful."

" And they have all had to be shored up and underpinned and tied together with steel," said Sunray, " because they were either so carelessly or so faithlessly built. And anyhow, these were not built in Sarnac's time."

" Mortimer Smith's time," Sarnac corrected.

" They were built hundreds of years earlier than that."

§ 3

" You must not judge the religion of an age by its temples and churches," said Sarnac. " An unhealthy body may have many things in it that it cannot clear away, and the weaker it is the less it can prevent abnormal and unserviceable growths. . . . Which sometimes may be in themselves quite bright and beautiful growths.

" But let me describe to you the religious life of my home and upbringing. There was a sort of State Church in England, but it had lost most of its official standing in regard to the community as a whole ; it had two buildings in Cherry Gardens —one an old one dating from the hamlet days with a square tower and rather small as churches went, and the other new and spacious with a spire. In addition there were the chapels of two other Christian communities, the Congregationalists and the Primitive Methodists, and also one belonging to the old Roman Catholic communion. Each professed to present the only true form of Christianity and each maintained a minister, except the larger Church of England place, which had two, the vicar and the curate. You might suppose that, like the museums of history and the Temples of Vision we set before our young people, these places would display in the most moving and beautiful forms possible the history of our race and the great adventure of life in which we are all engaged, they would remind us of our brotherhood and lift us out of selfish thoughts. . . . But let me tell you how I saw it :—

"I don't remember my first religious instruction. Very early I must have learnt to say a rhymed prayer to—

> " ' Gentle Jesus, meek and mild,
> Look on me, a little child.'

And also another prayer about 'Trespassing' which I thought referred to going into fields or woods where there was no public footpath, and which began with the entirely incomprehensible words, 'Our Father Charting Heaven, Haloed B thy Name.' Also one asked for one's 'daily bread' and that God's Kingdom should come. I learnt these two prayers from my mother at an incredibly early age, and said them every night and sometimes in the morning. She held these words in far too great reverence to explain them, and when I wanted to ask for my ' daily bread and butter,' she scolded me bitterly. I also wanted to ask what would happen to good Queen Victoria when God's Kingdom came, but I never mustered courage to ask my mother that. I had a curious idea that there could be a marriage but that nobody had thought of that solution. This must have been very early in my life, because Victoria the Good died when I was five, during the course of a long, far-away, and now almost-forgotten struggle called the Boer War.

" These infantile perplexities deepened and then gave way to a kind of self-protective apathy when I was old enough to go to church and Sunday school.

" Sunday morning was by far the most strenuous part of all the week for my mother. We had all had a sort of bath overnight in the underground kitchen, except my father and mother, who I don't think ever washed all over—I don't know for certain —and on Sunday morning we rose rather later than usual and put on our ' clean things ' and our best clothes. (Everybody in those days wore a frightful lot of clothes. You see, they were all so unhealthy they could not stand the least exposure to wet or cold.) Breakfast was a hurried and undistinguished meal on the way to greater things. Then we had to sit about, keeping out of harm's way, avoiding all crumpling or dirt, and pretending to be interested in one of the ten or twelve books our home possessed, until church time. Mother prepared the Sunday meal, almost always a joint of meat in a baking-dish which my elder sister took in to the baker's next door but one to be cooked while we worshipped. Father rosè later than anyone and appeared strangely transformed in a collar, dickey and cuffs and a black coat and his hair smoothed down and parted. Usually some unforeseen delay arose ; one of my sisters had a hole in her stocking, or my boots wouldn't button and nobody could find the button-hook, or a prayer-book was mislaid. This engendered an atmosphere of flurry. There were anxious moments when the church bell ceased to ring and began a monotonous ' tolling-in.'

" ' Oh ! we shall be late *again* ! ' said my mother. ' We shall be late *again*.'

" ' I'll go on with Prue ! ' my father would say.

" ' Me too ! ' said Fanny.

" ' Not till you've found that button-'ook, Miss Huzzy,' my mother would cry. ' For well I know you've 'ad it.'

" Fanny would shrug her shoulders.

" ' Why 'e carn't 'ave lace-up shoes to 'is feet like any other kid, I *carn't* understand,' my father would remark unhelpfully.

" My mother, ashen white with flurry, would wince and say, ' Lace-up shoes at *'is* age ! Let alone that 'e'd break the laces.'

" ' What's that on the chiffoneer ? ' Fanny would ask abruptly.

" ' Ah ! Naturally you know.'

" ' Naturally I use my eyes.'

" ' Tcha ! Got your answer ready ! Oh, you *wicked* girl ! '

"Fanny would shrug her shoulders again and stare out of the window. There was more trouble afoot than a mislaid buttonhook between her and my mother. Overnight 'Miss Huzzy' had been abroad long after twilight, a terrible thing from a mother's point of view, as I will make plain to you later.

"My mother, breathing hard, would button my boots in a punitive manner and then off we would go, Prue hanging on to father ahead, Fanny a little apart and scornful, and I trying to wriggle my little white-cotton-gloved hand out of my mother's earnest grip.

"We had what was called a 'sitting' at church, a long seat with some hassocks and a kind of little praying-ledge at the back of the seat in front. We filed into our sitting and knelt and rose up, and were ready for the function known as morning service."

§ 4

"And this service again was a strange thing. We read about these churches and their services in our histories and we simplify and idealise the picture ; · we take everything in the account, as we used to say in that old world, at its face value. We think that the people understood and believed completely the curious creeds of those old-world religions ; that they worshipped with a simple ardour ; that they had in their hearts a secret system of comforts and illusions which some of us even now try to recover. But life is always more complicated than any account or representation of it can be. The human mind in those days was always complicating and overlaying its ideas, forgetting

primary in secondary considerations, substituting
repetition and habit for purposive acts, and forgetting
and losing its initial intentions. Life has grown
simpler for men as the ages have passed because
it has grown clearer. We were more complicated
in our lives then because we were more confused.
And so we sat in our pews on Sunday, in a state
of conforming inattention, not really thinking out
what we were doing, feeling rather than knowing
significances and with our thoughts wandering like
water from a leaky vessel. We watched the people
about us furtively and minutely and we were acutely
aware that they watched us. We stood up, we half
knelt, we sat, as the ritual of the service required
us to do. I can still recall quite vividly the long
complex rustle of the congregation as it sat down
or rose up in straggling unison.

"This morning service was a mixture of prayers
and recitations by the priests—vicar and curate we
called them—and responses by the congregation,
chants, rhymed hymns, the reading of passages
from the Hebrew-Christian Bible, and at last a discourse. Except for this discourse all the service
followed a prescribed course set out in a prayer-
book. We hopped from one page of the prayer-
book to another, and 'finding your place' was a
terrible mental exercise for a small boy with a sedulous
mother on one side and Prue on the other.

"The service began lugubriously and generally
it was lugubrious. We were all miserable sinners,
there was no health in us ; we expressed our mild
surprise that our Deity did not resort to violent
measures against us. There was a long part called

the Litany in which the priest repeated with considerable gusto every possible human misfortune, war, pestilence, famine, and so on, and the congregation interjected at intervals, ' Good Lord deliver us ! ' although you might have thought that these were things within the purview of our international and health and food administrators rather than matters for the Supreme Being. Then the officiating priest went on to a series of prayers for the Queen, the rulers of the State, heretics, unfortunate people, travellers, and the harvest, all of which I concluded were being dangerously neglected by Divine Providence, and the congregation reinforced the priest's efforts by salvos of ' We beseech Thee to hear us, Good Lord.' The hymns were of very variable quality, but the greater part were effusive praises of our Maker, with frequent false rhymes and bad quantities. We thanked Heaven for our ' blessings,' and that without a thought of irony. Yet you would imagine that a Deity of Infinite Power might easily have excused our gratitude for the precarious little coal and green-grocery business in Cherry Gardens and all my mother's toil and anxieties and my father's worries.

" The general effect of this service beneath its surface adulation of the worshipped God, was to blame Him thoroughly and completely for every human misfortune and to deny the responsibility of mankind for its current muddle and wretchedness. Throughout the land and throughout most of the world, Sunday after Sunday, by chant and hymn and prayer and gesture, it was being dinned into the minds of young people, whenever for a moment the service broke through the surface of their protective instinctive inattention, that mankind was worthless and hopeless, the helpless plaything of a moody, impulsive, vain, and irresistible Being. This rain of suggestion came between their minds and the Sun of Life ; it hid the Wonderful from them ; it robbed them of access to the Spirit of Courage. But so alien was this doctrine of abasement from the heart of man, that for the most part the congregation sat or stood or knelt in rows in its pews repeating responses and singing mechanically, with its minds distracted to a thousand distant more congenial things, watching the deportment of its neighbours, scheming about business or pleasure, wandering in reverie.

"There would come at times into this service, sometimes but not always, parts of another service, the Communion Service. This was the reduced remainder of that Catholic Mass of which we have all learnt in our histories. As you know, the world of Christianity was still struggling, nineteen hundred years after Christianity had begun, to get rid of the obsession of a mystical blood sacrifice, to forget a traditional killing of a God-man, that was as old as agriculture and the first beginnings of human settlement. The English State Church was so much a thing of compromise and tradition that in the two churches it had in Cherry Gardens the teaching upon this issue was diametrically opposed ; one, the new and showy one, St. Jude's, was devoted to an exaggeration of the importance of the Communion, called it the Mass, called the table on which it was celebrated the Altar, called the Rev. Mr. Snapes the Priest, and generally emphasised the ancient pagan interpretation, while the other, the little old

43

church of St. Osyth, called its priest a Minister, its altar the Lord's Table, and the Communion the Lord's Supper, denied all its mystical importance, and made it merely a memorial of the life and death of the Master.   These age-long controversies between the immemorial temple worship of our race and the new life of intellectual and spiritual freedom that had then been dawning in the world for three or four centuries were far above my poor little head as I fretted and ' behaved myself ' in our sitting. To my youthful mind the Communion Service meant nothing more than a long addition to the normal tediums of worship.   In those days I had a pathetic belief in the magic of prayer, and oblivious of the unflattering implications of my request I would whisper throughout the opening prayers and recitations of the morning : ' Pray God there *won't* be a Communion Service.   Pray God there *won't* be a Communion Service.'

" Then would come the sermon, the original composition of the Rev. Mr. Snapes, and the only thing in the whole service that was not set and prescribed and that had not been repeated a thousand times before.

" Mr. Snapes was a youngish pinkish man with pinkish golden hair and a clean-shaven face ; he had small chubby features like a cluster of *champignons*, an expression of beatific self-satisfaction, and a plump voice. He had a way of throwing back the ample white sleeve of his surplice when he turned the pages of his manuscript, a sort of upthrow of the posed white hand, that aroused in me one of the inexplicable detestations of childhood. I used to hate this gesture, watch for its coming and squirm when it came.

44

THE BEGINNING OF THE DREAM

" The sermons were so much above my head that I cannot now tell what any of them were about. He would talk of things like the ' Comfort of the Blessed Eucharist' and the 'Tradition of the Fathers of the Church.' He would discourse too of what he called the Feasts of the Church, though a collection plate was the nearest approach to feasting we saw. He made much of Advent and Epiphany and Whitsuntide, and he had a common form of transition to modern considerations, ' And we too, dear Brethren, in these latter days have our Advents and our Epiphanies.' Then he would pass to King Edward's proposed visit to Lowcliff or to the recent dispute about the Bishop of Natal or the Bishop of Zanzibar. You cannot imagine how remote it was from anything of moment in our normal lives.

" And then suddenly, when a small boy was losing all hope of this smooth voice ever ceasing, came a little pause and then the blessed words of release : ' And now to God the Father, God the Son——'

" It was over ! There was a stir throughout the church. We roused ourselves, we stood up. Then we knelt for a brief moment of apparent prayer and then we scrabbled for hats, coats, and umbrellas, and so out into the open air, a great pattering of feet upon the pavement, dispersing this way and that, stiff greetings of acquaintances, Prue to the baker's for the Sunday dinner and the rest of us straight home.

" Usually there were delightful brown potatoes under the Sunday joint and perhaps there would be a fruit pie also. But in the spring came rhubarb, which I hated. It was held to be peculiarly good

for me, and I was always compelled to eat exceptionally large helpings of rhubarb tart.

"In the afternoon there was Sunday school or
else ' Children's Service,' and, relieved of the presence
of our parents, we three children went to the school-
house or to the church again to receive instruction
in the peculiarities of our faith. In the Sunday
school untrained and unqualified people whom we
knew in the weekdays as shop assistants and an
auctioneer's clerk and an old hairy deaf gentleman
named Spendilow, collected us in classes and dis-
coursed to us on the ambiguous lives and doings
of King David of Israel and of Abraham, Isaac,
and Jacob and the misbehaviour of Queen Jezebel
and the like topics. And we sang easy hymns in
unison. At times our teachers spoke of the Master
of Mankind, but they spoke without understanding ;
they spoke of him as a sort of trickster who worked
miracles and achieved jail delivery from the tomb.
And so had ' saved ' us—in spite of the manifest
fact that we were anything but saved. The teaching of the Master was, you know, buried under
these tales of Resurrection and Miracles for two
thousand years. He was a light shining in the
darkness and the darkness knew it not. And of
the great past of life, of the races of men and their
slow growth in knowledge, of fears and dark super-
stitions and the dawning victories of truth, of the
conquest and sublimation of human passions through
the ages, of the divinity of research and discovery,
of the latent splendour of our bodies and senses,
and the present dangers and possibilities amidst
which the continually more crowded masses of our

race were then blundering so tragically and yet with such bright gleams of hope and promise, we heard no talk at all. We were given no intimation that there was so much as a human community with a common soul and an ultimate common destiny. It would have been scandalous and terrifying to those Sunday-school teachers to have heard any such things spoken about in Sunday school.

"And mind you," said Sarnac, "there was no better preparation for life in all the world then than the sort of thing I was getting. The older church of St. Osyth was in the hands of the Rev. Thomas Benderton, who dispersed a dwindling congregation by bellowing sermons full of the threat of hell. He had scared my mother to the church of St. Jude by his frequent mention of the devil, and the chief topic of his discourse was the sin of idolatry ; he treated it always with especial reference to the robes adopted by Mr. Snapes when he celebrated Holy Communion and to something obscure that he did with small quantities of bread and wine upon his Communion table.

" Of what the Congregationalists and the Primitive Methodists did and taught in their places of resort, their chapels and Sunday schools, I do not know very exactly, because my mother would have been filled with a passion of religious terror if ever I had gone near those assemblies. But I know that their procedure was only a plainer version of our church experiences with still less of the Mass and still more of the devil. The Primitive Methodists, I know, laid their chief stress upon the belief that the greater portion of mankind, when once they had done with the privations and miseries of this life, would be tortured exquisitely for ever and ever in hell. I got this very clearly because a Primitive Methodist boy a little older than myself conveyed his anxieties to me one day when we had gone for a walk into Cliffstone.

" He was a bent sort of boy with a sniff and he wore a long white woollen comforter ; there hasn't been such a figure in the world now for hundreds of years. We walked along the promenade that followed the cliff edge, by the bandstand and by the people lounging in deck-chairs. There were swarms of people in their queer holiday clothes, and behind, rows of the pallid grey houses in which they lodged. And my companion bore his testimony. ' Mr. Molesly 'e says that the Day of Judgment might come any minute—come in fire and glory before ever we get to the end of these Leas. And all them people'd be tried.' . . .

" ' Jest as they are ? '

" ' Jest as they are. That woman there with the dog and that fat man asleep in 'is chair and— the policeman.'

" He paused, a little astonished at the Hebraic daring of his thoughts. ' The policeman,' he repeated. ' They'd be weighed and found wanting, and devils would come and torture them. Torture that policeman. Burn him and cut him about. And everybody. Horrible, horrible torture. . . .'

" I had never heard the doctrines of Christianity applied with such particularity before. I was dismayed.

" ' I sh'd 'ide,' I said.

" ' 'E'd see you. 'E'd see you and tell the devils,'

said my little friend. "'*E* sees the wicked thoughts in us now.'" . . .

"But did people really believe such stuff as that?" cried Sunray.

"As far as they believed anything," said Sarnac. "I admit it was frightful, but so it was. Do you realise what cramped distorted minds grew up under such teaching in our under-nourished, infected bodies?"

"Few people could have really believed so grotesque a fairy-tale as hell," said Radiant.

"More people believed than you would think," said Sarnac. "Few people, of course, held it actively for long—or they would have gone mad—but it was in the background of a lot of minds. And the others? The effect of this false story about the world upon the majority of minds was a sort of passive rejection. They did not deny, but they refused to incorporate the idea with the rest of their thoughts. A kind of dead place, a *scar*, was made just where there ought to have been a sense of human destiny, a vision of life beyond the immediate individual life . . .

"I find it hard to express the state of mind into which one grew. The minds of the young had been outraged by these teachings; they were no longer capable of complete mental growth, a possibility had been destroyed. Perhaps we never did really take into ourselves and believe that grotesque fairy-tale, as you call it, about hell but, because of what it had done to our minds we grew up without a living faith and without a purpose. The nucleus of our religious being was this suppressed fear of hell. Few of us ever had it out fairly into the light of day. It was considered to be bad taste to speak of any such things, or indeed of any of the primaries of life, either by way of belief or denial. You might allude circuitously. Or joke. Most of the graver advances in life were made under a mask of facetiousness.

" Mentally that world in the days of Mortimer Smith was a world astray. It was astray like a lost dog and with no idea of direction. It is true that the men of that time were very like the men of this time—in their possibilities—but they were unhealthy in mind as well as body, they were adrift and incoherent. Walking as we do in the light, and by comparison simply and directly, their confusion, the tortuous perplexity of their thoughts and conduct is almost inconceivable to us. There is no sort of mental existence left in our world now, to which it can be compared."

§ 5

" I think I mentioned the line of hills, the Downs that bounded the world of my upbringing to the north. What lay beyond them was a matter for wonder and speculation to me long before I was able to clamber to their crests. In summer time the sun set behind them to the north-west, often in a glow of gold and splendour, and I remember that among my fancies was a belief that the Day of Judgment was over there and that Celestial City to which Mr. Snapes would some day lead us—in procession, of course, and with a banner.

" My first ascent of this childhood's boundary must have occurred when I was eight or nine. I do not remember with whom I went or any other particulars, but I have a very acute memory of my disappointment at looking down a long, very gentle slope and seeing nothing but fields and hedges and groups of large sheep feeding. What I had expected to find I cannot now remember. I seem to have noted only the foreground then, and it must have been after many such excursions that I began to realise the variegated spaciousness of the country to the north. The view indeed went very far ; on a clear day we saw blue hills nearly twenty miles away ; there were woodlands and parklands, brown ridges of plough-land that became golden ridges of corn in summer time, village churches amidst clustering greenery, and the gleaming of ponds and lakes. Southward the horizon lifted as the Downs were ascended and the breadth of the sea-belt increased. It was my father drew my attention to that, on the first occasion of our crossing the Downs together.

"'Go as 'igh as you like, 'Arry,' he said, ' and the sea goes up as 'igh. There it is, you see—level with us and we ever so 'igh above Cherry Gardens. And yet it don't *drown'd* Cherry Gardens ! And why don't it drown'd Cherry Gardens seeing that it might ? Tell me that, 'Arry.'

" I couldn't.

"'Providence,' said my father triumphantly. 'Providence does it. 'Olds back the sea, Thus Far. And over there, see 'ow plain it is ! is France.'

" I saw France and it was exceptionally plain.

"' Sometimes you see France and sometimes you don't,' said my father. ' There's a lesson in that too, my boy, for those who care to take it.'

" It had always been the custom of my father

to go out after tea on Sundays, summer and winter alike, and walk right over the Downs to Chessing Hanger, six miles and more away. He went, I knew, to see my Uncle John, Uncle John Julip, my mother's brother, who was gardener to Lord Bramble of Chessing Hanger Park. But it was only when he began to take me with him that I realised that these walks had any other motive than fraternal (in law) affection and the natural desire of a pent-up shopkeeper for exercise. But from the first journey on I knew that the clue to these expeditions lay in the burthens with which we returned to Cherry Gardens. Always there was supper in the cosy little gardener's cottage, and always as we departed we picked up an unobtrusive load of flowers, fruit or vegetables, celery, peas, aubergines, mushrooms or what-not, and returned through the dusk or moon-light or darkness or drizzle as the season and the weather might determine to the little shop. And sometimes my father would be silent or whistle softly and sometimes he would improve our journey with a discourse on the wonders of nature, the beauty of goodness, and the beneficence of Providence to man.

"He talked of the moon one moonlight night. 'Look at it, 'Arry,' he said—'a dead world. Like a skull it is, up there, stripped of its soul which is its flesh so to speak and all its trees, which, if you take me, were its 'air and its whiskers—stripped and dead for ever and ever. Dry as a bone. And everyone who lived there gone too. Dust and ashes and gone.'

"'Where they gone, farver?' I would ask.

"'Gorn to their judgment,' he would explain

52

with gusto. 'Kings and greengroshers, all the lot of 'em, tried and made sheep and goats of, and gone to their bliss or their sufferings, 'Arry. According to their iniquities. Weighed and found wanting.'

" Long pause.

" ' It's a pity,' he said.

" ' What is, farver ? '

" ' Pity it's over. It 'ud be something to look at, them running about up there. Friendly-like it 'ud be. But that's questioning the ways of Providence, that is. I suppose we'd be always staring up and falling over things. . . . You never see a thing in this world, 'Arry, that you think isn't right but what when you come to think it out it isn't wiser than you knew. Providence is as deep as E is I and you can't get be'ind 'im. And don't go banging them pears against your side, my boy ; they'm Wi'yums, and they won't like it.'

" About the curious habits of animals and the ways and migrations of birds my father would also talk very freely.

" ' Me and you, 'Arry, we walk by the light of reason. We 'ave reasonable minds given us to do it with. But animals and birds and worms and things, they live by Instink ; they jus' feel they 'ave to do this or that and they do it. It's Instink keeps the whale in the sea and the bird in the air; but we go where our legs carry us as reason 'as directed. You can't ask an animal Why did you do this ? or Why did you do that ?—you just '*it* it ; but a man you ask and 'e 'as to answer, being a reasonable creature. That's why we 'as jails and punishment and are answerable for our sins, 'Arry. Every sin

we 'as to answer for, great or small. But an animal
don't 'ave to answer. It's innocent. You *'it* it or
else you leave it be. . . .'

"My father thought for a time. 'Except for
dogs and some *old* cats,' he said. He mused among
his memories for a time. 'I've known some *sinful*
cats, 'Arry,' he said.

"He would enlarge on the wonders of instinct.

"He would explain how swallows and starlings
and storks and such-like birds were driven by instinct
thousands of miles, getting drowned on the way and
dashed to pieces against lighthouses. 'Else they'd
freeze and starve where they was, 'Arry,' said my
father. And every bird knew by instinct what sort
of nest it had to build, no one ever showing it or telling
it. Kangaroos carried their young in pouches by
instinct, but man being a reasonable creature made
perambulators. Chickens ran about by instinct
directly they were born ; not like human children,
who had to be carried and taken care of until reason
came. And jolly lucky that was for the chicken,
'For 'ow a 'en would carry them,' said my father,
'I *carn't* imagine.'

"I remember that I put my father into a difficulty
by asking him why Providence had not given birds
an instinct against beating themselves against lighthouses and moths against the gas-jet and the candle-
flame. For in the room over the shop on a summer's
night it was quite unpleasant to read a book because
of the disabled flies and moths that fell scorched upon
its pages. 'It's to teach 'em some lesson,' said my
father at last. 'But what it's to teach them, 'Arry,
I don't rightly know.'

54

" And sometimes he would talk, with illustrative stories, of ill-gotten gold never staying with the getter, and sometimes he would talk of murders—for there were still many murders in the world—and how they always came out, ' hide them as you may.' And always he was ready to point out the goodness and wisdom, the cleverness, forethought, ingenuity, and kindlinesss of Providence in the most earnest and flattering manner.

" With such high discourse did we enliven our long trudges between Cherry Gardens and Chessing Hanger, and my father's tone was always so exalted that with a real shock I presently came to realise that every Sunday evening we were in plain English stealing and receiving stolen produce from Lord Bramble's gardens. Indeed, I cannot imagine how we should have got along without that weekly raid. Our little home at Cherry Gardens was largely supported by my father's share in the profits of these transactions. When the produce was too good and costly for Cherry Gardens' needs, he would take it down to Cliffstone and sell it to a friend there who had a fashionable trade."

Sarnac paused.

" Go on," said Radiant. " You are making us believe in your story. It sounds more and more as if you had been there. It is so circumstantial. Who was this Lord Bramble ? I have always been curious about Lords."

§ 6

" Let me tell my story in my own way," said Sarnac. " If I answer questions I shall get lost. You are all ready to ask a hundred questions already about things I have mentioned and points familiar to me but incomprehensible to you because our world has forgotten them, and if I weaken towards you you will trail me away and away further and further from my father and my Uncle Julip. We shall just talk about manners and customs and about philosophy and history. I want to tell my story."

"Go on with your story," said Sunray.

"This Uncle John Julip of mine, although he was my mother's brother, was a cynical, opinionated man. He was very short and fatter than was usual among gardeners. He had a smooth white face and a wise self-satisfied smile. To begin with, I saw him only on Sundays and in white shirt sleeves and a large straw hat. He made disparaging remarks about my physique and about the air of Cherry Gardens every time he saw me. His wife had been a dissenter of some sort and had become a church-woman under protest. She too was white-faced and her health was bad. She complained of pains. But my Uncle John Julip disparaged her pains because he said they were not in a reasonable place. There was stomachache and backache and heartburn and the wind, but her pains were neither here nor there ; they were therefore pains of the imagination and had no claim upon our sympathy.

"When I was nearly thirteen years old my father and uncle began planning for me to go over to the Chessing Hanger gardens and be an under-gardener. This was a project I disliked very greatly ; not only did I find my uncle unattractive, but I thought weed-ing and digging and most of the exercises of a garden extremely tiring and boring. I had taken very kindly to reading, I liked languages, I inherited something of my father's loquaciousness, and I had won a special prize for an essay in my school. This had fired the most unreasonable ambitions in me—to write, to write in newspapers, possibly even to write books. At Cliffstone was what was called a public library to which the householders of Cliffstone had access and from which members of their families could borrow books—during holidays I would be changing my book almost every day—but at Chessing Hanger there were no books at all. My sister Fanny encouraged me in my reading; she too was a voracious reader of novels, and she shared my dislike of the idea that I should become a gardener.

" In those days, you must understand, no attempt was made to gauge the natural capacity of a child. Human beings were expected to be grateful for any opportunity of 'getting a living.' Parents bundled their children into any employment that came handy, and so most people followed occupations that were misfits, that did not give full scope for such natural gifts as they possessed and which commonly cramped or crippled them. This in itself diffused a vague discontent throughout the community, and inflicted upon the great majority of people strains and restraints and suppressions that ate away their possibility of positive happiness. Most youngsters as they grew up, girls as well as boys, experienced a sudden tragic curtailment of freedom and discovered themselves forced into some unchosen specific drudgery from which it was very difficult to escape. One summer holiday came, when, instead of enjoying delightful long days of play and book-devouring in Cliffstone,

as I had hitherto done, I was sent off over the hills
to stay with Uncle John Julip, and 'see how I got
on' with him. I still remember the burning disgust,
the sense of immolation, with which I lugged my little
valise up the hills and over the Downs to the gardens.

"This Lord Bramble, Radiant, was one of the
landlords who were so important during the reigns
of the Hanoverian Kings up to the time of Queen
Victoria the Good. They owned large areas of
England as private property; they could do what
they liked with it. In the days of Victoria the Good
and her immediate predecessors these landlords who
had ruled the Empire through the House of Lords
made a losing fight for predominance against the
new industrialists, men who employed great masses
of people for their private gain in the iron and steel
industries, cotton and wool, beer and shipping, and
these again gave way to a rather different type who
developed advertisement and a political and financial
use of newspapers and new methods of finance. The
old land-holding families had to adapt themselves to
the new powers or be pushed aside. Lord Bramble
was one of those pushed aside, an indignant, old-
fashioned, impoverished landowner. He was in a
slough of debts. His estates covered many square
miles; he owned farms and woodlands, a great white
uncomfortable house, far too roomy for his shrunken
means, and two square miles of park. The park was
greatly neglected, it was covered with groups of old
trees infested and rotten with fungus; rabbits and
moles abounded, and thistles and nettles. There
were no young trees there at all. The fences and
gates were badly patched; and here and there ran

degenerating roads. But boards threatening tres-
passers abounded, and notices saying ' NO THOR-
OUGHFARE.' For it was the dearest privilege
of the British landlord to restrict the free movements of ordinary people, and Lord Bramble guarded
his wilderness with devotion. Great areas of good
land in England in those days were in a similar state
of picturesquely secluded dilapidation."

" Those were the lands where they did the shooting," said Radiant.

" How did you know ? "

" I have seen a picture. They stood in a line
along the edge of a copse, with brown-leaved trees and
a faint smell of decay and a touch of autumnal damp-
ness in the air, and they shot lead pellets at birds."

" They did. And the beaters—I was pressed
into that service once or twice—drove the birds, the
pheasants, towards them. Shooting parties used to
come to Chessing Hanger, and the shooting used to
go on day after day. It was done with tremendous
solemnity."

" But why ? " asked Willow.

" Yes," said Radiant. " Why did men do it ? "

" I don't know," said Sarnac. " All I know is
that at certain seasons of the year the great majority
of the gentlemen of England who were supposed to
be the leaders and intelligence of the land, who were
understood to guide its destinies and control its future,
went out into the woods or on the moors to massacre
birds of various sorts with guns, birds bred specially
at great expense for the purpose of this slaughter.
These noble sportsmen were marshalled by game-
keepers ; they stood in rows, the landscape was

animated with the popping of their guns. The
highest in the land participated gravely in this national
function and popped with distinction. The men of
this class were in truth at just that level above imbecility
where the banging of a gun and the thrill of seeing
a bird swirl and drop is inexhaustibly amusing. They
never tired of it. The bang of the gun seems to
have been essential to the sublimity of the sensations
of these sportsmen. It wasn't mere killing, because
in that case these people could also have assisted in
killing the sheep and oxen and pigs required by the
butchers, but this sport they left to men of an inferior
social class. Shooting birds on the wing was the
essential idea. When Lord Bramble was not killing
pheasants or grouse he shot in the south of France at
perplexed pigeons with clipped wings just let out of
traps. Or he hunted—not real animal hunting, not
a fair fight with bear or tiger or elephant in a jungle,
but the chasing of foxes—small stinking red animals
about the size of water-spaniels, which were sedu-
lously kept from extinction for this purpose of hunting ; they were hunted across cultivated land, and
the hunters rode behind a pack of dogs. Lord Bramble dressed himself up with extreme care in a red
jacket and breeches of pigskin to do this. For the
rest of his time the good man played a card game
called bridge, so limited and mechanical that anyone nowadays would be able to read out the results
and exact probabilities of every deal directly he saw
his cards. There were four sets of thirteen cards
each. But Lord Bramble, who had never learnt
properly to count up to thirteen, found it full of dramatic surprises and wonderful sensations. A large

part of his time was spent in going from race-course to race-course ; they raced a specially flimsy breed of horses in those days. There again he dressed with care. In the illustrated papers in the public library I would see photographs of Lord Bramble, with a silk hat—a top hat, *you* know—cocked very much on one side ' in the Paddock ' or ' snapped with a lady friend.' There was much betting and knowingness about this horse-racing. His Lordship dined with comparative intelligence, erring only a little on the excessive side with the port. People still smoked in those days, and Lord Bramble would consume three or four cigars a day. Pipes he thought plebeian and cigarettes effeminate. He could read a newspaper but not a book, being incapable of sustained attention ; after dinner in town he commonly went to a theatre or music-hall where women could be seen, more or less undraped. The clothing of that time filled such people as Lord Bramble with a coy covetousness for nakedness. The normal beauty of the human body was a secret and a mystery, and half the art and decoration of Chessing Hanger House played stimulatingly with the forbidden vision.

" In that past existence of mine I took the way of life of Lord Bramble as a matter of course, but now that I recall it I begin to see the enormous absurdity of these assassins of frightened birds, these supporters of horses and ostlers, these peepers at feminine thighs and shoulder-blades. Their women sympathised with their gunmanship, called their horses ' the dears,' cultivated dwarfed and crippled breeds of pet dogs, and yielded the peeps expected of them.

" Such was the life of the aristocratic sort of people

in those days. They set the tone of what was considered a hard, bright, healthy life. The rest of the community admired them greatly and imitated them to the best of its ability. The tenant farmer, if he could not shoot pheasants, shot rabbits, and if he could not bet twenty-pound notes at the fashionable race-meeting at Goodwood, put his half-crown upon his fancy at the Cliffstone races on Byford Downs—with his hat cocked over one eye as much like Lord Bramble and King Edward as possible.

" Great multitudes of people there were whose lives were shaped completely by the habits and traditions of these leaders. There was my Uncle John Julip for example. His father had been a gardener and his grandfather before him, and almost all his feminine ancestry and his aunts and cousins were, as the phrase went, ' in service.' None of the people round and about the downstairs of Chessing Hanger had natural manners ; all were dealing in some more or less plausible imitation of some real lady or gentleman. My Uncle John Julip found his ideal in a certain notorious Sir John ffrench-Cuthbertson. He sought similar hats and adopted similar attitudes.

"He bet heavily in imitation of his model, but he bet less fortunately. This my aunt resented, but she found great comfort in the way in which his clothing and gestures under-studied Sir John.

" ' If only he'd been *born* a gentleman,' said my aunt, ' everything ud a-been all right. 'E's a natural sportsman ; 'e eats 'is 'eart out in the gardens.'

" He certainly did not work his heart out. I do not remember ever seeing him dig or carry or wheel a barrow. My memory of him in the garden is of one who stood, one hand gripping a hoe as if it were a riding whip under the tail of his coat, and the other gesticulating or pointing out what had to be done.

" To my father and myself he was always consciously aristocratic, bearing himself in the grand manner. This he did, although my father was a third as tall again as he was and far more abundantly intelligent. He always called my father ' Smith.'

" ' What are you going to do with that boy, Smith ? ' he would ask. ' Seems to me, wants feedin' up and open air.'

" My father, who secretly shared the general view that my Uncle John under happier stars would have made a very fine gentleman, always tried, as he expressed it, ' to keep his end up ' by calling my uncle ' John.' He would answer, ' Carn't say as I've rightly settled that, John. 'E's a regular book-worm nowadays, say what you like to him.'

" ' Books ! ' said my Uncle John Julip with a concentrated scorn of books that was essentially English. ' You can't get anything out of books that 'asn't been put into them. It stands to reason. There's nothing in books that didn't first come out of the sile. Books is flattened flowers at the best, as 'is Lordship said at dinner only the other night.'

" My father was much struck by the idea. ' That's what I tell 'im,' he said—inexactly.

" ' Besides, who's going to put anything into a book that's worth knowing ? ' said my uncle. ' It's like expecting these here tipsters in the papers to give away something worth keeping to theirselves. Not it ! '

" ' 'Arf the time,' my father agreed, ' I expect they're

telling you lies in these books of yours and larfing at you. All the same,' he reflected with an abrupt lapse from speculation to reverence, 'there's One Book, John.'

" He had remembered the Bible.

" ' I wasn't speaking of that, Smith,' said my uncle sharply. 'Sufficient unto the day—— I mean, that's Sunday Stuff.'

" I hated my days of trial in the gardens. Once or twice during that unpleasant month I was sent with messages up to the kitchen and once to the pantry of the great house. There I said something unfortunate for my uncle, something that was to wipe out all possibility of a gardener's career for me.

" The butler, Mr. Petterton, was also a secondary aristocrat, but in a larger and quite different manner from that of my uncle. He towered up and looked down the slopes of himself, his many chins were pink and stabbed by his collar, and his hair was yellow and very shiny. I had to deliver into his hands a basket of cucumbers and a bunch of blue flowers called borage used in the mixing of summer drinks. He was standing at a table talking respectfully to a foxy little man in tweeds who was eating bread-and-cheese and drinking beer ; this I was to learn later was Lord Bramble's agent. There was also a young footman in this room, a subterranean room it was with heavily barred windows, and he was cleaning silver plate with exemplary industry.

" ' So you brought this from the gardens,' said Mr. Petterton with fine irony. 'And may I ask why Mr.—why *Sir John* did not condescend to bring them himself ? '

" ' 'E tole me to bring them,' I said.

" ' And pray who may you be ? '

" ' I'm 'Arry Smith,' I said. ' Mr. Julip, 'e's my uncle.'

" ' Ah ! ' said Mr. Petterton and was struck by a thought. ' That's the son of Smith who's a sort of greengrosher in Cliffstone.'

" ' Cherry Gardens, sir, we live at.'

" ' Haven't seen you over here before, my boy. Have you ever visited us before ? '

" ' Not 'ere, sir.'

" ' Not here ! But you come over to the gardens perhaps ? '

" ' Nearly every Sunday, sir.'

" ' Exactly. And usually I suppose, Master Smith, there's something to carry back ? '

" ' Almost always, sir.'

" ' Something a bit heavy ? '

" ' Not *too* heavy,' I said bravely.

" ' You see, sir ? ' said Mr. Petterton to the foxy little man in tweeds.

" I began to realise that something unpleasant was in the wind when this latter person set himself to cross-examine me in a rapid, snapping manner. What was it I carried ? I became very red about the face and ears and declared I did not know. Did I ever carry grapes ? I didn't know. Pears ? I didn't know. Celery ? I didn't know.

" ' Well, *I* know,' said the agent. ' *I* know. So why should I ask you further ? Get out of here.'

" I went back to my uncle and said nothing to him of this very disagreeable conversation, but I knew quite well even then that I had not heard the last of this matter."

Misfortunes come upon the Smith Family

§ 1

" AND now," said Sarnac, " I have to tell of a tornado of mischances that broke up our precarious little home at Cherry Gardens altogether. In that casual, planless, over-populated world there were no such things as security or social justice as we should understand these words nowadays. It is hard for us to imagine its universal ramshackle insecurity. Think of it. The whole world floated economically upon a cash and credit system that was fundamentally fictitious and conventional, there were no adequate protections against greedy abuses of those monetary conventions, no watch kept over world-production and world-consumption, no knowledge of the variations of climate year by year, and the fortunes not only of individuals but of states and nations fluctuated irrationally and uncontrollably. It was a world in which life was still almost as unsafe for men and women as life remains to-day for a field-mouse or a midge, which is never safe from one moment to another in a world of cats and owls and swallows and the like. People were born haphazard, gladdened, distressed, glorified or killed haphazard, and no one was ready for either their births or their deaths. Sudden death there is still in the world, a bright adventure—that lightning yesterday might have killed all or any of us, but such death is a rare thing and a clean thing. There is none of the distressful bearing-down to death through want, anxiety, and illness ill-tended and misunderstood, that was the common experience in the past. And one death does not devastate a dozen or more lives as deaths often did in the old days. A widow in the old days had lost not only her lover but her 'living.' Yet life is full of subtle compensations. We did not feel our endless dangers in those days. We had a wonderful power of disregard until the chances struck us.

"All children," said Sarnac, "start with an absolute confidence in the permanence of the things they find about them. Disillusionment about safety postulates clear-headedness. You could not realize your dangers unless you were clear-headed, and if you were clear-headed you had the fortitude to face your dangers. That old world was essentially a world of muddle-headed sophisticated children, blind to the universal catastrophe of the top-heavy and collapsing civilisation in which they played their parts. They thought that life was generally safe in a world of general insecurity. Misfortune astonished everyone in those days, though I cannot understand why they should have been astonished at any misfortune.

"The first blow fell without notice about six weeks after I had come back from Chessing Hanger to my last half year of schooling before I became a gardener. It was late afternoon and I was home from school. I was downstairs reading a book and my mother was clearing away tea and grumbling at Fanny who wanted to go out. The lamp was lit, and both I and my father who was having what he called 'a bit of a read at the noosepaper' were as close up to its insufficient light as we could get. We heard the shop bell jangle overhead.

THE DREAM

" ' Drat it ! ' said my father. ' Whaddey want this time o' day ? '

" He removed his spectacles. He had bought a pair haphazard at a pawnbroker's shop and always used them when he read. They magnified his large mild eyes very greatly. He regarded us protestingly. What *did* they want ? We heard the voice of Uncle John Julip calling down the staircase :

" ' Mort'mer,' he said in a voice that struck me as unusual. I had never heard him call my father anything but Smith before.

" ' That you, John ? ' said my father standing up.

" ' It's me. I want to speak to you.'

" ' Come down and 'ave some tea, John,' cried my father at the bottom of the stairs.

" ' Somethin' to tell you. You better come up here. Somethin' serious.'

" I speculated if it could be any misdeed of mine he had come over about. But my conscience was fairly clear.

" ' Now whatever can it be ? ' asked my father.

" ' You better go up and arst 'im,' my mother suggested.

" My father went.

" I heard my uncle say something about, ' We're busted. We've bin give away and we're busted,' and then the door into the shop closed. We all listened to the movements above. It sounded as though Uncle Julip was walking up and down as he talked. My sister Fanny in her hat and jacket flitted unobtrusively up the stairs and out. After a time Prue came in ; she had been helping teacher tidy up, she said, though I knew better. Then after a long interval my father came downstairs alone.

"He went to the hearthrug like one in a trance and stood, staring portentously in order to make my mother ask what was the matter. 'Why hasn't John come down for a bit of tea or something? Where's he gone, Morty?'

"' 'E's gorn for a van,' said my father; 'that's where 'e's gone. For a van.'

"' Whatever for?' asked my mother.

"' For a removal,' said my father. 'That's what for.'

"' Removal?'

"' We got to put 'em up 'ere for a night or so.'

"' Put 'em up! Who?'

"' 'Im and Adelaide. He's coming to Cherry Gardens.'

"' You done mean, Morty, 'e's lost 'is situation?'

"' I do. S'Lordship turned against 'im. Mischief 'as been made. Spying. And they managed to get 'im out of it. Turned out 'e is. Tole to go.'

"' But surely they give 'im notice!'

"' Not a bit of it. S'Lordship came down to the gardens 'ot and strong. "'Ere," 'e said, "get out of it!" Like that 'e said it. "You thank your lucky stars," 'e said, "I ain't put the 'tecs on to you and your snivellin' brother-in-law." Yes. S'Lordship said that.'

"' But what did 'e mean by it, Morty?'

"' Mean. 'E meant that certain persons who shall be nameless 'ad put a suspicion on John, told lies about 'im and *watched* 'im. Watched 'im they did and me. They've drawed me into it, Martha. They've drawed in young 'Arry. They've made up a tale about us. . . . I always said we was a

bit too regular. . . . There it is, 'e ain't a 'ead
gardener any more. 'E ain't going to 'ave references
give 'im ; 'e ain't ever going to 'ave another regular
job. 'E's been betrayed and ruined, and there we are !'

" ' But they say 'e took sompthing ?—my brother
John took sompthing ? '

" ' Surplus projuce. What's been a perquisite
of every gardener since the world began.' . . .

" I sat with burning ears and cheeks pretending
not to hear this dreadful conversation. No one
knew of my own fatal share in my uncle's downfall.
But already in my heart, like the singing of a lark
after a thunderstorm, was arising a realisation that
now I might never become a gardener. My mother
expressed her consternation brokenly. She asked
incredulous questions which my father dealt with
in an oracular manner. Then suddenly my mother
pounced savagely on my sister Prue, reproaching
her for listening to what didn't concern her instead
of washing up."

" This is a very circumstantial scene," said Radiant.

" It was the first great crisis of my dream life,"
said Sarnac. " It is very vivid in my memory. I
can see again that old kitchen in which we lived
and the faded table-cloth and the paraffin lamp with
its glass container. I think if you gave me time I
could tell you everything there was in that room."

" What's a hearthrug ? " asked Firefly suddenly.
" What sort of thing was your hearthrug ? "

" Like nothing on earth to-day. A hearthrug
was a sort of rug you put in front of a coal fire, next
to the fender, which prevented the ashes creeping
into the room. This one my father had made out

of old clothes, trousers and such-like things, bits of flannel and bits of coarse sacking, cut into strips and sewn together. He had made it in the winter evenings as he sat by the fireside, sewing industriously."

"Had it any sort of pattern?"

"None. But I shall never tell my story, if you ask questions. I remember that my uncle, when he had made his arrangements about the van, came in for a bread-and-cheese supper before he walked back to Chessing Hanger. He was very white and distressed looking, Sir John had all faded away from him ; he was like a man who had been dragged out from some hiding-place, he was a very distressed and pitiful man exposed to the light. I remember my mother asked him, ' 'Ow's Adelaide taking it ? '

" My uncle assumed an expression of profound resignation. ' Starts a new pain,' he said bitterly. ' At a time like this.'

" My father and mother exchanged sympathetic glances.

" ' I tell you——,' said my uncle, but did not say what he told us.

" A storm of weak rage wrung him. ' If I knew who'd done all this,' he said. ' That—that *cat* of a 'ousekeeper—cat I call her—she's got someone what wanted my place. If she and Petterton framed it up——'

" He struck the table, but half-heartedly.

" My father poured him out some beer.

" ' Ugh ! ' said my uncle and emptied the glass.

" ' Got to face it,' said my uncle, feeling better. ' Got to go through with it. I suppose with all these tuppenny-apenny villa gardens 'ere there's

jobbing work to be got. I'll get something all
right. . . . Think of it ! Jobbing gardener ! Me
—a Jobber ! By the Day ! It'll set up some of
these 'ere season-ticket clerks no end to 'ave Lord
Bramble's gardener dragging a lawn-mower for them.
I can see 'em showing me to their friends out of
the window. Bin 'ead-gardener to a Lord, they'll
say. Well, well—— !'

" ' It's a come-down,' said my father when my
uncle had departed. ' Say what you like, it's a
come-down.'

" My mother was preoccupied with the question
of their accommodation. ' She'll 'ave to 'ave the
sofa in the sitting-room I expect, and 'e'll 'ave a
bit of a shake-up on the floor. Don't suppose she'll
like it. They'll 'ave their own bedding of course.
But Adelaide isn't the sort to be comfortable on a sofa.'

" Poor woman ! she was not. Although my
uncle and my father and mother all pointed out to
her the untimeliness and inconsiderateness of her
conduct she insisted upon suffering so much that
a doctor had to be called in. He ordered a prompt
removal to a hospital for an immediate operation.

" Those were days," said Sarnac, " of the pro-
foundest ignorance about the body. The ancient
Greeks and the Arabs had done a little anatomy
during their brief phases of intellectual activity, but
the rest of the world had only been studying physiology in a scientific way for about three hundred
years. People in general still knew practically nothing of vital processes. As I have told you they
even bore children by accident. And living the
queer lives they did, with abnormal and ill-prepared

food in a world of unchecked infections, they found the very tissues of the bodies going wrong and breaking out into the queerest growths. Parts of these bodies would cease to do anything but change into a sort of fungoid proliferation——"

"Their bodies were like their communities !" said Radiant.

"The same sort of thing. They had tumours and cancers and such-like things in their bodies and Cherry-Garden urban-districts on their country-sides. But these growths !—they are dreadful even to recall."

"But surely," said Willow, "in the face of such a horrible possibility which might afflict anyone, all the world must have wanted to push on with physiological research."

"Didn't they see," said Sunray, "that all these things were controllable and curable ?"

"Not a bit of it," said Sarnac. "They didn't positively *like* these tumours and cancers, but the community was too under-vitalised to put up a real fight against these miseries. And everyone thought that he or she would escape—until it had them. There was a general apathy. And the priests and journalists and so forth, the common opinion makers, were jealous of scientific men. They did their best to persuade people that there was nothing hopeful in scientific research, they did all they could to discredit its discoveries, to ridicule its patient workers and set people against them."

"That's what puzzles me most," said Sunray.

"Their mental habits were different. Their minds hadn't been trained to comprehensive thinking. Their thinking was all in compartments and patches.

73

The morbid growths in their bodies were nothing
to the morbid growths in their minds."

§ 2

"My aunt in the hospital, with that lack of consideration for my uncle that had always distinguished
her, would neither recover nor die. She was a
considerable expense to him and no help ; she added
greatly to his distresses. After some days and at
the urgent suggestion of my mother he removed
himself from our sitting-room to a two-roomed lodging in the house of a bricklayer in an adjacent street ;
into this he crowded his furniture from Chessing
Hanger, but he frequented my father's shop and showed
a deepening attachment to my father's company.

"He was not so successful a jobbing gardener
as he had anticipated. His short contemptuous way
with his new clients in the villas of Cliffstone failed
to produce the respect he designed it to do ; he
would speak of their flower-beds as 'two penn'orths
of all-sorts' and compare their gardens to a table-
cloth or a window box ; and instead of welcoming
these home-truths, they resented them. But they
had not the manliness to clear up this matter by a
good straightforward argument in which they would
have had their social position very exactly defined ;
they preferred to keep their illusions and just ceased
to employ him. Moreover, his disappointment with
my aunt produced a certain misogyny, which took
the form of a refusal to take orders from the wives
of his patrons when they were left in sole charge
of the house. As many of these wives had a con-

siderable influence over their husbands, this too injured my uncle's prospects. Consequently there were many days when he had nothing to do but stand about our shop to discuss with my father as hearer the defects of Cliffstone villa-residents, the baseness of Mr. Petterton and that cat ('*cat*' he called her) and the probable unworthiness of any casual customer who strayed into range of comment.

"Nevertheless my uncle was resolved not to be defeated without a struggle. There was a process which he called 'keeping his pecker up,' which necessitated, I could not but perceive, periodic visits to the Wellington public-house at the station corner. From these visits he returned markedly more garrulous, more like Sir John ffrench-Cuthbertson, and exhaling a distinctively courageous smell when he coughed or breathed heavily. After a time, as his business difficulties became more oppressive, my father participated in these heartening excursions. They broadened his philosophical outlook but made it, I fancied, rather less distinct.

"My uncle had some indefinite sum of money in the Post Office Savings Bank, and in his determination not to be beaten without a struggle he did some courageous betting on what he called 'certs' at the race-meetings on Byford Downs."

"'Cert' beats me altogether," said Radiant.

"A 'cert' was a horse that was certain to win and never did. A 'dead cert' was an extreme form of the 'cert.' You cannot imagine how the prospects and quality of the chief race-horses were discussed throughout the land. The English were not a nomadic people, only a minority could ride horses,

but everybody could bet on them. The King was,
so to speak, head of the racing just as he was head
of the army. He went in person to the great race-
meetings as if to bless and encourage the betting
of his subjects. So that my Uncle John Julip was
upheld by the most loyal and patriotic sentiments
when he wasted his days and his savings on Byford
Downs. On several of these occasions my father
went with him and wrestled with fortune also. They
lost generally, finally they lost most of what they
had, but on one or two occasions, as my uncle put
it, they 'struck it rich.' One day they pitched
upon a horse called Rococo, although it was regarded
as the very reverse of a 'cert' and the odds were
heavy against it, but an inner light seems to have
guided my uncle ; it came in first and they won as
much as thirty-five pounds, a very large sum for
them. They returned home in a state of solemn
exaltation, which was only marred by some mechanical
difficulty in pronouncing the name of the winning
horse. They began well but after the first syllable
they went on more like a hen that had laid an egg
than like rational souls who had spotted a winner.
'Rocococo' they would say or 'Rocochohohoho.' Or
they would end in a hiccup. And though each
tried to help the other out, they were not really
helpful to each other. They diffused an unusually
powerful odour of cigars and courage. Never had they
smelt so courageous. My mother made them tea.

"'*Tea!*' said my uncle meaningly. He did
not actually refuse the cup she put before him, but
he pushed it a little aside.

"For some moments it seemed doubtful whether

he was going to say something very profound or whether he was going to be seriously ill. Mind triumphed over matter. 'Knew it would come, Marth,' he said. 'Knew allong it would come. Directly I heard name. Roc——' He paused.

" ' Cococo,' clucked my father.

" ' Cocococo—hiccup,' said my uncle. ' I knew ourour 'ad come. Some men, Smith, some men 'ave that instink. I would 'ave put my shirt on that 'orse, Marth—only. . . . They wouldn't 'ave took my shirt.'

" He looked suddenly very hard at me. 'They wouldn't 'ave took it, 'Arry,' he said. ' They done *take* shirts ! ' " ' No,' he said and became profoundly thoughtful.

" Then he looked up. ' Thirty-six to one against,' he said. ' We'd 'ave 'ad shirts for a lifetime.'

" My father saw it from a wider, more philosophical point of view. ' Might never 'ave been spared to wear 'em out,' he said. ' Better as it is, John.'

" ' And mind you,' said my uncle ; ' this is only a beginning. Once I start spotting 'em I go on spotting 'em—mind that. This Roc——'

" ' Cococo.'

" ' Cocococo—whatever it is, s'only a beginning. S'only the firs'-ray-sunlight 'v' a glorious day.'

" ' In that case,' said my mother, ' t'seems to me some of us might have a share.'

" ' Certainly,' said my uncle, ' certainly, Marth.' And amazingly he handed me a ten-shilling piece— in those days we had gold coins and this was a little disk of gold. Then he handed Prue the same. He gave a whole sovereign, a golden pound, to Fanny and a five-pound Bank of England note to my mother.

" ' Hold on ! ' said my father warningly.

" ' Tha's a' right, Smith,' said my uncle with a gesture of princely generosity. ' *You* share, seventeen pounce ten. Six pounce ten leaves 'leven. Lessee. One 'n' five six—seven—eight—nine—ten—'leven. *Here !* '

" My father took the balance of the money with a puzzled expression. Something eluded him. ' Yers,' he said ; ' but——'

" His mild eye regarded the ten-shilling piece I still held exposed in my hand. I put it away immediately but his gaze followed my hand towards my pocket until it met the table edge and got into difficulties.

" ' Thout the turf, Smith, there wouldn't be such a country as England,' said my Uncle John, and rounded his remarks off with, ' Mark my words.' "

" My father did his best to do so."

§ 3

" But this hour of success was almost the only bright interlude in a steady drift to catastrophe. In a little while I gathered from a conversation between my mother and my father that we were ' behind with the rent.' That was a quarterly payment we paid to the enterprising individual who owned our house. I know all that sounds odd to you, but that is the way things were done. If we got behind with our rent the owner could turn us out."

" But where ? " asked Firefly.

" Out of the house. And we weren't allowed to stay in the street. But it is impossible for me to explain everything of that sort in detail. We were behind with the rent and catastrophe impended. And then my sister Fanny ran away from us.

" In no other respect," said Sarnac, " is it so difficult to get realities over to you and make you understand how I thought and felt in that other life than in matters of sex. Nowadays sex is so simple. Here we are free and frank men and women ; we are trained so subtly that we scarcely know we are trained, not to be stupidly competitive, to control jealous impulses, to live generously, to honour the young. Love is the link and flower of our choicest friendships. We take love by the way as we take our food and our holidays, the main thing in our lives is our creative work. But in that dark tormented world in which I passed my dream life, all the business of love was covered over and netted in by restraints and put in fetters that fretted and tortured. I will tell you at last how I was killed. Now I want to convey to you something of the reality of this affair of Fanny.

" Even in this world," said Sarnac, " my sister Fanny would have been a conspicuously lovely girl. Her eyes could be as blue as heaven, or darken with anger or excitement so that they seemed black. Her hair had a brave sweep in it always. Her smile made you ready to do anything for her ; her laughter made the world clean and brightly clear about her even when it was touched with scorn. And she was ignorant—— I can hardly describe her ignorance.

" It was Fanny first made me feel that ignorance was shameful. I have told you the sort of school we had and of our religious teachers. When I was nine or ten and Fanny was fifteen, she was already scolding me for fumbling with the pronunciation of words and particularly with the dropping of the aspirate.

"'Harry,' she said, 'if you call me Fenny again it's war and pinching. My name's Fanny and your's is Harry and don't you forget it. It's not English we talk in this place ; it's mud.'

"Something had stung her. She had been talking with someone with a better accent and she had been humiliated. I think that someone may have mocked her. Some chance acquaintance it must have been, some ill-bred superior boy upon the Cliffstone promenade. But Fanny was setting out now to talk good English and make me do the same, with a fury all her own.

"'If only I could talk French,' she said. 'There's France in sight over there ; all its lighthouses winking at us, and all we've got to say is, " *Parley vous Francy,*" and grin as if it was a joke.' She brought home a sixpenny book which professed but failed to teach her French. She was reading voraciously, greedily, to know. She read endless novels but also she was reading all sorts of books, about the stars, about physiology (in spite of my mother's wild scoldings at the impropriety of reading a book 'with pictures of yer insides' in it), about foreign countries. Her passion that I should learn was even greater than her own passion for knowledge.

"At fourteen she left school and began to help earn her living. My mother had wanted her to go into 'service,' but she had resisted and resented this passionately. While that proposal was still hanging over her, she went off by herself to Cliffstone and got a job as assistant book-keeper in a pork-butcher's shop. Before a year was out she was book-keeper, for her mind was as neat as it was nimble. She earned enough money to buy books and drawing material for me and to get herself clothes that scandalised all my mother's ideas of what was becoming. Don't imagine she ' dressed well,' as we used to say ; she experimented boldly, and some of her experiments were cheap and tawdry.

" I could lecture to you for an hour," said Sarnac, " of what dress and the money to buy dresses meant for a woman in the old world.

" A large part of my sister's life was hidden from me ; it would have been hidden altogether but for the shameless tirades of my mother, who seemed to prefer to have an audience while she scolded Fanny. I can see now that my mother was bitterly jealous of Fanny because of her unexhausted youth, but at the time I was distressed and puzzled at the gross hints and suggestions that flew over my head. Fanny had a maddening way of not answering back or answering only by some minor correction. ' It's horrible, mother,' she would say. ' Not 'orrible.'

" Behind her defensive rudenesses, unlit, unguided, poor Fanny was struggling with the whole riddle of life, presented to her with an urgency no man can fully understand. Nothing in her upbringing had ever roused her to the passion for real work in the world ; religion for her had been a grimace and a threat ; the one great reality that had come through to her thoughts was love. The novels she read all told of love, elusively, partially, and an impatience in her imagination and in her body leapt to these hints. Love whispered to her in the light and beauty of things about her ; in the moonlight,

in the spring breezes. Fanny could not but know
that she was beautiful. But such morality as our
world had then was a morality of abject suppression.
Love was a disgrace, a leering fraud, a smutty joke.
She was not to speak about it, not to look towards
it until some good man—the pork butcher was a
widower and seemed likely to be the good man in
her case—came and spoke not of love indeed but
marriage. He would marry her and hurry home
with his prize and tear the wrappings from her loveliness, clumsily, stupidly, in a mood of morbidly
inflamed desire."

"Sarnac," said Firefly, "you are horrible."

"No," said Sarnac. "But that world of the
past was horrible. Most of the women, your ances-
tors, suffered such things. And that was only the
beginning of the horror. Then came the birth and
desecration of the children. Think what a delicate,
precious and holy thing a child is ! They were
begotten abundantly and abnormally, born reluctantly,
and dropped into the squalor and infection of an
overcrowded disordered world. Bearing a child was
not the jolly wholesome process we know to-day ;
in that diseased society it was an illness, it counted
as an illness, for nearly every woman. Which the
man her husband resented—grossly. Five or six
children in five or six years and a pretty girl was
a cross, worried wreck of a woman, bereft of any
shred of spirit or beauty. My poor scolding, worried
mother was not fifty when she died. And one saw
one's exquisite infants grow up into ill-dressed,
under-nourished, ill-educated children. Think of
the agony of shamed love that lay beneath my poor

82

mother's slaps and scoldings ! The world has forgotten now the hate and bitterness of disappointed
parentage. That was the prospect of the moral life
that opened before my sister Fanny ; that was the
antistrophe to the siren song of her imagination.

" She could not believe this of life and love. She
experimented with love and herself. She was, my
mother said, ' a bold, bad girl.' She began I know
with furtive kissings and huggings in the twilight,
with boy schoolfellows, with clerks and errand boys.
Some gleam of nastiness came into these adventures
of the dusk and made her recoil. At any rate she
became prim and aloof to Cherry Gardens, but only
because she was drawn to the bands and lights and
prosperity of Cliffstone. That was when she began
to read and correct her accent. You have heard of
our old social stratifications. She wanted to be like
a lady ; she wanted to meet a gentleman. She
imagined there were gentlemen who were really
gentle, generous, wise and delightful, and she imagined
that some of the men she saw on the cliff promenade
at Cliffstone were gentlemen. She began to dress
herself as I have told.

" There were scores of such girls in every town
in Europe," said Sarnac, " turning their backs on
their dreadful homes. In a sort of desperate hope.

" When you hear about the moral code of the
old world," Sarnac went on, " you are apt to think
of it as a rule that everyone respected in exactly
the same way that you think everyone believed the
professed religions. We have not so much a moral
code now as a moral training, and our religion involves
no strain on reason or instincts, and so it is difficult

for us to understand the tortuosity and evasions and defiances and general furtiveness and meanness of a world in which nobody really understood and believed the religious creeds, not even the priests, and nobody was really convinced to the bone of the sweetness and justice of the moral code. In that distant age almost everybody was sexually angry or uncomfortable or dishonest ; the restraints we had did not so much restrain as provoke people. It is difficult to imagine it now."

"Not if you read the old literature," said Sunray. "The novels and plays are pathological."

"So you have my pretty sister Fanny, drawn by impulses she did not understand, flitting like a moth out of our dingy home in Cherry Gardens to the lights, bright lights of hope they seemed to her, about the bandstand and promenade of Cliffstone. And there staying in the lodging-houses and boarding-houses and hotels were limited and thwarted people, keeping holiday, craving for bright excitements, seeking casual pleasures. There were wives who had tired of their husbands and husbands long weary of their wives, there were separated people who could not divorce and young men who could not marry because they could not afford to maintain a family. With their poor hearts full of naughtiness, rebellious suppressions, jealousies, resentments. And through this crowd, eager, provocative, and defenceless, flitted my pretty sister Fanny."

§ 4

"On the evening before Fanny ran away my father and my uncle sat in the kitchen by the fire

84

discoursing of politics and the evils of life. They had both been keeping up their peckers very resolutely during the day and this gave a certain rambling and recurrent quality to their review. Their voices were hoarse, and they drawled and were loud and emphatic and impressive. It was as if they spoke for the benefit of unseen listeners. Often they would both be talking together. My mother was in the scullery washing up the tea-things and I was sitting at the table near the lamp trying to do some homework my teacher had given me, so far as the distraction of this conversation so close to me and occasional appeals to me to 'mark' this or that, would permit. Prue was reading a book called *Ministering Children* to which she was much addicted. Fanny had been helping my mother until she was told she was more a hindrance than a help. Then she came and stood at my side looking over my shoulder at what I was doing.

" ' What's spoiling trade and ruining the country,' said my uncle, ' is these 'ere strikes. These 'ere strikes reg'ler destrushion—destruction for the country.'

" ' Stop everything,' said my father. ' It stands to reason.'

" ' They didn't ought to be allowed. These 'ere miners'r paid and paid 'andsomely. Paid 'andsomely they are. 'Andsomely. Why ! I'd be glad of the pay they get, glad of it. They 'as bulldogs, they 'as pianos. Champagne. Me and you, Smith, me and you and the middle classes generally ; we don't get pianos. We don't get champagne. Not-tit. . . .'

" ' Ought to be a Middle Classes Union,' said my father, ' keep these 'ere workers in their places.

85

They 'old up the country and stop trade. Trade !
Trade's orful. Why ! people come in now and
look at what you got and arst the price of this and
that. Think twice they do before they spend a
sixpence. . . . And the coal you're expected to
sell nowadays ! I tell 'em, if this 'ere strike comes
off this 's 'bout the last coal you're likely to see,
good *or* bad. Straight out, I tell 'em. . . . '

" ' You're not working, Harry,' said Fanny without troubling to lower her voice. ' Don't see how
you *can* work, with all this jawing going on. Come
out for a walk.'

" I glanced up at her and rose at once. It wasn't
often Fanny asked me to go for a walk with her.
I put my books away.

" ' Going out for a bit of fresh air, mother,' said
Fanny, taking her hat down from its peg.

" ' No, you don't—not at this time,' cried my mother
from the scullery. ' Ain't I said, once and for all——? '

" ' It's all right, mother, Harry's going with me.
He'll see no one runs away with me and ruins me.
. . . You've said it once and for all—times enough.'

" My mother made no further objection, but she
flashed a look of infinite hate at my sister.

" We went upstairs and out into the street.

" For a time we said nothing, but I had a sense
that I was going to be ' told things.'

" ' I've had about enough of all this,' Fanny began
presently. ' What's going to become of us ? Father
and uncle 've been drinking all day ; you can see
they're both more than half-screwed. Both of 'em.
It's every day now. It's worse and worse and worse.
Uncle hasn't had a job these ten days. Father's

always with him. The shop's getting filthy. He doesn't sweep it out now for days together.'

"'Uncle seems to have lost 'eart,' I said, 'since he heard that Aunt Adelaide would have to have that second operation.'

"'Lost heart! He never had any heart to lose.' My sister Fanny said no more of my uncle—by an effort. '*What* a home!' she cried.

"She paused for a moment. 'Harry,' she said, 'I'm going to get out of this. Soon.'

"I asked what she meant by that.

"'Never mind what I mean. I've got a situation. A different sort of situation. . . . Harry, you—you care for me, Harry?'

"Professions of affection are difficult for boys of thirteen. 'I'd do anything for you, Fanny,' I said after a pause. 'You know I would.'

"'And you wouldn't tell on me?'

"'Whad you take me for?'

"'Nohow?'

"'No'ow.'

"'I knew you wouldn't,' said Fanny. 'You're the only one of the whole crew I'll be sorry to leave. I *do* care for you, Harry. Straight, I do. I used to care for mother. Once. But that's different. She's scolded me and screamed at me till it's gone. Every bit of it. I can't help it,—it's gone. I'll think of you, Harry—often.'

"I realised that Fanny was crying. Then when I glanced at her again her tears were over.

"'Look here, Harry,' she said, 'would you do—something—for me. Something—not so very much—and not tell? Not tell afterwards, I mean.'

" ' I'd do anything, Fanny.'

" ' It's not so very much really. There's that little old portmanteau upstairs. I've put some things in it. And there's a little bundle. I've put 'em both under the bed at the back where even Prying Prue won't think of looking. And to-morrow—when father's out with uncle like he is now every day, and mother's getting dinner downstairs and Prue's pretending to help her and sneaking bits of bread—if you'd bring those down to Cliffstone to Crosby's side-door. . . . They aren't so very heavy.'

" ' I ain't afraid of your portmanteau, Fanny. I'd carry it more miles than that for you. But where's this new situation of yours, Fanny? and why ain't you saying a word about it at home?'

" ' Suppose I asked you something harder than carrying a portmanteau, Harry?'

" ' I'd do it, Fanny, if I could do it. You know that, Fanny.'

" ' But if it was just to ask no questions of where I am going and what I am going to do. It's—it's a good situation, Harry. It isn't hard work.'

" She stopped short. I saw her face by the yellow light of a street lamp and I was astonished to see it radiant with happiness. And yet her eyes were shining with tears. What a Fanny it was, who could pass in a dozen steps from weeping to ecstasy!'

" ' Oh! I wish I could tell you all about it, Harry,' she said. ' I wish I could tell you all about it. Don't you worry about me, Harry, or what's going to happen to me. You help me, and after a bit I'll write to you. I will indeed, Harry.'

" ' You aren't going to run away and marry?'

I asked abruptly. 'It'd be like you, Fanny, to do that.'

"'I won't say I am ; I won't say I'm not ; I won't say anything, Harry. But I'm as happy as the sunrise, Harry ! I could dance and sing. If only I can do it, Harry.'

"'There's one thing, Fanny.'

"She stopped dead. 'You're not going back on me, Harry ?'

"'No. I'll do what I've promised, Fanny. But ——' I had a moral mind. I hesitated. 'You're not doing anything wrong, Fanny ?'

"She shook her head and did not answer for some moments. The look of ecstasy returned.

"'I'm doing the rightest thing that ever I did, Harry, the rightest thing. If only I can do it. And you are a dear to help me, a perfect dear.'

"And suddenly she put her arms about me and drew my face to hers and kissed me and then she pushed me away and danced a step. 'I love al the world to-night,' said Fanny. 'I love all the world. Silly old Cherry Gardens ! You thought you'd got me ! You thought I'd never get away !'

"She began a sort of chant of escape. 'To-morrow's my last day at Crosby's, my very last day. For ever and ever. Amen. He'll never come too near me again and breathe down my neck. He'll never put his fat hand on my bare arm and shove his face close to mine while he looks at my cash-sheet. When I get to ——, wherever I'm going, Harry, I'll want to send him a post card. Good-bye, Mr. Crosby, good-bye, *dear* Mr. Crosby. For ever and ever. Amen !' She made what I knew to be

her imitation of Mr. Crosby's voice. ' You're the
sort of girl who ought to marry young and have a
steady husband older than yourself, my dear. Did
I ought ? And who said you might call me your
dear, dear Mr. Crosby ? Twenty-five shillings a
week and pawings about and being called *dear*, thrown
in. . . . I'm wild to-night, Harry—wild to-night.
I could laugh and scream, and yet I want to cry,
Harry, because I'm leaving you. And leaving them
all ! Though why I care I don't know. Poor,
boozy, old father ! Poor, silly, scolding mother !
Some day perhaps I may help them if only I get
away. And you—you've got to go on learning and
improving, Harry, learning, learning. Learn and
get out of Cherry Gardens. Never drink. Never
let drink cross your lips. Don't smoke. For why
should anyone smoke ? Take the top side of life,
for it's easier up there. Indeed, it's easier. Work
and read, Harry. Learn French—so that when I
come back to see you, we can both talk together.'

" ' You're going to learn French ? You're going
to France ? '

" ' Farther than France. But not a word, Harry.
Not a word of it. But I wish I could tell you everything. I can't. I mustn't. I've given my promise.
I've got to keep faith. All one has to do in the
world is to love and keep faith. But I wish mother
had let me help wash-up to-night, my last night.
She hates me. She'll hate me more yet. . . . I
wonder if I'll keep awake all night or cry myself
to sleep. Let's race as far as the goods-station, Harry,
and then walk home.' "

§ 5

" The next night Fanny did not come home at all. As the hours passed and the emotion of my family deepened I began to realise the full enormity of the disaster that had come upon our home."

Sarnac paused and smiled. " Never was there so *clinging* a dream. I am still half Harry Mortimer Smith and only half myself. I am still not only in memory but half in feeling also that young English barbarian in the Age of Confusion. And yet all the time I am looking at my story from our point of view and telling it in Sarnac's voice. Amidst this sunshine. . . . Was it really a dream ? . . . I don't believe I am telling you a dream."

" It isn't a bit like a dream," said Willow. " It is a story—a real story. Do you think it was a dream?"

Sunray shook her head. " Go on," she said to Sarnac. " Whatever it is, tell it. Tell us how your family behaved when Fanny ran away."

" You must keep in mind that all these poor souls were living in a world of repressions such as seem almost inconceivable now. You think they had ideas about love and sex and duty different from our ideas. We are taught that they had different ideas. But that is not the truth ; the truth is that they had no clear, thought-out ideas about such things at all. They had fears and blank prohibitions and ignorances where we have ideas. Love, sex, these were things like the enchanted woods of a fairy tale. It was forbidden even to go in. And— none of us knew to what extent—Fanny had gone in.

" So that evening was an evening of alarm deepening to a sort of moral panic for the whole household. It seemed to be required of my family that they should all behave irrationally and violently. My mother began to fret about half-past nine. ' I've tole 'er, once for all,' she said, partly to herself but also for my benefit. ' It's got to stop.' She cross-examined me about where Fanny might be. Had she said anything about going on the pier ? I said I didn't know. My mother fumed and fretted. Even if Fanny had gone on the pier she ought to be home by ten. I wasn't sent to bed at the usual hour so that I saw my father and uncle come in after the public-house had closed. I forget now why my uncle came in to us instead of going straight home, but it was not a very unusual thing for him to do so. They were already disposed to despondency and my mother's white face and anxious tidings deepened their gloom.

" ' Mortimer,' said my mother, ' that gal of yours 'as gone a bit too far. Sarf-pars' ten and she isn't 'ome yet.'

" ' Aven't I tole 'er time after time,' said my father, ' she's got to be in by nine ? '

" ' Not times enough you 'aven't,' said my mother, ' and 'ere's the fruit ! '

" ' I've tole 'er time after time,' said my father. ' Time after time.' And he continued to repeat this at intervals throughout the subsequent discussion until another refrain replaced it.

" My uncle said little at first. He took up his position on the hearthrug my father had made and stood there, swaying slightly, hiccoughing at intervals behind his hand, frowning and scrutinising the faces of the speakers. At last he delivered his judgment. 'Somethin'sappened to that girl,' he said. 'You mark my words.'

" Prue had a mind apt for horrors. 'She's bin in 'naccident per'aps,' she said. 'She may've bin knocked down.'

" ' I've tole 'er,' said my father, ' time after time.'

" ' If there's bin 'naccident,' said my uncle sagely. ' Well . . . 'nything ma've 'appened.' He repeated this statement in a louder firmer voice. ''Nything ma've 'appened.'

" ''Stime you went to bed, Prue,' said my mother, ' 'igh time. N you too, 'Arry.'

" My sister got up with unusual promptitude and went out of the room. I think she must have had an idea then of looking for Fanny's things. I lingered.

" ' May've been 'naccident, may not,' said my mother darkly. ' Sworse things than accidents.'

" ' Whaddyoumean by that, Marth ? ' asked my uncle.

" ' Never mind what I mean. That girl's worried me times and oft. There's worse things than accidents.'

" I listened thrilled. ' You be orf to bed, 'Arry,' said my mother.

" ' Whaddyou got to do,—simple,' said my uncle, leaning forward on his toes. ' Telephone 'ospitals. Telephone plice. Old Crow at the *Wellington* won't-'ve gone to bed. 'Sgot telephone. Good customers. 'E'll telephone. Mark my words—s'snaccident.'

" And then Prue reappeared at the top of the stairs.

" ' *Mother !* ' she said in a loud whisper.

" ' You be orf to bed, miss,' said my mother. ' 'Aven't I got worries enough ? '

" ' Mother,' said Prue. ' You know that little old portmantle of Fanny's ? '

" Everyone faced a new realisation.

" ' Sgorn,' said Prue, ' And her two best 'ats and all 'er undercloe's and 'er other dress—gorn too.'

" ' Then she's took 'em ! ' said my father.

" ' And 'erself ! ' said my mother.

" ' Time after time I tole her,' said my father.

" ' She's run away ! ' said my mother with a scream in her voice. ' She's brought shame and disgrace on us ! She's run away ! '

" ' Someone's got 'old of 'er,' said my father.

" My mother sat down abruptly. ' After all I done for 'er ! ' she cried, beginning to weep. ' With an honest man ready to marry 'er ! Toil and sacrifice, care and warnings, and she's brought us to shame and dishonour ! She's run away ! That I should 'ave lived to see this day ! Fanny ! '

" She jumped up suddenly to go and see with her own eyes that Prue's report was true. I made myself as inconspicuous as possible, for I feared some chance question might reveal my share in our family tragedy. But I didn't want to go to bed ; I wanted to hear things out.

" ' Sanny good my going to the plice-station for you on my way 'ome ? ' my uncle asked.

" ' Plice ! ' said my father. ' What good's plice ? Gaw ! If I 'ad my 'ands on that villain's throat —I'd plice 'im ! Bringing shame on me and mine ! *Plice !* 'Ere's Fanny, my little daughter Fanny, beguiled and misled and carried away ! . . . I'm 'asty. . . . Yes, John. You go in and tell the plice. It's on your way. Tell 'em from me. I

won't leave not a single stone unturned so's to bring
'er back.'

"My mother came back whiter than ever. 'It's
right enough,' she said. 'She's gorn! She's off.
While we stand 'ere, disgraced and shamed, she's away.'

"'Who with?' said my father. 'That's the
question, who with? 'Arry, 'ave you ever seen
anyone about with your sister? Anyone 'anging
about? Any suspicious-looking sort of dressed-up
fancy man? 'Ave you ever?'

"I said I hadn't.

"But Prue had evidence. She became voluble.
About a week ago she had seen Fanny and a man
coming along from Cliffstone, talking. They hadn't
seen her; they had been too wrapped up in each
other. Her description of the man was very vague
and was concerned chiefly with his clothes; he had
worn a blue serge suit and a grey felt hat; he was
'sort of a gentleman like.' He was a good lot
older than Fanny—Prue wasn't sure whether he
had a moustache or not.

"My father interrupted Prue's evidence by a
tremendous saying which I was to hear him repeat
time after time during the next week. 'Sooner'n
this sh'd've 'appened,' said my father, 'I'd 've seen
'er lying dead at my feet—*gladly* I'd've seen 'er
lying dead at my feet!'

"'Poor girl!' said my uncle. 'Sabitter lesson
she 'as before 'er. A *bitter* lesson! Poo' chile!
Poo' little Fanny!'

"'Poor Fanny indeed!' cried my mother vindic-
tively, seeing it all, I perceived, from an entirely
different angle. 'There she is prancin' about with

'er fancy gentleman now in all 'er fallals ; dinners
and wine she'll 'ave, flowers she'll 'ave, dresses and
everything ! Be took about and shown things !
Shown off and took to theayters. The shame of
it ! And us 'ere shamed and disgraced and not a
word to say when the neighbours ask us questions !
'Ow can I look 'em in the face ? 'Ow can I look
Mr. Crosby in the face ? That man was ready to
go down on 'is bended knees to 'er and worship 'er.
Stout though 'e was. 'E'd 'ave given 'er anything
she arst for—in reason. What 'e could see in 'er,
I could never make out. But see it 'e did. And
now I've got to face 'im and tell 'im I've told 'im
wrong. Time after time I've said to 'im—" *You wait.
You wait, Mr. Crosby.*" And that 'uzzy !—sly and
stuck-up and deep ! Gorn ! '

" My father's voice came booming over my mother's
shrill outcry. 'Sooner'n this should've 'appened I'd
've seen 'er dead at my feet ! '

" I was moved to protest. But for all my thirteen
years I found myself weeping. ' 'Ow d'you *know*,'
I blubbered, ' that Fanny 'asn't gone away and got
married ? 'Ow d'you know ? '

" ' Married ! ' cried my mother. ' Why should
she run away to be married ! If it was merridge,
what was to prevent 'er bringing 'im 'ome and having
'im interjuced to us all, right and proper ? Isn't her
own father and mother and 'ome good enough for her,
that she 'as to run away and get married ? When she
could 'ave 'ad it 'ere at St. Jude's nice and respectable
with your father and your uncle and all of us and white
favours and a carriage and all. I wish I could 'ope
she was merried ! I wish there was a chance of it ! '

" My uncle shook his head in confirmation.

" ' Sooner 'n this should 've 'appened,' boomed my father, ' I'd 've seen 'er dead at my feet ! '

" ' Last night,' said Prue, ' she said 'er prayers.'

" ' Didn't she *always* say 'er prayers ? ' asked my uncle, shocked.

" ' Not kneeling down,' said Prue. ' But last night she was kneeling quite a long time. She thought I was asleep but I watched 'er.'

" ' That looks bad,' said my uncle. ' Y'know, Smith ; that looks bad. I don't like that praying. Sominous. I don't like it.'

" And then suddenly and violently Prue and I were packed off upstairs to bed.

" For long the sound of their voices went on ; the three of them came up into the shop and stood at the front door while my uncle gradually took leave, but what further things they said I did not hear. But I remember that suddenly I had a brilliant idea, suggested no doubt by Prue's scrap of evidence. I got out of bed and knelt down and said, ' Pray God, be kind to my Fanny ! Pray God not to be hard on Fanny ! I'm sure she means to get married. For ever and ever. Amen.' And after putting Providence upon his honour, so to speak, in this fashion, I felt less mentally distracted and got back into bed and presently I fell asleep."

Sarnac paused.

" It's all rather puzzling," said Willow.

" It seemed perfectly natural at the time," said Sarnac.

" That pork butcher was evidently a repulsive creature," said Firefly. " Why didn't they object to him ? "

" Because the importance of the marriage ceremonial was so great in those days as to dominate the entire situation. I knew Crosby quite well ; he was a cunning-faced oily-mannered humbug with a bald head, fat red ears, a red complexion and a paunch. There are no such people in the world now ; you must recall some incredible gross old-world caricature to imagine him. Nowadays you would as soon think of coupling the life of a girl with some gross heavy animal as with such a man. But that mattered nothing to my father or my mother. My mother I suspect rather liked the idea of the physical humiliation of Fanny. She no doubt had had her own humiliations—for the sexual life of this old world was a tangle of clumsy ignorances and secret shames. Except for my mother's real hostility to Fanny I remember scarcely a scrap of any simple natural feeling, let alone any reasonable thinking, in all that terrible fuss they made. Men and women in those days were so much more complex and artificial than they are now ; in a muddled way they were amazingly intricate. You know that monkeys, even young monkeys, have old and wrinkled faces, and it is equally true that in the Age of Confusion life was so perplexing and irrational that while we were still children our minds were already old and wrinkled. Even to my boyish observation it was clear that my father was acting the whole time ; he was behaving as he imagined he was expected to behave. Never for a moment either when drunk or sober did he even attempt to find out, much less to express, what he was feeling naturally about Fanny. He was afraid to do so. And that night we were all acting—all of us. We were all afraid to do anything but act in what we imagined would be regarded as a virtuous rôle."

"But what were you afraid of?" asked Radiant. "Why did you act?"

"I don't know. Afraid of blame. Afraid of the herd. A habit of fear. A habit of inhibition."

"What was the objection to the real lover?" asked Firefly. "I don't understand all this indignation."

"They guessed rightly enough that he did not intend to marry Fanny."

"What sort of a man was he?

"I never saw him until many years afterwards. But I will tell you about that when I come to it."

"Was he—the sort of man one could love?"

"Fanny loved him. She had every reason to do so. He took care of her. He got her the education she craved for. He gave her a life full of interest. I believe he was an honest and delightful man."

"They stuck to each other?"

"Yes."

"Then why didn't he marry her—if it was the custom?"

"He was married already. Marriage had embittered him. It embittered many people. He'd been cheated. He had been married by a woman who pretended love to impose herself upon him and his fortunes and he had found her out."

"Not a very difficult discovery," said Firefly.

"No."

"But why couldn't they divorce?"

"In those days it took two to make a divorce. She wouldn't let him loose. She just stuck on and lived on his loneliness. If he had been poor he would probably have tried to murder her, but as it happened he had the knack of success and he was rich. Rich people could take liberties with marriage-restrictions that were absolutely impossible for the poor. And he was, I should guess, sensitive, affectionate and energetic. Heaven knows what sort of mind he was in when he came upon Fanny. He 'picked her up,' as people used to say casually. The old world was full of such pitiful adventures in encounter. Almost always they meant disaster, but this was an exceptional case. Perhaps it was as lucky for him that he met her as it was for her that she met him. Fanny you know was one of those people you have to be honest with ; she was acute and simple ; she cut like a clean sharp knife. They were both in danger and want ; the ugliest chances might have happened to her and he was far gone on the way to promiscuity and complete sexual degradation. . . . But I can't go off on Fanny's story. In the end she probably married him. They were going to marry. In some way the other woman did at last make it possible."

" But why don't you know for certain ? "

" Because I was shot before that happened. If it happened at all."

§ 6

" *No !* " cried Sarnac, stopping a question from Willow by a gesture.

" I shall never tell my story," said Sarnac, " if you interrupt with questions. I was telling you of the storm of misfortunes that wrecked our household at Cherry Gardens. . . .

"My father was killed within three weeks of Fanny's elopement. He was killed upon the road between Cherry Gardens and Cliffstone. There was a young gentleman named Wickersham with one of the new petrol-driven motor-cars that were just coming into use ; he was hurrying home as fast as possible, he told the coroner, because his brakes were out of order and he was afraid of an accident. My father was walking with my uncle along the pavement, talking. He found the pavement too restricted for his subject and gestures, and he stepped off suddenly into the roadway and was struck by the car from behind and knocked headlong and instantly killed.

"The effect upon my uncle was very profound. For some days he was thoughtful and sober and he missed a race-meeting. He was very helpful over the details of the funeral.

"'You can't say 'e wasn't prepared, Marth,' he told my mother. 'You can't say 'e wasn't prepared. Very moment 'e was killed, 'e 'ad the name 'v' Providence on 'is lips. 'E'd been saying 'ow sorely 'e'd been tried by this and that.'

"''E wasn't the only one,' said my mother.

"''E was saying 'e knew it was only to teach 'im some lesson though he couldn't rightly say what the lesson was. 'E was convinced that everything that 'appened to us, good though it seemed or bad though it seemed, was surely for the best. . . .'

"My uncle paused dramatically.

"'And then the car 'it 'im,' said my mother, trying to picture the scene.

"''Then the car 'it 'im,' said my uncle."

The Widow Smith moves to London

§ I

" IN those days," said Sarnac, " the great majority of the dead were put into coffins and buried underground. Some few people were burnt, but that was an innovation and contrary to the very materialistic religious ideas of the time. This was a world in which you must remember people were still repeating in perfect good faith a creed which included ' the resurrection of the body and the life everlasting.' Intellectually old Egypt and her dreaming mummies still ruled the common people of the European world. The Christian creeds were themselves mummies from Lower Egypt. As my father said on one occasion when he was discussing this question of cremation : ' It might prove a bit orkward at the Resurrection. Like not 'aving a proper wedding garment so to speak. . . .

" ' Though there's sharks,' said my father, whose mental transitions were sometimes abrupt. ' And them as 'ave been eat by lions. Many of the best Christian martyrs in their time was eat by lions. . . . They'd *certainly* be given bodies. . . .

" ' And if *one* is given a body why not another ? ' said my father, lifting mild and magnified eyes in enquiry.

" ' It's a difficult question,' my father decided.

" At any rate there was no discussion of cremation in his case. We had a sort of hearse-coach with a place for the coffin in front to take him to the cemetery, and in this vehicle my mother and Prue travelled also ; my elder brother Ernest, who had come down from London for the occasion, and my uncle and I walked ahead and waited for it at the cemetery gates and followed the coffin to the grave-side. We were all in black clothes, even black gloves, in spite of the fact that we were wretchedly poor.

" ' 'Twon't be my last visit to this place this year,' said my uncle despondently, ' not if Adelaide goes on as she's doing.'

" Ernest was silent. He disliked my uncle and was brooding over him. From the moment of his arrival he had shown a deepening objection to my uncle's existence.

" ' There's luck they say in funerals,' said my uncle presently, striking a brighter note. ' Fi keep my eye open I dessay I may get a 'int of somethin'.'

" Ernest remained dour.

" We followed the men carrying the coffin towards the cemetery chapel in a little procession led by Mr. Snapes in his clerical robes. He began to read out words that I realised were beautiful and touching and that concerned strange and faraway things : ' I am the Resurrection and the Life. He that believeth in Me though he were dead yet shall he live. . . .'

" ' I know that my Redeemer liveth and that He shall stand at the latter day upon the earth. . . .'

" ' We brought nothing into this world, and it is certain we can carry nothing out. The Lord gave, and the Lord hath taken away ; blessed be the Name of the Lord.'

" Suddenly I forgot the bickerings of my uncle and brother and was overcome with tenderness and grief for my father. A rush from my memory of many clumsy kindlinesses, a realisation of the loss of his companionship came to me. I recalled the happiness of many of my Sunday tramps by his side in spring-time, on golden summer evenings, in winter when the frost had picked out every twig in the downland hedgerows. I thought of his endless edifying discourses about flowers and rabbits and hill-sides and distant stars. And he was gone. I should never hear his voice again. I should never see again his dear old eyes magnified to an immense wonder through his spectacles. I should never have a chance of telling him how I cared for him. And I had never told him I cared for him. Indeed, I had never realised I cared for him until now. He was lying stiff and still and submissive in that coffin, a rejected man. Life had treated him badly. He had never had a dog's chance. My mind leapt forward beyond my years and I understood what a tissue of petty humiliations and disappointments and degradations his life had been. I saw then as clearly as I see now the immense pity of such a life. Sorrow possessed me. I wept as I stumbled along after him. I had great difficulty in preventing myself from weeping aloud."

§ 2

"After the funeral my brother Ernest and my uncle had a violent wrangle about my mother's future. Seeing that my Aunt Adelaide was for all practical purposes done for, my uncle suggested that he should sell up most of his furniture, ' bring his

capital' into the greengrocery business and come
and live with his sister. But my brother declared
that the greengrocery business was a dying concern,
and was for my mother moving into a house in Cliffstone when she might let lodgings. Prue would
be 'no end of a 'elp' in that. At first this was
opposed by my uncle and then he came round to
the idea on condition that he participated in the bene-
fits of the scheme, but this Ernest opposed, asking
rather rudely what sort of help my uncle supposed
he would be in a lodging-house. 'Let alone you're
never out of bed before ten,' he said, though how
he knew of this fact did not appear.

"Ernest had been living in London, working at
a garage ; he drove hired cars by the month or job,
and his respect for the upper classes had somehow
disappeared. The dignity of Sir John ffrench-Cuthbertson at secondhand left him cold and scornful.
'You ain't going to 'ave *my* mother to work for you
and wait on you, no'ow,' he said.

"While this dispute went on my mother with
the assistance of Prue was setting out the cold colla-
tion which in those days was the redeeming feature
of every funeral. There was cold ham and chicken.
My uncle abandoned his position of vantage on my
father's rag hearthrug and we all sat down to our
exceptional meal.

"For some little time the cold ham and chicken
made a sort of truce between my brother Ernest
and my uncle, but presently my uncle sighed, drank
off his beer and reopened the argument. 'You
know I think, Marth,' he said spearing a potato
from the dish neatly with his fork, '*you* ought to

'ave some voice in what is going to become of you. Me and this young man from London 've been 'aving a bit of a difference 'bout what you ought to do.'

" I realised abruptly from the expression of my mother's white face, a sort of white intentness which her widow's cap seemed to emphasise, that she was quite determined to have not only some voice but a decisive voice in this matter, but before she could say anything my brother Ernest had intervened.

" ' It's like this, mother,' he said, ' you got to do something, 'aven't you ? '

" My mother was about to reply when Ernest snatched a sort of assent from her and proceeded : ' Well, naturally I ask, what sort of thing can you do ? And *as* naturally, I answer Lodgings. You carn't expect to go on being a greengrocer, because that ain't natural for a woman, considering the weights and coal that 'as to be lifted.'

" ' And could be lifted easy, with a man to 'elp 'er,' said my uncle.

" ' If 'e *was* a man,' said my brother Ernest with bitter sarcasm.

" ' Meaning—— ? ' asked my uncle with cold hauteur.

" ' What I say,' said brother Ernest. ' No more, no less. So if you take my advice, mother, what you'll do is this. You go down early to-morrow to Cliffstone to look for a suitable little 'ouse big enough to 'old lodgers and not so big as to break your back, and I'll go and talk to Mr. Bulstrode about ending up your tenancy 'ere. Then we'll be able to see where we are.'

" Again my mother attempted to speak and was overborne.

" ' 'Fyou think I'm going to be treated as a nonentity,' said my uncle, 'you're making the biggest mistake you ever made in your life. See? Now you listen to me, Marth——'

" ' You shut up ! ' said my brother. ' Mother's *my* business first and foremost.'

" ' *Shut up !* ' echoed my uncle. ' Wot *manners !* At a funeral. From a chap not a third my age, a mere 'azardous empty boy ! *Shut* up ! You shut up yourself, my boy, and listen to those who know a bit more about life than you do. I've smacked your 'ed before to-day. Not once or twice either. And I warmed your 'ide when you stole them peaches —and much good it did you ! I oughter've took yer skin off ! You and me 'ave never got on much, and unless you keep a civil tongue in your head we ain't going to get on now.'

" ' Seeing which,' said brother Ernest with a dangerous calmness ; ' the sooner you make yourself scarce the better for all concerned.'

" ' Not to leave my on'y sister's affairs in the 'ands of a cub like you.'

" Again my mother essayed to speak, but the angry voices disregarded her.

" ' I tell you you're going to get out, and if you can't get out of your own discretion I warn you I'll 'ave to 'elp you.'

" ' Not when you're in mourning,' said my mother. ' Not wearing your mourning. And besides——'

" But they were both too heated now to attend to her.

" ' You're pretty big with your talk,' said my uncle, ' but don't you preshume too far on my forbearance. I've 'ad about enough of this.'

" ' So've I,' said my brother Ernest and stood up.

" My uncle stood up too and they glared at one another.

" ' That's the door,' said my brother darkly.

" My uncle walked back to his wonted place on the hearthrug. 'Now don't let's 'ave any quarrelling on a day like this,' he said. 'If you 'aven't any consideration for your mother you might at least think of 'Im who has passed beyond. My objec' 'ere is simply to try n'range things so's be best for all. And what I say is this, the ideer of your mother going into a lodging-'ouse alone, without a man's 'elp, is ridiculous, perfectly ridiculous, and only a first-class inconsiderate young fool——'

" My brother Ernest went and stood close to my uncle. 'You've said enough,' he remarked. 'This affair's between me and my mother and your motto is Get Out. See?'

" Again my mother had something to say and again she was silenced. "'This is man's work, mother,' said Ernest. 'Are you going to shift it, uncle?'

" My uncle faced up to this threat of Ernest. 'I've a juty to my sister——'

" And then I regret to say my brother laid hands on him. He took him by the collar and by the wrist and for a moment the two black-clad figures swayed.

"'Lea' go my coat,' said my uncle. 'Lea' go my coat collar.'

" But a thirst for violence had taken possession of Ernest. My mother and Prue and I stood aghast.

"'Ernie!' cried my mother. 'You forget yourself!'

"''Sall *right*, mother,' said Ernie, and whirled my

uncle violently from the hearthrug to the bottom
of the staircase. Then he shifted his grip from
my uncle's wrist to the seat of his tight black trousers
and partly lifted and partly impelled him up the
staircase. My uncle's arms waved wildly as if he
clutched at his lost dignity.

"' John ! ' cried my mother. ' 'Ere's your 'at ! '

" I had a glimpse of my uncle's eye as he vanished
up the staircase. He seemed to be looking for his
hat. But he was now offering no serious opposition
to my brother Ernest's handling of him.

"'Give it 'im, 'Arry,' said my mother. 'And
there's 'is gloves too.'

" I took the black hat and the black gloves and
followed the struggle upstairs. Astonished and unre-
sisting my uncle was propelled through the front
door into the street and stood there panting and
regarding my brother. His collar was torn from its
stud and his black tie disarranged. Ernest was
breathing heavily. 'Now you be orf and mind
your own business,' said Ernie.

" Ernie turned with a start as I pushed past him.
''Ere's your 'at and gloves, uncle,' I said, handing
them to him. He took them mechanically, his eyes
still fixed on Ernest.

"' And you're the boy I trained to be 'onest,'
said my uncle to my brother Ernest, very bitterly.
' Leastways I tried to. You're the young worm
I fattened up at my gardens and showed such kindness to ! *Gratitood !* '

" He regarded the hat in his hand for a moment
as though it was some strange object, and then by
a happy inspiration put it on his head.

THE DREAM

" ' God 'elp your poor mother,' said my Uncle John Julip. ' God 'elp 'er.'

" He had nothing more to say. He looked up the street and down and then turned as by a sort of necessity in the direction of the *Wellington* public-house. And in this manner was my Uncle John Julip on the day of my father's funeral cast forth into the streets of Cherry Gardens, a prospective widower and a most pathetic and unhappy little man. That dingy little black figure in retreat still haunts my memory. Even from the back he looked amazed. Never did a man who has not been kicked look so like a man who has been. I never saw him again. I have no doubt that he carried his sorrows down to the *Wellington* and got himself thoroughly drunk, and I have as little doubt that he missed my father dreadfully all the time he was doing so.

" My brother Ernest returned thoughtfully to the kitchen. He was already a little abashed at his own violence. I followed him respectfully.

" ' You didn't ought t'ave done that,' said my mother.

" ' What right 'as 'e to plant 'imself on you to be kept and waited on ? '

" ' 'E wouldn't 'ave planted 'imself on me,' my mother replied. ' You get 'eated, Ernie, same as you used to do, and you won't listen to anything.'

" ' I never did fancy uncle,' said Ernie.

" ' When you get 'eated, Ernie, you seem to forget everything,' said my mother. ' You might've remembered 'e was my brother.'

" ' Fine brother ! ' said Ernie. ' Why !—who started all that stealing ? Who led poor father to drink and bet ? '

" ' All the same,' said my mother, ' you 'adn't no right to 'andle 'im as you did. And your poor father 'ardly cold in 'is grave ! ' She wept. She produced a black-bordered handkerchief and mopped her eyes. ' I did 'ope your poor father would 'ave a nice funeral—all the trouble and expense—and now you've spoilt it. I'll never be able to look back on this day with pleasure, not if I live to be a 'undred years, I'll always remember 'ow you spoilt your own father's funeral—turning on your uncle like this.'

" Ernest had no answer for her reproaches. ' He shouldn't 've argued and said what he did,' he objected.

" ' And all so unnecessary ! All along I've been trying to tell you you needn't worry about me. I don't want no lodging-'ouse in Cliffstone—*with* your uncle or *without* your uncle. I wrote to Matilda Good a week come Tuesday and settled everything with 'er—everything. It's settled.'

" ' What d'you mean ? ' asked Ernest.

" ' Why, that 'ouse of hers in Pimlico. She's been wanting trusty 'elp for a long time, what with her varicose veins up and downstairs and one thing 'nother, and directly she got my letter about your poor dear father she wrote orf to me. " You need never want a 'ome," she says, " so long as I got a lodger. You and Prue are welcome," she says, " welcome 'elp, and the boy can easy find work up 'ere—much easier than 'e can in Cliffstone." All the time you was planning lodging-'ouses and things for me I was trying to tell you——'

" ' You mean it's settled ? '

" ' It's settled.'

" ' And what you going to do with your bits of
furniture 'ere ? '

" ' Sell some and take some. . . . '

" ' It's feasible,' said Ernest after reflection.

" And so we needn't reely 'ave 'ad that—bit
of a' argument ? ' said Ernest after a pause. ' Not
me and uncle ? '

' ' Not on *my* account you needn't,' said my mother.

" ' Well—we *'ad* it,' said Ernest after another
pause and without any visible signs of regret."

§ 3

" If my dream was a dream," said Sarnac, " it
was a most circumstantial dream. I could tell you
a hundred details of our journey to London and how
we disposed of the poor belongings that had furnished
our home in Cherry Gardens. Every detail would
expose some odd and illuminating difference between
the ideas of those ancient days and our own ideas.
Brother Ernest was helpful, masterful and irascible.
He got a week's holiday from his employer to help
mother to settle up things, and among other things
that were settled up I believe my mother persuaded
him and my uncle to ' shake hands,' but I do not
know the particulars of that great scene, I did not
see it, it was merely mentioned in my hearing during
the train journey to London. I would like to tell
you also of the man who came round to buy most
of our furniture, including that red and black sofa
I described to you, and how he and my brother had
a loud and heated argument about some damage to

one of its legs, and how Mr. Crosby produced a bill,
that my mother understood he had forgiven us on
account of Fanny long ago. There was also some
point about something called 'tenant's fixtures'
that led my brother and the landlord, Mr. Bulstrode,
to the verge of violence. And Mr. Bulstrode, the
landlord, brought accusations of damage done to
the fabric of his house that were false, and he made
extravagant claims for compensation based thereon
and had to be rebutted with warmth. There was
also trouble over carting a parcel of our goods to
the railway-station, and when we got to the terminus
of Victoria in London it was necessary, I gathered,
that Ernest should offer to fight a railway porter
—you have read of railway porters ?—before we received proper attention.

"But I cannot tell you all these curious and typical
incidents now because at that rate I should never
finish my story before our holidays are over. I
must go on now to tell you of this London, this
great city, the greatest city it was in the world in
those days, to which we had transferred our fates.
All the rest of my story, except for nearly two years
and a half I spent in the training camp and in France
and Germany during the First World War, is set
in the scenery of London. You know already what
a vast congestion of human beings London was ;
you know that within a radius of fifteen miles a population of seven and a half million people were gathered
together, people born out of due time into a world
unready for them and born mostly through the sheer
ignorance of their procreators, gathered together
into an area of not very attractive clay country by

an urgent need to earn a living, and you know the
terrible fate that at last overwhelmed this sinfully
crowded accumulation ; you have read of west-end
and slums, and you have seen the cinema pictures
of those days showing crowded streets, crowds gaping
at this queer ceremony or that, a vast traffic of clumsy
automobiles and distressed horses in narrow unsuitable streets, and I suppose your general impression
is a nightmare of multitudes, a suffocating realisation
of jostling discomfort and uncleanness and of an
unendurable strain on eye and ear and attention.
The history we learn in our childhood enforces that
lesson.

"But though the facts are just as we are taught
they were, I do not recall anything like the distress
at London you would suppose me to have felt, and
I do remember vividly the sense of adventure, the
intellectual excitement and the discovery of beauty
I experienced in going there. You must remember
that in this strange dream of mine I had forgotten
all our present standards ; I accepted squalor and
confusion as being in the nature of things, and the
aspects of this city's greatness, the wonder of this
limitless place and a certain changing and evanescent
beauty, rise out of a sea of struggle and limitation
as forgetfully as a silver birch rises out of the swamp
that bears it.

"The part of London in which we took up our
abode was called Pimlico. It bordered upon the
river, and once there had been a wharf there to which
ships came across the Atlantic from America. This
word Pimlico had come with other trade in these
ships ; in my time it was the last word left alive

of the language of the Algonquin Red Indians, who had otherwise altogether vanished from the earth. The Pimlico wharf had gone, the American trade was forgotten, and Pimlico was now a great wilderness of streets of dingy grey houses in which people lived and let lodgings. These houses had never been designed for the occupation of lodgers ; they were faced with a lime-plaster called stucco which made a sort of pretence of being stone ; each one had a sunken underground floor originally intended for servants, a door with a portico and several floors above which were reached by a staircase. Beside each portico was a railed pit that admitted light to the front underground room. As you walked along these Pimlico streets these porticos receded in long perspectives and each portico of that endless series represented ten or a dozen misdirected, incomplete and rather unclean inhabitants, infected mentally and morally. Over the grey and dingy architecture rested a mist or a fog, rarely was there a precious outbreak of sunlight ; here and there down the vista a grocer's boy or a greengrocer's boy or a fish hawker would be handing in food over the railings to the subterranean members of a household, or a cat (there was a multitude of cats) would be peeping out of the railings alert for the danger of a passing dog. There would be a few pedestrians, a passing cab or so, and perhaps in the morning a dust-cart collecting refuse filth—set out for the winds to play with in boxes and tin receptacles at the pavement edge—or a man in a uniform cleaning the streets with a hose. It seems to you that it must have been the most depressing of spectacles.

It wasn't, though I doubt if I can make clear to you that it wasn't. I know I went about Pimlico thinking it rather a fine place and endlessly interesting. I assure you that in the early morning and by my poor standards it had a sort of grey spaciousness and dignity. But afterwards I found the thing far better done, that London architectural aquatint, in Belgravia and round about Regent's Park.

" I must admit that I tended to drift out of those roads and squares of lodging-houses either into the streets where there were shops and street-cars or southward to the Embankment along the Thames. It was the shops and glares that drew me first as the lights began to fail and, strange as it may seem to you, my memories of such times are rich with beauty. We feeble children of that swarming age had I think an almost morbid gregariousness ; we found a subtle pleasure and reassurance in crowds and a real disagreeableness in being alone ; and my impressions of London's strange interest and charm are I confess very often crowded impressions of a kind this world no longer produces, or impressions to which a crowded foreground or background was essential. But they were beautiful.

" For example there was a great railway-station, a terminus, within perhaps half a mile of us. There was a great disorderly yard in front of the station in which hackney automobiles and omnibuses assembled and departed and arrived. In the late twilight of an autumn day this yard was a mass of shifting black shadows and gleams and lamps, across which streamed an incessant succession of bobbing black heads, people on foot hurrying to catch the trains :

as they flitted by the lights one saw their faces gleam and vanish again. Above this foreground rose the huge brown-grey shapes of the station buildings and the façade of a big hotel, reflecting the flares below and pierced here and there by a lit window : then very sharply came the sky-line and a sky still blue and luminous, tranquil and aloof. And the innumerable sounds of people and vehicles wove into a deep, wonderful and continually varying drone. Even to my boyish mind there was an irrational conviction of unity and purpose in this spectacle.

" The streets where there were shops were also very wonderful and lovely to me directly the too-lucid and expository daylight began to fade. The variously coloured lights in the shop windows which displayed a great diversity of goods for sale splashed the most extraordinary reflections upon the pavements and roadway, and these were particularly gem-like if there had been rain or a mist to wet the reflecting surfaces. One of these streets—it was called Lupus Street, though why it had the name of an abominable skin disease that has long since vanished from the earth I cannot imagine—was close to our new home and I still remember it as full of romantic effectiveness. By daylight it was an exceedingly sordid street, and late at night empty and echoing, but in the magic hours of London it was a bed of black and luminous flowers, the abounding people became black imps and through it wallowed the great shining omnibuses, the ships of the street, filled with light and reflecting lights.

" There were endless beauties along the river bank. The river was a tidal one held in control by a stone embankment, and the roadway along the embankment was planted at the footway edge with plane trees and lit by large electric lights on tall standards. These planes were among the few trees that could flourish in the murky London air, but they were unsuitable trees to have in a crowded city because they gave off minute specules that irritated people's throats. That however I did not know ; what I did know was that the shadows of the leaves on the pavements thrown by the electric glares made the most beautiful patterings I had ever seen. I would walk along on a warm night rejoicing in them, more particularly if now and then a light breeze set them dancing and quivering.

" One could walk from Pimlico along this Thames Embankment for some miles towards the east. One passed little black jetties with dangling oil lamps ; there was a traffic of barges and steamers on the river altogether mysterious and romantic to me ; the frontages of the houses varied incessantly, and ever and again were cleft by crowded roadways that brought a shining and twinkling traffic up to the bridges. Across the river was a coming and going of trains along a railway viaduct ; it contributed a restless *motif* of clanks and concussion to the general drone of London, and the engines sent puffs of firelit steam and sudden furnace-glows into the night. One came along this Embankment to the great buildings at Westminster, by daylight a pile of imitation Gothic dominated by a tall clock-tower with an illuminated dial, a pile which assumed a blue dignity with the twilight and became a noble portent standing at attention, a forest of spears, in the night. This was the Parliament House, and in its chambers a formal King, an ignoble nobility and a fraudulently elected gathering of lawyers, financiers and adventurers took upon themselves, amidst the general mental obscurity of those days, a semblance of wisdom and empire. As one went on beyond Westminster along the Embankment came great grey-brown palaces and houses set behind green gardens, a railway bridge and then two huge hotels, standing high and far back, bulging with lit windows ; there was some sort of pit or waste beneath them, I forget what, very black, so that at once they loomed over one and seemed magically remote. There was an Egyptian obelisk here, for all the European capitals of my time, being as honest as magpies and as original as monkeys, had adorned themselves with obelisks stolen from Egypt. And farther along was the best and noblest building in London, St. Paul's Cathedral ; it was invisible by night, but it was exceedingly serene and beautiful on a clear, blue, windy day. And some of the bridges were very lovely with gracious arches of smutty grey stone, though some were so clumsy that only night could redeem them.

"As I talk I remember," said Sarnac. "Before employment robbed me of my days I pushed my boyish explorations far and wide, wandering all day and often going without any meal, or, if I was in pocket, getting a bun and a glass of milk in some small shop for a couple of pennies. The shop windows of London were an unending marvel to me ; and they would be to you too if you could remember them as I do ; there must have been

hundreds of miles of them, possibly thousands of
miles. In the poorer parts they were chiefly food-
shops and cheap clothing shops and the like, and one
could exhaust their interest, but there were thorough-
fares like Regent Street and Piccadilly and narrow
Bond Street and Oxford Street crammed with all
the furnishings of the life of the lucky minority,
the people who could spend freely. You will find
it difficult to imagine how important a matter the
mere buying of things was in the lives of those people.
In their houses there was a vast congestion of objects
neither ornamental nor useful ; *purchases* in fact ;
and the women spent large portions of every weekday in buying things, clothes, table-litter, floor-
litter, wall-litter. They had no work ; they were too
ignorant to be interested in any real thing ; they had
nothing else to do. That was the world's reward,
the substance of success—purchases. Through them
you realised your well-being. As a shabby half-
grown boy I pushed my way among these spenders,
crowds of women dressed, wrapped up rather, in
layer after layer of purchases, scented, painted.
Most of them were painted to suggest a health-flushed
face, the nose powdered a leprous white.

" There is one thing to be said for the old fashion
of abundant clothing ; in that crowded jostling
world it saved people from actually touching each
other.

" I would push through these streets eastward
to less prosperous crowds in Oxford Street and
to a different multitude in Holborn. As you went
eastward the influence of women diminished and
that of young men increased. Cheapside gave you

all the material for building up a twentieth-century young man from the nude. In the shop windows he was disarticulated and priced : hat five and sixpence, trousers eighteen shillings, tie one and six ; cigarettes tenpence an ounce ; newspaper a halfpenny, cheap novel sevenpence ; on the pavement outside there he was put together and complete and the cigarette burning, under the impression that he was a unique immortal creature and that the ideas in his head were altogether his own. And beyond Cheapside there was Clerkenwell with curious little shops that sold scarcely anything but old keys or the parts of broken-up watches or the like detached objects. Then there were great food markets at Leadenhall Street and Smithfield and Covent Garden, incredible accumulations of raw stuff. At Covent Garden they sold fruits and flowers that we should think poor and undeveloped, but which everyone in those days regarded as beautiful and delicious. And in Caledonian Market were innumerable barrows where people actually bought and took away every sort of broken and second-hand rubbish, broken ornaments, decaying books with torn pages, secondhand clothing—a wonderland of litter for any boy with curiosity in his blood. . . .

" But I could go on talking endlessly about this old London of mine and you want me to get on with my story. I have tried to give you something of its endless, incessant, multitudinous glittering quality and the way in which it yielded a thousand strange and lovely effects to its changing lights and atmosphere. I found even its fogs, those dreaded fogs of which the books tell, romantic. But then I was a boy at the adventurous age. The fog was often very thick in Pimlico. It was normally a soft creamy obscurity that turned even lights close at hand into luminous blurs. People came out of nothingness within six yards of you, were riddles and silhouettes before they became real. One could go out and lose oneself within ten minutes of home and perhaps pick up with a distressed automobile driver and walk by his headlights, signalling to him where the pavement ended. That was one sort of fog, the dry fog. But there were many sorts. There was a sort of yellow darkness, like blackened bronze, that hovered about you and did not embrace you and left a clear nearer world of deep browns and blacks. And there was an unclean wet mist that presently turned to drizzle and made every surface a mirror."

"And there was daylight," said Willow, "sometimes surely there was daylight."

"Yes," Sarnac reflected ; "there was daylight. At times. And sometimes there was quite a kindly and redeeming sunshine in London. In the spring, in early summer or in October. It did not blaze, but it filled the air with a mild warmth, and turned the surfaces it lit not indeed to gold but to amber and topaz. And there were even hot days in London with skies of deep blue above, but they were rare. And sometimes there was daylight without the sun. . . .

"Yes," said Sarnac and paused. "At times there was a daylight that stripped London bare, showed its grime, showed its real ineffectiveness, showed the pitiful poverty of intention in its buildings, showed the many coloured billstickers' hoardings for the crude and leprous things they were, brought out the shabbiness of unhealthy bodies and misfitting garments, . . .

"Those were terrible, veracious, unhappy days. When London no longer fascinated but wearied and offended, when even to an uninstructed boy there came some intimation of the long distressful journey that our race had still to travel before it attained even to such peace and health and wisdom as it has to-day."

§ 4

Sarnac stopped short in his talk and rose with something between a laugh and a sigh. He stood facing westward and Sunray stood beside him.

"This story will go on for ever if I digress like this. See! the sun will be behind that ridge in another ten minutes. I cannot finish this evening, because most of the story part still remains to be told."

"There are roast fowls with sweet corn and chestnuts," said Firefly. "Trout and various fruits."

"And some of that golden wine?" said Radiant.

"Some of that golden wine."

Sunray, who had been very still and intent, awoke. "Sarnac dear," she said, slipping her arm through his. "What became of Uncle John Julip?"

Sarnac reflected. "I forget," he said.

"Aunt Adelaide Julip died?" asked Willow.

"She died quite soon after we left Cherry Gardens. My uncle wrote, I remember, and I remember my mother reading the letter at breakfast like a proclamation and saying, 'Seems if she was reely ill after all.'

If she had not been ill then surely she had carried malingering to the last extremity. But I forget any particulars about my uncle's departure from this world. He probably outlived my mother, and after her death the news of his end might easily have escaped me."

"You have had the most wonderful dream in the world, Sarnac," said Starlight, "and I want to hear the whole story and not interrupt, but I am sorry not to hear more of your Uncle John Julip."

"He was such a perfect little horror," said Firefly. . . .

Until the knife-edge of the hills cut into the molten globe of the sun, the holiday-makers lingered watching the shadows in their last rush up to the mountain crests, and then, still talking of this particular and that in Sarnac's story, the six made their way down to the guest-house and supper.

"Sarnac was shot," said Radiant. "He hasn't even begun to get shot yet. There is no end of story still to come."

"Sarnac," asked Firefly, "you weren't killed in the Great War, were you? Suddenly? In some inconsequent sort of way?"

"Not a bit of it," said Sarnac. "I am really beginning to be shot in this story though Radiant does not perceive it. But I must tell my story in my own fashion."

At supper what was going on was explained to the master of the guest-house. Like so many of these guest-house-keepers he was a jolly, convivial, simple soul, and he was amused and curious at Sarnac's alleged experience. He laughed at the impatience

of the others ; he said they were like children in a
Children's Garden, agog for their go-to-bed fairy
tale. After they had had coffee they went out for
a time to see the moonlight mingle with the ruddy
afterglow above the peaks : and then the guest-master
led the way in, made up a blazing pinewood fire and
threw cushions before it, set out an after-dinner wine,
put out the lights and prepared for a good night's
story-telling.

Sarnac remained thoughtful looking into the flames
until Sunray set him off again by whispering : " Pimlico ? "

§ 5

" I will tell you as briefly as I can of the household
in Pimlico where we joined forces with my mother's
old friend, Matilda Good," said Sarnac ; "but I
confess it is hard to be reasonably brief when one's
mind is fuller of curious details than this fire is of
sparks."

" That's excellent ! " said the master of the guest-
house. " That's a perfect story-teller's touch ! "
and looked brightly for Sarnac to continue.

" But we are all beginning to believe that he has
been there," whispered Radiant, laying a restraining
hand on the guest-master's knee. " And he "—
Radiant spoke behind his hand—" he believes it
altogether."

"Not *really* ? " whispered the guest-master. He
seemed desirous of asking difficult questions and
then subsided into an attention that was at first a
little constrained and presently quite involuntary.

" These houses in Pimlico were part of an enormous

proliferation of houses that occurred between a hundred years and seventy years before the Great War. There was a great amount of unintelligent building enterprise in those decades in London, and all the building, as I have already told you I think, was done on the supposition that there was an endless supply of fairly rich families capable of occupying a big house and employing three or four domestic servants. There were underground kitchens and servants' rooms, there was a dining-room and master's study at the ground level, there was a 'drawing-room floor' above, two rooms convertible into one by a device known as folding doors, and above this were bedrooms on a scale of diminishing importance until one came to attics without fire-places in which the servants were to sleep. In large areas and particularly in Pimlico, these fairly rich families of the builder's imagination, with servile domestics all complete, never appeared to claim the homes prepared for them, and from the first, poorer people, for whom of course no one had troubled to plan houses, adapted these porticoed plaster mansions to their own narrower needs. My mother's friend, Matilda Good, was a quite typical Pimlico householder. She had been the trusted servant of a rich old lady in Cliffstone who had died and left her two or three hundred pounds of money——"

The master of the guest-house was endlessly perplexed and made an interrogative noise.

"Private property," said Radiant very rapidly. "Power of bequest. Two thousand years ago. Made a Will, you know. Go on, Sarnac."

"With that and her savings," said Sarnac, "she

was able to become tenant of one of these Pimlico houses and to furnish it with a sort of shabby gentility, She lived herself in the basement below and in the attic above, and all the rest of the house she had hoped to let in pieces, floor by floor or room by room to rich or at least prosperous old ladies, and to busy herself in tending them and supplying their needs and extracting a profit and living out of them, running up and down her staircase as an ant runs up and down a rose stem tending its aphides. But old ladies of any prosperity did not come into Pimlico. It was low and foggy, the children of its poorer streets were rough and disrespectful, and it was close to the river embankment over which rich, useless, old ladies naturally expected to be thrown. So Matilda Good had to console herself with less succulent and manageable lodgers.

" I remember Matilda Good giving us an account of those she had as we sat in her front downstairs room having a kind of tea supper on the evening of our arrival. Ernest had declined refreshment and departed, his task as travel conductor done, but there were my mother and Prue and myself, all in dingy black and all a little stiff and strange, thawing slowly to tea and hot buttered toast with a poached egg each, our mouths very full and our eyes and ears very attentive to Matilda Good.

" She appeared quite a grand lady to me that night. She was much larger than any lady I had hitherto been accustomed to ; she had a breadth and variety of contour like scenery rather than a human being ; the thought of her veins being varicose, indeed of all her anatomy being varicose and fantastic, seemed

a right and proper one. She was dressed in black
with outbreaks of soiled lace, a large gold-rimmed
brooch fastened her dress at the neck and she had
a gold chain about her, and on her head was what
was called a ' cap,' an affair like the lower shell of
an oyster inverted, made of layers of dingy lace
and adorned with a black velvet bow and a gold
buckle. Her face had the same landscape unanato-
mical quality as her body ; she had a considerable
moustache, an overhung slightly mischievous mouth
and two different large dark-grey eyes with a slightly
vertical cast in them and very marked eyelashes.
She sat sideways. One eye looked at you rather
sidelong, the other seemed to watch something over
your head. She spoke in a whisper which passed
very easily into wheezy, not unkindly laughter.

" ' You'll get no end of exercise on these stairs,
my dear,' she said to sister Prue, ' no end of exercise.
There's times when I'm going up to bed when I
start counting 'em, just to make sure that they aren't
taking in lodgers like the rest of us. There's no
doubt this 'ouse will strengthen your legs, my dear.
Mustn't get 'em too big and strong for the rest
of you. But you can easy manage that by carrying
something, carrying something every time you go
up or down. Ugh—ugh. That'll equalise you.
There's always something to carry, boots it is, hot
water it is, a scuttle of coals or a parcel.'

" ' I expect it's a busy 'ouse,' said my mother,
eating her buttered toast like a lady.

" ' It's a toilsome 'ouse,' said Matilda Good. ' I
don't want to deceive you, Martha ; it's a toilsome
'ouse.

" ' But it's a 'ouse that keeps full,' said Matilda Good, challenging me with one eye and ignoring me with the other. ' Full I am now, and full I've been since last Michaelmas, full right up ; two permanents I've 'ad three years on end and those my best floors. I've something to be thankful for, all things considered, and now I got 'elp of a sort that won't slide downstairs on a tea tray or lick the ground-floor's sugar lump by lump knowing the lumps was counted and never thinking that wetness tells, the slut ! we'll get on swimmingly. The sluts I've 'ad, Martha ! These board-schools turn them out a 'orror to God and a danger to men. I can't tell you. It's a comfort to set eyes on any girl as I can see at once 'as been brought up to take a pride in 'erself. 'Ave a little of that watercress with your toast, my dear. It'll do that complexion of yours good.'

" My sister Prue reddened and took some watercress.

" ' The drawing-room floor,' said Matilda Good, ' is a lady. It isn't often you keep a lady three years, what with the things they know and the things they fancy they know, but I've kept her. She's a real lady—born. Bumpus 'er name is—Miss Beatrice Bumpus. I don't know whether you'll like her, Martha, when you set eyes on her, but she's got to be studied. She's a particular sort of Warwickshire Bumpus that hunts. She'll ask you if you want the vote, Martha, directly she sees you're a fresh face. It isn't *a* vote or *any* old vote she asks you to want, it's *the* vote.' The whispering voice grew thicker and richer and a persuasive smile spread far and wide over the face. ' If it's all the same to you, Martha, you better say you do.'

" My mother was sipping her fourth cup of tea. ' I don't know,' she said, ' as I altogether 'old with this vote.'

" Matilda Good's great red hands which had been lying apparently detached in her lap, produced short arms and lace cuffs and waved about in the air, waving my mother's objections away. ' 'Old with it on the drawing-room floor,' wheezed Matilda. ' 'Old with it on the drawing-room floor.'

" ' But if she arsts questions ? '

" ' She won't wait to have them answered. It won't be difficult, Martha. I wouldn't put you into a position of difficulty, not if I could 'elp it. You just got to 'old with 'er quietly and she'll do the rest.'

" ' Mother,' said Prue, who was still too overawed by Matilda Good to address her directly. ' Mother, what *is* this here vote ? '

" ' Vote for Parliament, my dear,' said Matilda Good.

" ' When shall we get it ? ' asked my mother.

" ' You won't get it,' said Matilda Good.

" ' But if we did, what should we have to do with it, like ? '

" ' *Nothing*,' said Matilda Good with bottomless contempt. ' All the same it's a great movement, Martha, and don't you forget it. And Miss Bumpus she works night and day, Martha, gets 'it about by policemen, and once she was actually in prison a night, getting you and me the vote.'

" ' Well, it shows a kind nature,' said my mother.

" ' My ground-floor's a gentleman. The worst

of 'im is the books there are to dust, books *and*
books. Not that 'e ever reads 'em much. . . .
Very likely you'll 'ear 'im soon playing his pianola.
You can 'ear it down 'ere almost as if you were
inside it. Mr. Plaice, 'e's an Oxford gentleman and
he works at a firm of publishers, Burrows and Graves,
they're called ; a very 'igh-class firm I'm told—
don't go in for advertisements or anything vulgar.
He's got photographs of Greek and Latin statues
and ruins round above his bookshelves and shields
with College arms. Naked some of the statues are,
but for all that none of them are anything but quite
nice and genteel, *quite* genteel. You can see at once
he's a University gentleman. And photographs of
Switzerland he's got. He goes up mountains in
Switzerland and speaks the language. He's a smoker ;
sets with a pipe writing or reading evening after
evening and marking things with his pencil. Manu-
scripts he reads and proofs. Pipes he has with a
pipe for every day in the week, and a smoker's outfit all made with bee-utiful stone, serpentine they
call it, sort of bloodshot green it is ; tobacco-jar
and a pot for feathers to clean his pipes, little places
for each day's pipe, everything all of stone ; it's a
regular monument. And when you're dusting it—
remember if you drop this here serpentine it breaks
like earthenware. Most of the maids I've 'ad 'ave
'ad a chip at that tobacco graveyard of 'is. And
mind you——' Matilda Good leant forward and
held out her hand to arrest any wandering of my
mother's attention. *''E don't 'old with Votes for
Women !* See ? '

"' One's got to be careful,' said my mother.

" ' One has. He's got one or two little whims, has Mr. Plaice, but if you mind about them he don't give you much trouble. One of 'is whims is to pretend to 'ave a bath every morning. Every morning he 'as a shallow tin bath put out in his room and a can of cold water and a sponge, and every morning he pretends to splash about in it something fearful and makes a noise like a grampus singing a hymn—calls it 'is Tub, he does ; though it's a lot more like a canary's saucer. Says he must have it as cold as possible even if there's ice on it. Well——'

" Matilda Good performed a sort of landslide over the arm of her chair, her head nodded, and the whisper became more confidential. ' He *doesn't*,' wheezed Matilda Good.

" ' You mean he doesn't get into the bath ? '

" ' Not-tit,' said Matilda Good. ' You can see when he's really been in by his wet footmarks on the floor. Not 'arf the time does he have that bath. Per'aps 'e used to have it when he was a young man at College. I wonder. But it's always got to be put out and the can always got to be lugged up and poured out and poured away again, and nobody's ever to ask if he'd like the chill taken off. Not the sort of thing you ask a University gentleman. No. All the same,' said Matilda Good, ' all the same I've caught 'im pouring his hand and shaving water into that water-splash in the winter, after he'd been going dirty for a week. But have a can of warm ? Have the chill taken off his water ? Not Tim ! It's curious, ain't it ? But that's one of his whims.

"'I sometimes think,' said Matilda Good still more extravagantly confidential, 'that perhaps he climbs all those mountains in Switzerland same way as he takes his bath. . . .'

"She rolled back large portions of her person into a less symmetrical attitude. 'This Mr. Plaice you must know,' she said, 'has a voice between a clergyman's and a schoolmaster's, sort of hard and superior, and when you say anything to him he's apt to make a noise, "Arrr . . . Arrr . . . Arrr," a sort of slow neighing it is, as though he doesn't think much of you but doesn't want to blame you for that and anyhow can't attend to you properly. You mustn't let it annoy you. It's the way he's been brought up. And he has a habit of using long condescending sort of words to you. And calling you insulting names. He'll think nothing of calling you "My worthy Abigail," or "Come in, my rosy fingered Aurora," when you knock in the morning. Just as though a girl could keep 'er 'ands pink and clean with all these fires to light! He'll ask of me "How's the Good Matilda? How's honest Matilda Good to-day?"—sort of fiddling about with your name. Of course he don't mean to be rude; it's just his idea of being pleasant and humorous, and making you feel you're being made fun of in a gentle sort of way instead of being terrible like he might be, and—seeing he's good pay and very little trouble, Martha—it's no good getting offended with him. All the same I can't help thinking at times of how he'd get on if I answered 'im back, and which of us two would be left alive if we had a fair match of it, making fun of one another. The

things—the things I could say ! But that,' said
Matilda Good, breaking into an ingratiating smile
of extraordinary extent and rolling one eye at me
—'is just a dream. It isn't the sort of dream to
indulge in in this 'ouse. I've rehearsed it a bit, I
admit. Says 'e—but never mind what 'e says or
what I says back to him. . . . Ugh ! Ugh ! . . .
He's good pay and regular, my dear ; he ain't likely
to lose his job and he ain't likely ever to get another,
and in this Vale anyhow we got to put up with 'is
whims. And——'

" Matilda Good spoke as one who confesses to
a weakness. ' His pianola cheers me up at times.
I will say that for 'im. It's almost the only noise
one hears from him. Except when he takes off his
boots.

" ' Well, up above my drawing-room at present
is my second floor front, the Reverend Moggeridge
and his good lady. They been here five months
now and they seem like taking root.'

" ' Not a clergyman ? ' said my mother respectfully.

" ' A very poor clergyman,' said Matilda, ' but a
clergyman. So much to our credit, Martha. Oh !
but they're poor old things ! Poor old things !
Been curate or something all his life in some out-
of-the-world place. And lost his job. Somebody
had the heart to turn 'em out. Or something happened. I wonder. 'E's a funny old man. . . .

" ' He dodders off nearly every Saturday on supply,
they call it, to take services somewhere over the
Sunday, and like as not he comes back with his cold
worse than ever, sniffing and sniffing. It's cruel
how they treat these poor old parsons on supply,

fetch 'em from the station in open traps they do, in the worst of weather, and often the rectory teetotal without a drop of anything for a cold. Christianity ! I suppose it's *got* to be. . . . The two of them just potter about upstairs and make shift to get their meals, such as they are, over the bedroom fire. She even does a bit of her own washing. Dragging about. Poor old things ! Old and forgotten and left about. But they're very little trouble and there it is. And as I say—anyhow—he's a clergyman. And in the other room at the back there's a German lady who teaches—well, anything she can persuade anyone to be taught. She hasn't been here more than a month, and I don't know whether I like her or not, but she seems straight enough and she keeps herself pretty much to herself and when one has a room to let one can't always pick and choose.'

" ' And that's the lot, my dear. To-morrow we'll have to begin. You'll go up presently and settle into your two rooms at the top. There's a little one for Mortimer and a rather bigger one for you and Prue. There's pegs and curtains for your things. I'm next door to you. I'll give you my little old alarum clock and show you all about it and to-morrow at seven sharp down we come, you and me and Prue. My Lord, I suppose, has the privilege of his sex and doesn't come down until half-past ! Oh ! I'm a suffragette, Martha,—same as Miss Bumpus. First thing is this fire, and unless we rake the ashes well forward the boiler won't heat. Then there's fires and boots, dust the front rooms and breakfasts : Mr. Plaice at eight sharp and mind it is, and Miss Bumpus at eight-thirty, and get away with Mr. Plaice if you can first because of the shortness of tablespoons. Five I got altogether and before I lost my last third floor back I 'ad seven. 'E was a nice lot ; 'e was. The old people get their own breakfast when they want it, and Frau Buchholz has a tray, just bread and butter and tea, whenever we can manage it after the drawing-room's been seen to. That's the programme, Martha.'

" ' I'll do my best, 'Tilda," said my mother. ' *As* you know.'

" ' Hullo ! ' said Matilda indicating the ceiling, ' the concert's going to begin. That bump's him letting down the pianola pedals.'

" And then suddenly through the ceiling into our subterranean tea party came a rush of Clavier notes —I can't describe it.

" One of the few really good things of that age was the music. Mankind perfected some things very early ; I suppose precious-stone work and gold work have never got very much beyond the levels it reached under the Seventeenth Dynasty in Egypt, ages ago, and marble statuary came to a climax at Athens before the conquests of Alexander. I doubt if there has ever come very much sweeter music into the world than the tuneful stuff we had away back there in the Age of Confusion. This music Mr. Plaice was giving us was some bits of Schumann's *Carnaval* music ; we hear it still played on the Clavier ; and it was almost the first good music I ever heard. There had been brass bands on Cliffstone promenade, of course, but they simply made a glad row. I don't know if you understand what a pianola was. It was an instrument for playing the Clavier with hammers directed by means of perforated rolls, for the use of those who lacked the intelligence and dexterity to read music and play the Clavier with their hands. Because everyone was frightfully unhandy in those days. It thumped a little and struck undiscriminating chords, but Mr. Plaice managed it fairly well and the result came, filtered through the ceiling—— As we used to say in those days, it might have been worse.

"At the thought of that music I recall—and whenever I hear Schumann as long as I live I shall recall—the picture of that underground room, the little fire-place with the kettle on a hob, the kettle-holder and the toasting fork beside the fire-place jamb, the steel fender, the ashes, the small blotched looking-glass over the mantel, the little china figures of dogs in front of the glass, the gaslight in a frosted glass globe hanging from the ceiling and lighting the tea-things on the table. (Yes, the house was lit by coal-gas ; electric light was only just coming in. . . . My dear Firefly ! can I possibly stop my story to tell you what coal-gas was ? A good girl would have learnt that long ago.)

"There sat Matilda Good reduced to a sort of imbecile ecstasy by these butterflies of melody. She nodded her cap, she rolled her head and smiled ; she made appreciative rhythmic gestures with her hands ; one eye would meet you in a joyous search for sympathy while the other contemplated the dingy wall-paper beyond. I too was deeply stirred. But my mother and sister Prue sat in their black with an expression of forced devotion, looking very refined and correct, exactly as they had sat and listened to my father's funeral service five days before.

" ' Sputiful,' whispered my mother, like making a response in church, when the first piece came to an end. . . .

" I went to sleep that night in my little attic with fragments of Schumann, Bach and Beethoven chasing elusively about my brain. I perceived that a new phase of life had come to me. . . .

" Jewels," said Sarnac. " Some sculpture, music —just a few lovely beginnings there were already of what man could do with life. Such things I see now were the seeds of the new world of promise already there in the dark matrix of the old."

§ 6

" Next morning revealed a new Matilda Good, active and urgent, in a loose and rather unclean mauve cotton wrapper and her head wrapped up in a sort of turban of figured silk. This costume she wore most of the day except that she did her hair and put on a cotton lace cap in the afternoon. (The black dress and the real lace cap and the brooch, I was to learn, were for Sundays and for weekday evenings of distinction.) My mother and Prue were arrayed in rough aprons which Matilda had very thoughtfully bought for them. There was a great bustle in the basement of the house, and Prue a little before eight went up with Matilda to learn how to set out breakfast for Mr. Plaice. I made his acquaintance later in the day when I took up the late edition of the *Evening Standard* to him. I found him a stooping, tall gentleman with a cadaverous face that was mostly profile, and he made great play with my Christian name.

"'Mortimer,' he said and neighed his neigh. 'Well—it might have been Norfolk-Howard.'

"There was an obscure allusion in that : for once upon a time, ran the popular legend, a certain Mr. Bugg seeking a less entomological name had changed his to Norfolk-Howard, which was in those days a very aristocratic one. . . . Whereupon vulgar people had equalised matters by calling the offensive bed-bugs that abounded in London, 'Norfolk-Howards.'

"Before many weeks were past it became evident that Matilda Good had made an excellent bargain in her annexation of our family. She had secured my mother's services for nothing, and it was manifest that my mother was a born lodging-house woman. She behaved like a partner in the concern, and the only money Matilda ever gave her was to pay her expenses upon some specific errand or to buy some specific thing. Prue however, with unexpected firmness, insisted upon wages, and enforced her claim by going out and nearly getting employment at a dressmaker's. In a little while Matilda became to the lodgers an unseen power for righteousness in the basement and all the staircase work was left to my mother and Prue. Often Matilda did not go up above the ground level once all day until, as she said, she 'toddled up to bed.'

"Matilda made some ingenuous attempts to utilize me also in the service of the household : I was exhorted to carry up scuttles of coal, clean boots

and knives and make myself useful generally. She
even put it to me one day whether I wouldn't like
a nice suit with buttons—in those days they still
used to put small serving boys in tight suits of green
or brown cloth, with rows of gilt buttons as close
together as possible over their little chests and
stomachs. But the very thought of it sent my mind
to Chessing Hanger, where I had conceived an
intense hatred and dread of 'service' and 'livery,'
and determined me to find some other employment
before Matilda Good's large and insidious will
enveloped and overcame me. And oddly enough
a talk I had with Miss Beatrice Bumpus helped me
greatly in my determination.

" Miss Bumpus was a slender young woman of
about five and twenty I suppose. She had short
brown hair, brushed back rather prettily from a
broad forehead, and she had freckles on her nose
and quick red-brown eyes. She generally wore a
plaid tweed costume rather short in the skirt and
with a coat cut like a man's ; she wore green
stockings and brown shoes—I had never seen green
stockings before—and she would stand on her hearthrug in exactly the attitude Mr. Plaice adopted on
his hearthrug downstairs. Or she would be sitting
at a writing-desk against the window, smoking cigarettes. She asked me what sort of man I intended
to be, and I said with the sort of modesty I had
been taught to assume as becoming my station, that
I hadn't thought yet.

" To which Miss Bumpus answered, 'Liar.'

" That was the sort of remark that either kills
or cures. I said, ' Well, Miss, I want to get educated

and I don't know how to do it. And I don't know
what I ought to do.'

"Miss Bumpus held me with a gesture while
she showed how nicely she could send out smoke
through her nose. Then she said, 'Avoid Blind
Alley Occupations.'

"'Yes, Miss.'

"'But you don't know what Blind Alley Occupations are ?'

"'No, Miss.'

"'Occupations that earn a boy wages and lead
nowhere. One of the endless pitfalls of this silly
man-made pseudo-civilisation. Never do anything
that doesn't lead somewhere. Aim high. I must
think your case out, Mr. Harry Mortimer. I might
be able to help you. . . .'

"This was the opening of quite a number of
conversations between myself and Miss Bumpus.
She was a very stimulating influence in my adolescence. She pointed out that although it was now
late in the year there were many evening classes
of various sorts that I might attend with profit.
She told me of all sorts of prominent and successful
people who had begun their careers from beginnings
as humble and hopeless as mine. She said I was
'unhampered' by my sex. She asked me if I was
interested in the suffrage movement, and gave me
tickets for two meetings at which I heard her speak,
and she spoke, I thought, very well. She answered
some interrupters with extreme effectiveness, and I
cheered myself hoarse for her. Something about
her light and gallant attitude to life reminded me
of Fanny. I said so one day, and found myself,

before I knew it, telling her reluctantly and shame-
fully the story of our family disgrace. Miss Bumpus
was much interested.

" ' She wasn't like your sister Prue ? '

" ' No, Miss.'

" ' Prettier ? '

" ' A lot prettier. Of course—you could hardly
call Prue *pretty*, Miss.'

" ' I hope she's got on all right,' said Miss Bumpus. ' I
don't blame her a bit. But I hope she got the best of it.'

" ' I'd give anything, Miss, to hear Fanny was
all right. . . . I did care for Fanny, Miss. . . .
I'd give anything almost to see Fanny again. . . .
You won't tell my mother, Miss, I told you anything
about Fanny ? It kind of slipped out like.'

" ' Mortimer,' said Miss Bumpus, ' you're a sticker.
I wish I had a little brother like you. There ! I
won't breathe a word.'

" I felt we had sealed a glorious friendship. I
adopted Votes for Women as the first plank of my
political platform. (No, Firefly, I *won't* explain. I
won't explain anything. You must guess what a
political platform was and what its planks were.)
I followed up her indications and found out about
classes in the district where I could learn geology
and chemistry and how to speak French and German.
Very timidly I mooted the subject of my further
education in the basement living-room."

§ 7

Sarnac looked round at the fire-lit faces of his
listeners.

" I know how topsy-turvy this story must seem
to you, but it is a fact that before I was fourteen
I had to plead for education against the ideas and
wishes of my own family. And the whole household from top to bottom was brought into the discussion by Matilda or my mother. Except for Miss
Bumpus and Frau Buchholz everyone was against
the idea.

" ' Education,' said Matilda, shaking her head
slowly from side to side and smiling deprecatingly.
' Education ! That's all very well for those who
have nothing better to do, but *you* want to get on in
the world. You've got to be earning, young man.'

" ' But if I have education I'll be able to earn more.'

" Matilda screwed up her mouth in a portentous
manner and pointed to the ceiling to indicate Mr.
Plaice. '*That's* what comes of education, young
man. A room frowsty with books and just enough
salary not to be able to do a blessed thing you want
to do. And giving yourself Airs. Business is what
you want, young man, not education.'

" ' And who's to pay for all these classes ? ' said
my mother. ' That's what *I* want to know.'

" ' That's what we all want to know,' said Matilda
Good.

" ' If I can't get education——' I said, and left
the desperate sentence unfinished. I am afraid I was
near weeping. To learn nothing beyond my present
ignorance seemed to me then like a sentence of
imprisonment for life. It wasn't I who suffered
that alone. Thousands of poor youngsters of fourteen or fifteen in those days knew enough to see
clearly that the doors of practical illiteracy were

closing in upon them, and yet did not know enough to find a way of escape from this mental extinction.

" 'Look here !' I said, 'if I can get some sort of job during the day, may I pay for classes in the evening ?'

" 'If you can earn enough,' said Matilda. ' It's no worse I suppose than going to these new cinema shows or buying sweets for girls.'

" 'You've got to pay in for your room here and your keep, Morty, first,' said my mother. ' It isn't fair on Miss Good if you don't.'

" 'I know,' I said, with my heart sinking. ' I'll pay in for my board and lodging. Some'ow. I don't want to be dependent.'

" 'What good you think it will do you,' said Matilda Good, 'I *don't* know. You'll pick up a certain amount of learning perhaps, get a certificate or something and ideas above your station. You'll give all the energy you might use in shoving your way up in some useful employment. You'll get round-shouldered and near-sighted. And just to grow up a discontented misfit. Well—have it your own way if you must. If you earn the money yourself it's yours to spend.'

" Mr. Plaice was no more encouraging. ' Well, my noble Mortimer,' he said, 'they tell me *Arr* that you aspire to university honours.'

" 'I want to learn a little more than I know, Sir.'

" 'And join the ranks of the half-educated proletariat ?'

" It sounded bad. ' I hope not, Sir,' I said.

" 'And what classes do you propose to attend, Mortimer ?'

" ' Whatever there are.'

" ' No plan ?   No aim ? '

" ' I thought they'd know.'

" ' Whatever they give you—eh ?   A promiscuous appetite. And while you—while you *Arr* indulge in this mixed feast of learning, this futile rivalry with the children of the leisured classes, somebody I suppose will have to keep *you*. Don't you think it's a bit hard on that kind mother of yours who toils day and night for you, that you shouldn't work and do *your* bit, eh ?   One of the things, Mortimer, we used to learn in our much-maligned public schools, was something we called *playing cricket*. Well, I ask you, is this—this disinclination to do a bit of the earning, *Arr*, is it playing cricket ?   I could expect such behaviour from an 'Arry, you know, but not from a Mortimer. *Noblesse oblige*. You think it over, my boy. There's such a thing as learning, but there's such a thing as Duty. Many of us have to be content with lives of unassuming labour. Many of us.   Men who under happier circumstances might have done great things. . . .'

" The Moggeridges were gently persuasive in the same strain.   My mother had put her case to them also.   Usually I was indisposed to linger in the Moggeridge atmosphere ;   they had old-fashioned ideas about draughts, and there was a peculiar aged flavour about them ;   they were, to be plain, a very dirty old couple indeed. With declining strength they had relaxed by imperceptible degrees from the not very exacting standards of their youth.   I used to cut into their room and out of it again as quickly as I could.

" But half a century of the clerical life among

yielding country folk had given these bent, decaying, pitiful creatures a wonderful way with their social inferiors. ' Morning, Sir and Mam,' I said, and put down the coals I had brought and took up the empty scuttle-lining I had replaced.

" Mrs. Moggeridge advanced shakily so as to intercept my retreat. She had silvery hair, a wrinkled face and screwed-up red-rimmed eyes ; she was short-sighted and came peering up very close to me whenever she spoke to me, breathing in my face. She held out a quivering hand to arrest me ; she spoke with a quavering voice. ' And how's Master Morty this morning ? ' she said, with kindly condescending intonations.

" ' Very well thank you, Mam,' I said.

" ' I've been hearing rather a sad account of you, Morty, rather a sad account.'

" ' Sorry, Mum,' I said, and wished I had the courage to tell her that my life was no business of hers.

" ' They say you're discontented, Morty. They say you complain of God's Mercies.'

" Mr. Moggeridge had been sitting in the arm-chair by the fire-place. He was in his slippers and shirt-sleeves and he had been reading a newspaper. Now he looked at me over his silver-rimmed spectacles and spoke in a rich succulent voice.

" ' I'm sorry you should be giving trouble to that dear mother of yours,' he said. ' Very sorry. She's a devoted saintly woman.'

" ' Yessir,' I said.

" ' Very few boys nowadays have the privilege of such an upbringing as yours. Some day you may understand what you owe her.'

("'I begin to,'" interjected Sarnac.)

"'It seems you want to launch out upon some extravagant plan of classes instead of settling down quietly in your proper sphere. Is that so?'

"'I don't feel I know enough yet, Sir,' I said. 'I feel I'd like to learn more.'

"'Knowledge isn't always happiness, Morty,' said Mrs. Moggeridge close to me—much too close to me.

"'And what may these classes be that are tempting you to forget the honour you owe your dear good mother?' said Mr. Moggeridge.

"'I don't know yet, Sir. They say there's classes in geology and French and things like that.'

"Old Mr. Moggeridge waved his hand in front of himself with an expression of face as though it was I who emitted an evil odour. 'Geology!' he said. 'French—the language of Voltaire. Let me tell you one thing plainly, my boy, your mother is quite right in objecting to these classes. Geology —geology is—All Wrong. It has done more harm in the last fifty years than any other single influence whatever. It undermines faith. It sows doubt. I do not speak ignorantly, Mortimer. I have seen lives wrecked and destroyed and souls lost by this same geology. I am an old learned man, and I have examined the work of many of these so-called geologists—Huxley, Darwin and the like; I have examined it very very carefully and very very tolerantly, and I tell you they are all, all of them, *hopelessly mistaken men.* . . . And what good will such knowledge do you? Will it make you happier? Will it make you better? No, my lad. But I know of something that will. Something older than geology. Older and better. Sarah dear, give me that book there, please. Yes '—reverentially—' *the* Book.'

"His wife handed him a black-bound Bible, with its cover protected against rough usage by a metal edge. 'Now, my boy,' he said, 'let me give you this—this old familiar book, with an old man's blessing. In that is all the knowledge worth having, all the knowledge you will ever need. You will always find something fresh in it and always something beautiful.' He held it out to me.

"Accepting it seemed the shortest way out of the room, so I took it. 'Thank you, Sir,' I said.

"'Promise me you will read it.'

"'Oh yes, Sir.'

"I turned to go. But giving was in the air.

"'Now, Mortimer,' said Mrs. Moggeridge, 'do please promise me to seek strength where strength is to be found and try to be a better son to that dear struggling woman.' And as she spoke she proffered for my acceptance an extremely hard, small, yellow orange.

"'Thank you, Mam,' I said, made shift to stow her gift in my pocket, and with the Bible in one hand and the empty coal-scuttle-lining in the other escaped.

"I returned wrathfully to the basement and deposited my presents on the window-sill. Some impulse made me open the Bible, and inside the cover I found, imperfectly erased, the shadowy outlines of these words, printed in violet ink : 'Not to be Removed from the Waiting-Room.' I puzzled over the significance of this for some time."

"And what did it signify ? " asked Firefly.

"I do not know to this day," said Sarnac. "But apparently the reverend gentleman had acquired

that Book at a railway-station during one of his
journeys as a Sunday supply."

" You mean—— ? " said Firefly.

" No more than I say. He was in many ways
a peculiar old gentleman, and his piety was I fancy
an essentially superficial exudation. He was—I will
not say ' dishonest,' but ' spasmodically acquisitive.'
And like many old people in those days he preferred
his refreshment to be stimulating rather than nutri-
tious, and so he may have blurred his ethical per-
ceptions. An odd thing about him—Matilda Good
was the first to point it out—was that he rarely took
an umbrella away with him when he went on supply
and almost always he came back with one—and
once he came back with two. But he never kept
his umbrellas ; he would take them off for long
walks and return without them, looking all the
brighter for it. I remember one day I was in the
room when he returned from such an expedition,
there had been a shower and his coat was wet. Mrs.
Moggeridge made him change it and lamented that
he had lost his umbrella *again*.

" ' Not *lost*,' I heard the old man say in a voice of
infinite gentleness. ' Not lost, dear. Not lost ; but
gone before. . . . Gone before the rain came. . . .
The Lord gave. . . . Lord hath taken 'way.'

" For a time he was silent, coat in hand. He
stood with his shirt-sleeve resting on the mantel-
shelf, his foot upon the fender, and his venerable
hairy face gazing down into the fire. He seemed
to be thinking deep, sad things. Then he remarked
in a thoughtful, less obituary tone : ' Ten'n-sixpence.
A jolly *goo*' 'mbrella."

§ 8

" Frau Buchholz was a poor, lean, distressful woman of five and forty or more, with a table littered with the documents of some obscure litigation. She did not altogether discourage my ambitions but she laid great stress on the hopelessness of attempting Kultur without a knowledge of German, and I am inclined to think that her attitude was determined mainly by a vague and desperate hope that I might be induced to take lessons in German from her.

" Brother Ernest was entirely against my ambition. He was shy and vocally inexpressive, and he took me to the Victoria Music Hall and spent a long evening avoiding the subject. It was only as we drew within five minutes of home that he spoke of it.

" ' What's all this about your not being satisfied with your education, 'Arry ? ' he asked. ' I thought you'd had a pretty decent bit of schooling.'

" ' I don't feel I know anything,' I said. ' I don't know history or geography or anything. I don't even know my own grammar.'

" ' You know enough,' said Ernest. ' You know enough to get a job. Knowing more would only make you stuck-up. We don't want any more stuck-ups in the family, God knows.'

" I knew he referred to Fanny, but of course neither of us mentioned her shameful name.

" ' Anyhow, I suppose I'll have to chuck it,' I said bitterly.

" ' That's about it, 'Arry. I know you're a sensible chap—at bottom. You got to be what you got to be.'

" The only encouragement I got to resist mental

extinction was from Miss Beatrice Bumpus, and after a time I found even that source of consolation was being cut off from me. For my mother began to develop the most gross and improbable suspicions about Miss Bumpus. You see I stayed sometimes as long as ten or even twelve minutes in the drawing-room, and it was difficult for so good a woman as my mother, trained in the most elaborate precautions of separation between male and female, to understand that two young people of opposite sex could have any liking for each other's company unless some sort of gross familiarity was involved. The good of those days, living as they did in a state of inflamed restraint, had very exaggerated ideas of the appetites, capacities and uncontrollable duplicity of normal human beings. And so my mother began to man-œuvre in the most elaborate way to replace me by Prue as a messenger to Miss Bumpus. And when I was actually being talked to—and even talking—in the drawing-room I had an increasing sense of that poor misguided woman hovering upon the landing outside, listening in a mood of anxious curiosity and ripening for a sudden inrush, a disgraceful exposure, wild denunciation of Miss Bumpus, and the rescue of the vestiges of my damaged moral nature. I might never have realised what was going on if it had not been for my mother's direct questionings and warnings. Her conception of a proper upbringing for the young on these matters was a carefully preserved ignorance hedged about by shames and foul terrors. So she was at once extremely urgent and extraordinary vague with me. What was I up to—staying so long with that woman?

I wasn't to listen to anything she told me. I was
to be precious careful what I got up to up there.
I might find myself in more trouble than I thought.
There were women in this world of a shamelessness
it made one blush to think of. She'd always done
her best to keep me from wickedness and nastiness."

" But she was mad ! " said Willow.

" All the countless lunatic asylums of those days
wouldn't have held a tithe of the English people
who were as mad in that way as she was."

" But the whole world was mad ? " said Sunray.
" *All* those people, except perhaps Miss Bumpus,
talked about your education like insane people !
Did none of them understand the supreme wickedness
of hindering the growth of a human mind ? "

" It was a world of suppression and evasion. You
cannot understand anything about it unless you
understand that."

" But the whole world ! " said Radiant.

" Most of it. It was still a fear-haunted world.
' Submit,' said the ancient dread, ' do nothing—lest
you offend. And from your children—*hide*.' What
I am telling you about the upbringing of Harry Mortimer Smith was generally true of the upbringing of
the enormous majority of the inhabitants of the earth.
It was not merely that their minds were starved and
poisoned. Their minds were stamped upon and
mutilated. That world was so pitiless and confused,
so dirty and diseased because it was cowed and dared
not learn of remedies. In Europe in those days
we used to be told the most extraordinary stories
of the wickedness and cruelty of the Chinese, and one
favourite tale was that little children were made to

grow up inside great porcelain jars in order to distort their bodies to grotesque shapes so that they could be shown at fairs or sold to rich men. The Chinese certainly distorted the feet of young women for some obscure purpose, and this may have been the origin of this horrible legend. But our children in England were mentally distorted in exactly the same fashion except that for porcelain jars we used mental tin-cans and dustbins. . . . My dears! when I talk of this I cease to be Sarnac! All the rage and misery of crippled and thwarted Harry Mortimer Smith comes back to me."

"Did you get to those classes of yours?" asked Sunray. "I hope you did."

"Not for a year or two—though Miss Bumpus did what she could for me. She lent me a lot of books—in spite of much ignorant censorship on the part of my mother—and I read voraciously. But, I don't know if you will understand it, my relations with Miss Bumpus were slowly poisoned by the interpretations my mother was putting upon them. I think you will see how easy it was for a boy in my position to fall in love, fall into a deep emotional worship of so bright and friendly a young woman. Most of us young men nowadays begin by adoring a woman older than ourselves. Adoring is the word rather than loving. It's not a mate we need at first but the helpful kindly goddess who stoops to us. And of course I loved her. But I thought much more of serving her or dying for her than of embracing her. When I was away from her my imagination might go so far as to dream of kissing her hands.

"And then came my mother with this hideous

obsession of hers, jealous for something she called my purity, treating this white passion of gratitude and humility as though it was the power that drags a blow-fly to some heap of offal. A deepening shame and ungraciousness came into my relations with Miss Bumpus. I became red-eared and tongue-tied in her presence. Possibilities I might never have thought of but for my mother's suggestions grew disgustingly vivid in my mind. I dreamt about her grotesquely. When presently I found employment for my days my chances of seeing her became infrequent. She receded as a personality and friend, and quite against my will became a symbol of femininity.

' Among the people who called to see her a man of three or four and thirty became frequent. My spirit flamed into an intense and impotent jealousy on account of this man. He would take tea with her and stay for two hours or more. My mother took care to mention his visits in my hearing at every opportunity. She called him Miss Bumpus' ' fancy man,' or alluded to him archly : ' A certain person called again to-day, Prue. When good-lookin' young men are shown in at the door, votes flies out of the winder.' I tried to seem indifferent but my ears and cheeks got red and hot. My jealousy was edged with hate. I avoided seeing Miss Bumpus for weeks together. I sought furiously for some girl, any girl, who would serve to oust her image from my imagination."

Sarnac stopped abruptly and remained for a time staring intently into the fire. His expression was one of amused regret. "How little and childish

it seems now ! " he said ; "and how bitter—oh !
how bitter it was at the time ! "

"Poor little errand-boy ! " said Sunray, stroking
his hair. "Poor little errand-boy in love."

"What an uncomfortable distressful world it
must have been for all young things ! " said Willow.

"Uncomfortable and pitiless," said Sarnac.

§ 9

"My first employment in London was as an
errand-boy—'junior porter' was the exact phrase
—to a draper's shop near Victoria Station : I packed
parcels and carried them to their destinations ; my
next job was to be boy in general to a chemist named
Humberg in a shop beyond Lupus Street. A chemist
then was a very different creature from the kind of
man or woman we called a chemist to-day ; he was
much more like the Apothecary we find in Shakespeare's plays and such-like old literature ; he was
a dealer in drugs, poisons, medicines, a few spices,
colouring matters and such-like odd commodities.
I washed endless bottles, delivered drugs and medicines,
cleared up a sort of backyard, and did anything else that
there was to be done within the measure of my capacity.

"Of all the queer shops one found in that old-world
London, the chemists' shops were I think the queerest.
They had come almost unchanged out of the Middle
Ages, as we used to call them, when Western Europe,
superstitious, dirty, diseased and degenerate, thrashed
by the Arabs and Mongols and Turks, afraid to
sail the ocean or fight out of armour, cowered behind
the walls of its towns and castles, stole, poisoned,
assassinated and tortured, and pretended to be the

Roman Empire still in being. Western Europe
in those days was ashamed of its natural varieties
of speech and talked bad Latin ; it dared not look
a fact in the face but nosed for knowledge among
riddles and unreadable parchments ; it burnt men
and women alive for laughing at the absurdities
of its Faith, and it thought the stars of Heaven were
no better than a greasy pack of cards by which fortunes
were to be told. In those days it was that the tradition of the 'Pothecary was made ; you know him
as he figures in *Romeo and Juliet* ; the time in which
I lived this life was barely four centuries and a half
from old Shakespeare. The 'Pothecary was in a
conspiracy of pretentiousness with the almost equally
ignorant doctors of his age, and the latter wrote and
he ' made up ' prescriptions in occult phrases and
symbols. In our window there were great glass
bottles of red- and yellow- and blue-tinted water,
through which our gas-lamps within threw a mystical
light on the street pavement."

" Was there a stuffed alligator ? " asked Firefly.

" No. We were just out of the age of stuffed
alligators, but below these coloured bottles in the
window we had stupendous china jars with gilt caps
mystically inscribed—let me see ! Let me think !
One was *Sem. Coriand.* Another was *Rad. Sarsap.*
Then—what was the fellow in the corner ? *Mar-
ant. Ar.* And opposite him—*C. Cincordif.* And
behind the counter to look the customer in the face
were neat little drawers with golden and precious
letters thereon ; *Pil. Rhubarb.* and *Pil. Antibil.* and
many more bottles, *Ol. Amyg.* and *Tinct. Iod.*, rows
and rows of bottles, mystic, wonderful. I do not

remember ever seeing Mr. Humberg take anything, much less sell anything, from all this array of erudite bottles and drawers ; his normal trade was done in the bright little packets of an altogether different character that were piled all over the counter, bright unblushing little packets that declared themselves to be Gummidge's Fragrant and Digestive Tooth Paste, Hooper's Corn Cure, Luxtone's Lady's Remedy, Tinker's Pills for All Occasions, and the like. Such things were asked for openly and loudly by customers ; they were our staple trade. But also there were many transactions conducted in undertones which I never fully understood. I would be sent off to the yard on some specious pretext whenever a customer was discovered to be of the *sotto voce* variety, and I can only suppose that Mr. Humberg was accustomed at times to go beyond the limits of his professional qualification and to deal out advice and instruction that were legally the privileges of the qualified medical man. You must remember that in those days many things that we teach plainly and simply to everyone were tabooed and made to seem occult and mysterious and very very shameful and dirty.

"My first reaction to this chemist's shop was a violent appetite for Latin. I succumbed to its suggestion that Latin was the key to all knowledge, and that indeed statements did not become knowledge until they had passed into the Latin tongue. For a few coppers I bought in a second-hand bookshop an old and worn Latin *Principia* written by a namesake Smith ; I attacked it with great determination and found this redoubtable language far more understandable, reasonable and straightforward than

the elusive irritable French and the trampling cough-
ing German I had hitherto attempted. This Latin
was a dead language, a skeleton language plainly
articulated ; it never moved about and got away
from one as a living language did. In a little while
I was able to recognize words I knew upon our bottles
and drawers and in the epitaphs upon the monu-
ments in Westminster Abbey, and soon I could even
construe whole phrases. I dug out Latin books
from the second-hand booksellers' boxes, and some
I could read and some I could not. There was a
war history of that first Cæsar, Julius Cæsar, the adven-
turer who extinguished the last reek of the decaying
Roman republic, and there was a Latin New Testa-
ment ; I got along fairly well with both. But
there was a Latin poet, Lucretius, I could not construe ;
even with an English verse translation on the opposite
page I could not construe him. But I read that
English version with intense curiosity. It is an
extraordinary thing to note, but that same Lucretius, an old Roman poet who lived and died two
thousand years before my time, four thousand years
from now, gave an account of the universe and of
man's beginnings, far truer and more intelligible
than the old Semitic legends I had been taught in
my Sunday school.

"One of the queerest aspects of those days was
the mingling of ideas belonging to different ages and
phases of human development due to the irregularity
and casualness of such educational organisation as
we had. In school and church alike, obstinate
pedantry darkened the minds of men. Europeans
in the twentieth Christian century mixed up the

theology of the Pharaohs, the cosmogony of the priest-kings of Sumeria, with the politics of the seventeenth century and the ethics of the cricket-field and prize-ring, and that in a world which had got to aeroplanes and telephones.

" My own case was typical of the limitations of the time. In that age of ceaseless novelty there was I, trying to get back by way of Latin to the half knowledge of the Ancients. Presently I began to struggle with Greek also, but I never got very far with that. I found a chance of going once a week on what was called early-closing night, after my day's work was done, to some evening classes in chemistry. And this chemistry I discovered had hardly anything in common with the chemistry of a chemist's shop. The story of matter and force that it told belonged to another and a newer age. I was fascinated by these wider revelations of the universe I lived in, I ceased to struggle with Greek and I no longer hunted the dingy book-boxes for Latin classics but for modern scientific works. Lucretius I found was hardly less out of date than Genesis. Among the books that taught me much were one called *Physiography* by a writer named Gregory, Clodd's *Story of Creation* and Lankester's *Science from an Easy Chair*. I do not know if they were exceptionally good books ; they were the ones that happened to come to my hand and awaken my mind. But do you realise the amazing conditions under which men were living at that time, when a youngster had to go about as eager and furtive as a mouse seeking food, to get even such knowledge of the universe and himself as then existed ? I still remem-

ber how I read first of the differences and resem-
blances between apes and men and speculations
arising thencefrom about the nature of the sub-men
who came before man. It was in the shed in the
yard that I sat and read. Mr. Humberg was on
the sofa in the parlour behind the shop sleeping
off his midday meal with one ear a-cock for the shop-
bell, and I, with one ear a-cock for the shop-bell
and the other for any sounds of movement in the
parlour, read for the first time of the forces that had
made me what I was—when I ought to have been
washing out bottles.

" At one point in the centre of the display behind
the counter in the shop was a row of particularly
brave and important-looking glass jars wearing
about their bellies the gold promises of *Aqua Fortis*,
Amm. Hyd. and such-like names, and one day as I
was sweeping the floor I observed Mr. Humberg
scrutinising these. He held one up to the light and
shook his head at its flocculent contents. ' Harry,'
he said, ' see this row of bottles ? '

" ' Yessir.'

" ' Pour 'em all out and put in fresh water.'

" I stared, broom in hand, aghast at the waste.
' They won't blow up if I mix 'em ? ' I said.

" ' Blow up ! ' said Mr. Humberg. ' It's only
stale water. There's been nothing else in these
bottles for a score of years. Stuff I want is behind
the dispensary partition—and it's different stuff
nowadays. Wash 'em out—and then we'll put in
some water from the pump. We just have 'em for
the look of 'em. The old women wouldn't be happy
if we hadn't got 'em there.' "

Part 2

THE LOVES AND DEATH OF HARRY MORTIMER SMITH

Fanny Discovers Herself

§ I

" AND now," said Sarnac, " I can draw near
to the essentials of life and tell you the sort
of thing love was in that crowded, dingy, fear-ruled
world of the London fogs and the amber London
sunshine. It was a slender, wild-eyed, scared and
daring emotion in a dark forest of cruelties and repressions. It soon grew old and crippled, bitter-spirited
and black-hearted, but as it happened, death came
early enough for me to die with a living love still in
my heart. . . ."

" To live again," said Sunray very softly.

" And love again," said Sarnac, patting her knee.
" Let me see——. . . ."

He took a stake that had fallen from the fire and
thrust it into the bright glow at the centre and watched
it burst into a sierra of flames.

" I think that the first person I was in love with
was my sister Fanny. When I was a boy of eleven
or twelve I was really in love with her. But somehow
about that time I was also in love with an undraped
plaster nymph who sat very bravely on a spouting dol-
phin in some public gardens near the middle of Cliffstone. She lifted her chin and smiled and waved
one hand and she had the sweetest smile and the
dearest little body imaginable. I loved her back
particularly, and there was a point where you looked
at her from behind and just caught the soft curve of
her smiling cheek and her jolly little nose-tip and chin
and the soft swell of her breast under her lifted arm.

I would sneak round her furtively towards this particular view-point, having been too well soaked in shame about all such lovely things to look openly. But I never seemed to look my fill.

" One day as I was worshipping her in this fashion, half-turned to her and half-turned to a bed of flowers and looking at her askance, I became aware of an oldish man with a large white face, seated on a garden seat and leaning forward and regarding me with an expression of oafish cunning as if he had found me out and knew my secret. He looked like the spirit of lewdness incarnate. Suddenly panic overwhelmed me and I made off—and never went near that garden again. Angels with flaming shames prevented me. Or a terror of again meeting that horrible old man. . . .

" Then with my coming to London Miss Beatrice Bumpus took control of my imagination and was Venus and all the goddesses, and this increased rather than diminished after she had gone away. For she went away and, I gather, married the young man I hated ; she went away and gave up her work for the Vote and was no doubt welcomed back by those Warwickshire Bumpuses (who hunted) with the slaughter of a fatted fox and every sort of rejoicing. But her jolly frank and boyish face was the heroine's in a thousand dreams. I saved her life in adventures in all parts of the world and sometimes she saved mine ; we clung together over the edges of terrific precipices until I went to sleep, and when I was the conquering Muhammad after a battle, she stood out among the captive women and answered back when I said I would never love her, with two jets of cigarette smoke and the one word, ' Liar ! '

" I met no girls of my own age at all while I was errand-boy to Mr. Humberg, my evening classes and my reading kept me away from the facile encounters of the streets. Sometimes, however, when I could not fix my attention upon my books, I would slip off to Wilton Street and Victoria Street where there was a nocturnal promenade under the electric lamps. There schoolgirls and little drabs and errand-boys and soldiers prowled and accosted one another. But though I was attracted to some of the girlish figures that flitted by me I was also shy and fastidious. I was drawn by an overpowering desire for something intense and beautiful that vanished whenever I drew near to reality."

§ 2

" Before a year was over there were several changes in the Pimlico boarding-house. The poor old Moggeridges caught influenza, a variable prevalent epidemic of the time, and succumbed to inflammation of the lungs following the fever. They died within three days of each other, and my mother and Prue were the only mourners at their dingy little funeral. Frau Buchholz fades out of my story ; I do not remember clearly when she left the house nor who succeeded her. Miss Beatrice Bumpus abandoned the cause of woman's suffrage and departed, and the second floor was taken by an extremely intermittent couple who roused my mother's worst suspicions and led to serious differences of opinion between her and Matilda Good.

"You see these new-comers never settled in with any grave and sober luggage ; they would come and stay for a day or so and then not reappear for a week or more, and they rarely arrived or departed together. This roused my mother's moral observation, and she began hinting that perhaps they were not properly married after all. She forbade Prue ever to go to the drawing-room floor, and this precipitated a conflict with Matilda. 'What's this about Prue and the drawing-room?' Matilda asked. 'You're putting ideas into the girl's head.'

"'I'm trying to keep them from 'er,' said my mother. 'She's got eyes.'

"'*And* fingers,' said Matilda with dark allusiveness. 'What's Prue been seeing now?'

"'Marks,' said my mother.

"'What marks?' said Matilda.

"'Marks enough,' said my mother. ''*Is* things are marked one name and 'Er's another, and neither of them Milton, which is the name they've given us. And the way that woman speaks to you, as though she felt you might notice sumpthing— friendly like and a bit afraid of you. And that ain't all ! By no means all ! I'm not blind and Prue isn't blind. There's kissing and making love going on at all times in the day ! Directly they've got 'ere sometimes. Hardly waiting for one to get out of the room. I'm not a perfect fool, Matilda. I been married.'

"'What's that got to do with us ? We're a lodging-'ouse, not a set of Nosey Parkers. If Mr. and Mrs. Milton like to have their linen marked a *hundred* different names, what's that to us ? Their book's always marked *paid in advance with thanks, Matilda Good*, and that's married enough for me. See? You're an uneasy woman to have in a lodging-house, Martha, an uneasy woman. There's no give and take about you. No save-your-fare. There was that trouble you made about the boy and Miss Bumpus—ridiculous it was—and now seemingly there's going to be more trouble about Prue and Mrs. Milton—who's a lady, mind you, say what you like, and—what's more—a gentlewoman. I wish you'd mind your own business a bit more, Martha, and let Mr. and Mrs. Milton mind theirs. If they aren't properly married it's they've got to answer for it in the long run, not you. You'll get even with them all right in the Last Great Day. Meanwhile do they do 'arm to anyone? A quieter couple and less trouble to look after I've never had in all my lodging-house days.'

" My mother made no answer.

" ' Well ? ' challenged Matilda.

" ' It's hard to be waiting on a shameless woman,' said my mother, obstinate and white-lipped.

" ' It's harder still to be called a shameless woman because you've still got your maiden name on some of your things,' said Matilda Good. 'Don't talk such Rubbish, Martha.'

" ' I don't see why 'E should 'ave a maiden name too—on 'is pyjamas,' said my mother rallying after a moment.

" ' You don't know Anything, Martha,' said Matilda, fixing her with one eye of extreme animosity and regarding the question in the abstract with the other. ' I've often thought it of you and now I

say it to you. You don't know Anything. I'm
going to keep Mr. and Mrs. Milton as long as I
can, and if you're too pernikkety to wait on them,
there's those who will. I won't have my lodgers
insulted. I won't have their underclothes dragged
up against them. Why! Come to think of it!
Of course! He *borrowed* those pyjamas of 'is! Or
they was given him by a gentleman friend they didn't
fit. Or he's been left money and had to change
his name sudden like. It often happens. Often.
You see it in the papers. And things get mixed
in the wash. Some laundries, they're regular Ex-
changes. Mr. Plaice, he once had a collar with
Fortescue on it. Brought it back after his summer
holiday. Fortescue! There's evidence for you.
You aren't going to bring up something against
Mr. Plaice on account of that, Martha? You
aren't going to say he's been living a double life
and isn't properly a bachelor. Do think a little
clearer, Martha. And don't think so much evil.
There's a hundred ways round before you think evil.
But you *like* to think evil, Martha. I've noticed it
times and oft. You fairly wallow in it. You haven't
the beginnings of a germ of Christian charity.'

" ' One can't help seeing things,' said my mother
rather shattered.

" ' *You* can't,' said Matilda Good. ' There's those
who can't see an inch beyond their noses, and yet
they see too much. And the more I see of you the
more I'm inclined to think you're one of that sort.
Anyhow, Mr. and Mrs. Milton stay here—whoever
else goes. Whoever else goes. That's plain, I
hope, Martha.'

" My mother was stricken speechless. She bridled and subsided and then, except for necessary and unavoidable purposes, remained hurt and silent for some days, speaking only when she was spoken to. Matilda did not seem to mind. But I noticed that when presently Matilda sent Prue upstairs with the Miltons' tea my mother's stiffness grew stiffer, but she made no open protest."

§ 3

" And then suddenly Fanny reappeared in my world.

" It was a mere chance that restored Fanny to me. All our links had been severed when we removed from Cliffstone to London. My brother Ernest was her herald.

" We were at supper in the basement room and supper was usually a pleasant meal. Matilda Good would make it attractive with potatoes roasted in their jackets, or what she called a 'frying-pan' of potatoes and other vegetables in dripping or such-like heartening addition to cold bacon and bread and cheese and small beer. And she would read bits out of the newspaper to us and discuss them, having a really very lively intelligence, or she would draw me out to talk of the books I'd been reading. She took a great interest in murders and such-like cases, and we all became great judges of motive and evidence under her stimulation. ' You may say it's morbid, Martha, if you like,' she said ; ' but there never was a murder yet that wasn't brimful of humanity. Brimful. I doubt sometimes if we know what anyone's capable of until they've committed a murder or two.'

"My mother rarely failed to rise to her bait. 'I can't think 'ow you can say such things, Matilda,' she would say. . . .

"We heard the sound of a motor-car in the street above. Brother Ernest descended by the area steps and my sister Prue let him in. He appeared in his chauffeur's uniform, cap in hand, leather jacket and gaiters.

"'Got a night off?' asked Matilda.

"'Court Theatre at eleven,' said Ernest. 'So I thought I'd come in for a bit of a warm and a chat.'

"'Have a snack?' said Matilda. 'Prue, get him a plate and a knife and fork and a glass. One glass of *this* beer won't hurt your driving. Why! we haven't seen you for ages!'

"'Thank you, Miss Good,' said Ernest, who was always very polite to her, 'I *will* 'ave a snack. I bin' here, there and everywhere, but it isn't that I haven't wanted to call on you.'

"Refreshment was administered and conversation hung fire for awhile. One or two starts were made and came to an early end. Ernest's manner suggested preoccupation and Matilda regarded him keenly. 'And what have you got to tell us, Ernie?' she said suddenly.

"'We-el,' said Ernest, 'it's a curious thing you should say that, Miss Good, for I 'ave got something to tell you. Something—well, I don't know 'ow to put it—curious like.'

"Matilda refilled his glass.

" ' I seen Fanny,' said Ernest, coming to it with violent abruptness.

" ' *No !* ' gasped my mother, and for a moment no one else spoke.

" ' So ! ' said Matilda, putting her arms on the table and billowing forward, ' you've seen Fanny ! Pretty little Fanny that I used to know. And where did you see her, Ernie ? '

" Ernest had some difficulty in shaping out his story. ' It was a week last Tuesday,' he said after a pause.

" ' She wasn't—not one of Them—about Victoria Station ? ' panted my mother.

" ' Did you see her first or did she see you ? ' asked Matilda.

" ' A week ago last Tuesday,' my brother repeated.

" ' And did you speak to her ? '

" ' Not at the time I didn't. No.'

" ' Did she speak to you ? '

" ' No.'

" ' Then 'ow d'you know it was our Fanny ? ' asked Prue, who had been listening intently.

" ' I thought she'd gone to 'er fate in some foreign country—being so near Boulogne,' my mother said. ' I thought them White Slave Traders 'ad the decency to carry a girl off right away from 'er 'ome. . . . Fanny ! On the streets of London ! Near 'ere. I told 'er what it would come to. Time and again I told 'er. Merry an 'onest man I said, but she was greedy and 'eadstrong. . . . 'Eadstrong and vain. . . . She didn't try to follow you, Ernie, to find out where we were or anything like that ? '

" My brother Ernest's face displayed his profound perplexity. ' It wasn't at all like that, mother,' he said. ' It wasn't—that sort of thing. You see——'

" He began a struggle with the breast pocket of his very tightly fitting leather jacket and at last produced a rather soiled letter. He held it in his hand, neither attempting to read it nor offering it to us. But holding it in his hand seemed to crystallise his very rudimentary narrative powers. ' I better tell you right from the beginning,' he said. ' It isn't at all what you'd suppose. Tuesday week it was ; last Tuesday week.'

" Matilda Good laid a restraining hand on my mother's arm. 'In the evening I suppose?' she helped.

" ' It was a dinner and fetch,' said my brother. ' Of course you understand I 'adn't set eyes on Fanny for pretty near six years. It was 'er knew me.'

" ' You had to take these people to a dinner and fetch them back again ? ' said Matilda.

" ' Orders,' said Ernest, ' was to go to one-oh-two Brantismore Gardens Earl's Court top flat, to pick up lady and gentleman for number to be given in Church Row Hampstead and call there ten-thirty and take home as directed. Accordingly I went to Brantismore Gardens and told the porter in the 'all—it was one of these 'ere flat places with a porter in livery—that I was there to time waiting. 'E telephoned up in the usual way. After a bit, lady and gentleman came out of the house and I went to the door of the car as I usually do and held it open. So far nothing out of the ornary. He was a gentleman in evening dress, like most gentlemen ; she'd got a wrap with fur, and her hair, you know, was done up nice for an evening party with something that sparkled. Quite the lady.'

" ' And it was Fanny ? ' said Prue.

" Ernest struggled mutely with his subject for some moments. ' Not yet, like,' he said.

" ' You mean you didn't recognise her then ? ' said Matilda.

" ' No. But she just looked up at me and seemed kind of to start and got in. I saw her sort of leaning forward and looking at me as 'E got in. Fact is, I didn't think much of it. I should have forgotten all about it if it 'adn't been for afterwards. But when I took them back something happened. I could see she was looking at me. . . . We went first to one-oh-two Brantismore Gardens again and then he got out and says to me, " Just wait a bit here " and then he helped her out. It sort of seemed as though she was 'arf-inclined to speak to me and then she didn't. But this time I thinks to myself : " I seen you before, somewhere, my Lady." Oddly enough I never thought of Fanny then at all. I got as near as thinking she was a bit like ' Arry 'ere. But it never entered my 'ead it might be Fanny. Strordinary ! They went up the steps to the door ; one of these open entrances it is to several flats, and seemed to have a moment's confabulation under the light, looking towards me. Then they went on up to the flat.'

" ' You didn't know her even then ? ' said Prue.

" ' 'E came down the steps quarternour after perhaps, looking thoughtful. White wescoat, 'e 'ad, and coat over 'is arm. Gave me an address near Sloane Street. Got out and produced his tip, rather on the large side it was, and stood still kind of thoughtful. Seemed inclined to speak and didn't know what to say. " I've an account at the garage," 'e says, "you'll book the car," and then : "You're not my usual driver," 'e says. "What's your name?" "Smith," I says. "Ernest Smith," he says. "Yes sir," I says, and it was only as I drove off that I asked myself 'Ow the 'Ell—I reely beg your pardon, Miss Good.'

" ' Don't mind me,' said Matilda. ' Go on.'

" ' 'Ow the Juice d'e know that my name was Ernest? I nearly 'it a taxi at the corner of Sloane Square I was so took up puzzling over it. And it was only about three o'clock in the morning, when I was lying awake still puzzling over it, that it came into my 'ead——'

" Ernest assumed the manner of a narrator who opens out his culminating surprise. ' —that that young lady I'd been taken out that evening was——'

" He paused before his climax.

" ' Fenny,' whispered Prue.

" ' Sister Fanny,' said Matilda Good.

" ' Our Fanny,' said my mother.

" ' *No less a person than Fanny!* ' said my brother Ernest triumphantly and looked round for the amazement proper to such a surprise.

" ' I thought it was going to be Fenny,' said Prue.

" ' Was she painted up at all?' asked Matilda.

" ' Not nearly so much painted as most of 'em are,' said my brother Ernest. 'Pretty nearly everyone paints nowadays. Titled people. Bishops' ladies. Widows. Everyone. She didn't strike me —well, as belonging to the painted sort particularly, not in the least. Kind of fresh and a little pale —like Fanny used to be.'

" ' Was she dressed like a lady—quiet-like?'

"'Prosperous,' said Ernest. 'Reely prosperous. But nothing what you might call extravagant.'

"'And the house you took 'em to—noisy? Singing and dancing and the windows open?'

"'It was a perfectly respectable quiet sort of 'ouse. Blinds down and no row whatever. A private 'ouse. The people who came to the door to say good night might 'ave been any gentleman and any lady. I see the butler. 'E came down to the car. 'E wasn't 'ired for the evening. 'E was a *real* butler. The other guests had a private limousine with an oldish careful sort of driver. Whadyou'd speak of as nice people.'

"'Hardly what you might call being on the streets of London,' said Matilda, turning to my mother. 'What was the gentleman like?'

"'I don't want to 'ear of 'im,' said my mother.

"'Dissipated sort of man about town—and a bit screwed?' asked Matilda.

"''E was a lot soberer than most dinner fetches,' said Ernest. 'I see that when 'e 'andled 'is money. Lots of 'em—oh! quite 'igh-class people get—'ow shall I say it?—just a little bit funny. 'Umerous like. Bit 'nnacurate with the door. 'E wasn't. That's what I can't make out. . . . And then there's this letter.'

"'Then there's this letter,' said Matilda. 'You better read it, Martha.'

"'How did you get that letter?' asked my mother, not offering to touch it. 'You don't mean to say she gave you a letter!'

"'It came last Thursday. By post. It was addressed to me, Ernest Smith, Esq., at the Garage.

It's a curious letter—asking about us. I can't make
'ead or tail of the whole business. I been thinking
about it and thinking about it. Knowing 'ow .set
mother was about Fanny—I 'esitated.'

" His voice died away.

" ' Somebody,' said Matilda in the pause that
followed, ' had better read that letter.'

" She looked at my mother, smiled queerly with
the corners of her mouth down, and then held out
her hand to Ernest."

§ 4

" It was Matilda who read that letter ; my mother's
aversion from it was all too evident. I can still
remember Matilda's large red face thrust forward
over the supper things and a little on one side so
as to bring the eye she was using into focus and
get the best light from the feeble little gas-bracket.
Beside her was Prue, with a slack curious face and
a restive glance that went ever and again to my
mother's face, as a bandsman watches the conductor's
baton. My mother sat back with a defensive expression on her white face, and Ernest was posed, wide
and large, in a non-committal attitude, ostentatiously
unable to ' make 'ead or tail ' of the affair.

" ' Let's see,' said Matilda, and took a preliminary
survey of the task before her. . . .

" ' *My dear Ernie*,' she says. . . .

" ' *My dear Ernie :*

" ' *It was wonderful seeing you again. I could
hardly believe it was you even after Mr.—Mr.——*
She's written it and thought better of it and scratched

it out again, Mr. Somebody—Mr. Blank—*had asked your name. I was beginning to fear I'd lost you all. Where are you living and how are you getting on? You know I went to France and Italy for a holiday— lovely lovely places—and when I came back I slipped off at Cliffstone because I wanted to see you all again and couldn't bear leaving you as I had done without a word.'*

"'She should've thought of that before,' said my mother.

"'*She told me, Mrs. Bradley did, about poor father's accident and death—the first I heard of it. I went to his grave in the cemetery and had a good cry. I couldn't help it. Poor old Daddy! It was cruel hard luck getting killed as he did. I put a lot of flowers on his grave and arranged with Ropes the Nurseryman about having the grass cut regularly.'*

"'And 'im,' said my mother, 'lying there! 'E'd 've rather seen 'er lying dead at 'is feet, 'e said, than 'ave 'er the fallen woman she was. And she putting flowers over 'im. 'Nough to make 'im turn in 'is grave.'

"'But very likely he's come to think differently now, Martha,' said Matilda soothingly. 'There's no knowing really, Martha. Perhaps in heaven they aren't so anxious to see people dead at their feet. Perhaps they get sort of kind up there. Let me see,—where was I? Ah?—*grass cut regularly.*

"'*Nobody knew where mother and the rest of you were. Nobody had an address. I went on to London very miserable, hating to have lost you. Mrs. Bradley*

*said that mother and Prue and Morty had gone to London
to friends, but where she didn't know. And then behold!
after nearly two years, you bob up again! It's too good
to be true. Where are the others? Is Morty getting
educated? Prue must be quite grown up? I would
love to see them again and help them if I can. Dear
Ernie, I do want you to tell mother and all of them that
I am quite safe and happy. I am being helped by a
friend. The one you saw. I'm not a bit fast or bad.
I lead a very quiet life. I have my tiny little flat here
and I read a lot and get educated. I work quite hard.
I've passed an examination, Ernie, a university examination. I've learnt a lot of French and Italian and
some German and about music. I've got a pianola
and I'd love to play it to you or Morty. He was always
the one for music. Often and often I think of you.
Tell mother, show her this letter, and let me know soon
about you all and don't think unkind things of me.
'Member the good times we had, Ernie, when we dressed
up at Christmas and father didn't know us in the shop,
and how you made me a doll's house for my birthday.
Oh! and cheese pies, Ernie! Cheese pies!'*

"'What were cheese pies?' asked Matilda.

"'It was a sort of silly game we had—passing
people. I forget exactly. But it used to make us
laugh—regular roll about we did.'

"'Then she gets back to you, Morty,' said Matilda.

"'*I'd love to help Morty if he still wants to be educated.
I could now. I could help him a lot. I suppose he's
not a boy any longer. Perhaps he's getting educated
himself. Give him my love. Give mother my love
and tell her not to think too badly of me. Fanny.*'

"'Fanny. Embossed address on her notepaper. That's all.'

"Matilda dropped the letter on the table. 'Well?' she said in a voice that challenged my mother. 'Seems to me that the young woman has struck one of the Right Sort—the one straight man in ten thousand . . . seems to have taken care of her almost more than an ordinary husband might've done. . . . What'r you going to do about it, Martha?'

"Matilda collected herself slowly from the table and leant back in her chair, regarding my mother with an expression of faintly malevolent irony."

§ 5

"I turned from Matilda's quizzical face to my mother's drawn intentness.

"'Say what you like, Matilda, that girl is living in sin.'

"'Even that isn't absolutely proved,' said Matilda.

"'Why should 'e——?' my mother began and stopped.

"'There's such things as feats of generosity,' said Matilda. 'Still——'

"'No,' said my mother. 'We don't want 'er 'elp. I'd be ashamed to take it. While she lives with that man——'

"'Apparently she doesn't. But go on.'

"'Stainted money,' said my mother. 'It's money she 'as from 'im. It's the money of a Kep Woman.'

"Her anger kindled. 'I'd sooner die than *touch* 'er money.'

"Her sense of the situation found form and expression. 'She leaves 'er 'ome. She breaks 'er father's 'eart. Kills 'im, she does. 'E was never the same man after she'd gone ; never the same. She goes off to shamelessness and luxury. She makes 'er own brother drive 'er about to 'er shame.'

"'Hardly—*makes*,' protested Matilda.

"''Ow was *'E* to avoid it? And then she writes this—this letter. Impudent I call it. Impudent! Without a word of repentance—not a single word of repentance. Does she 'ave the decency to say she's ashamed of 'erself? Not a word. Owns she's still living with a fancy man and means to go on doing it, glories in it. And offers us 'er kind assistance—us, what she's disgraced and shamed. Who was it that made us leave Cherry Gardens to 'ide our 'eads from our neighbours in London? *'Er!* And now she's to come 'ere in 'er moty-car and come dancing down these steps, all dressed up and painted, to say a kind word to poor mother. 'Aven't we suffered enough about 'er without 'er coming 'ere to show 'erself off at us? It's topsy-turvy. Why! if she comes 'ere at all, which I doubt—if she comes 'ere at all she ought to come in sackcloth and ashes and on 'er bended knees.'

"'She won't do that, Martha,' said Matilda Good.

"'Then let 'er keep away. We don't want the disgrace of 'er. She's chosen 'er path and let 'er abide by it. But *'ere!* To come *'ere!* 'Ow'r you going to explain it?'

"'*I'd* explain it all right,' said Matilda unheeded.

"''Ow am *I* going to explain it? And here's Prue! Here's this Mr. Pettigrew she's met at the

Week day Evening Social and wants to bring to
tea ! 'Ow's she going to explain 'er fine lady sister
to 'im ? Kep Woman ! Yes, Matilda, I say it.
It's the name for it. That's what she is. A Kep
Woman ! Nice thing to tell Mr. Pettigrew. 'Ere's
my sister, the Kep Woman ! 'E'd be off in a jiffy.
Shocked 'e'd be out of 'is seven senses. 'Ow would
Prue ever 'ave the face to go to the Week day Evening Social again after a show-up like that ? And
Ernie. What's 'E going to say about it to the
other chaps at the garage when they throw it up
at him that 'is sister's a Kep Woman ? '

" ' Don't you worry about *that*, mother,' said
Ernest gently but firmly. 'There's nobody ever
throws anything up against me at the garage anyhow
—and there won't be. Nohow. Not unless 'E
wants to swaller 'is teeth.'

" ' Well, there's 'Arry. 'E goes to 'is classes,
and what if someone gets 'old of it there ? 'Is
sister, a Kep Woman. They'd 'ardly let 'im go
on working after such a disgrace.'

" ' Oh I'd soon——' I began, following in my
brother's wake. But Matilda stopped me with a
gesture. Her gesture swept round and held my
mother, who was indeed drawing near the end of
what she had to say.

" ' I can see, Martha,' said Matilda, ' just 'ow
you feel about Fanny. I suppose it's all natural.
Of course, this letter——'

" She picked up the letter. She pursed her great
mouth and waggled her clumsy head slowly from
side to side. ' For the life of me I can't believe
the girl who wrote this is a bad-hearted girl,' she

said. 'You're bitter with her, Martha. You're bitter.'

" 'After all——' I began, but Matilda's hand stopped me again.

" 'Bitter !' cried my mother. 'I *know* 'er. She can put on that in'cent air just as though nothing 'ad 'appened and try and make you feel in the wrong——'

" Matilda ceased to waggle and began to nod. ' I see,' she said. ' I see. But why should Fanny take the trouble to write this letter, if she hadn't a real sort of affection for you all ? As though she need have bothered herself about the lot of you ! You'r no sort of help to her. There's kindness in the letter, Martha, and something more than kindness. Are you going to throw it back at her ? Her and her offers of help ? Even if she doesn't crawl and repent as she ought to do ! Won't you even answer her letter ? '

"' I won't be drawn into a correspondence with 'er,' said my mother. ' No ! So long as she's a Kep Woman, she's no daughter of mine. I wash my 'ands of 'er. And as for 'er 'Elp ! 'Elp indeed ! It's 'Umbug ! If she'd wanted 'elp us she could have married Mr. Crosby, as fair and honest a man as any woman could wish for.'

" ' So that's *that*,' said Matilda Good conclusively.

" Abruptly she swivelled her great head round to Ernest. ' And what are you going to do, Ernie ? Are *you* for turning down Fanny ? And letting the cheese pies just drop into the mud of Oblivium, as the saying goes, and be forgotten for ever and ever and ever ? '

" Ernest sat back, put his hand in his trouser pockets and remained thoughtful for some moments. ' It's orkward,' he said.

" Matilda offered him no assistance.

" ' There's my Young Lady to consider,' said Ernest and flushed an extreme scarlet.

" My mother turned her head sharply and looked at him. Ernest with a stony expression did not look at my mother.

" ' O—oh ! ' said Matilda. ' Here's something new. And who may your Young Lady be, Ernie ? '

" ' Well, I 'adn't proposed to discuss 'er 'ere just yet. So never mind what 'er name is. She's got a little millinery business. I'll say that for 'er. And a cleverer nicer girl never lived. We met at a little dance. Nothing isn't fixed up yet beyond a sort of engagement. There's been presents. Given 'er a ring and so forth. But naturally I've never told 'er anything about Fanny. I 'aven't discussed family affairs with 'er much, not so far. Knows we were in business of some sort and 'ad losses and father died of an accident ; that's about all. But Fanny—— Fanny's certainly going to be orkward to explain. Not that I want to be *'ard* on Fanny ! '

" ' I see,' said Matilda. She glanced a mute interrogation at Prue and found her answer in Prue's face. Then she picked up the letter again and read very distinctly : ' One hundred and two, Brantismore Gardens, Earl's Court.' She read this address slowly as though she wanted to print it on her memory. ' Top flat, you said it was, Ernie ? ' . . .

" She turned to me. ' And what are you going to do, Harry, about all this ? '

" ' I want to see Fanny for myself,' I said. ' I don't believe——'

" ' 'Arry,' said my mother, ' now—once for all —I forbid you to go near 'er. I won't 'ave you corrupted.'

" ' Don't forbid him, Martha,' said Matilda. ' It's no use forbidding him. *Because he will!* Any boy with any heart and spunk in him would go and see her after that letter. One hundred and two, Brantismore Gardens, Earl's Court,'—she was very clear with the address—'it's not very far from here.'

" ' I forbid you to go near 'er, 'Arry,' my mother reiterated. And then realising too late the full importance of Fanny's letter, she picked it up. ' I won't 'ave this answered. I'll burn it as it deserves. And forget about it. Banish it from my mind. *There.*'

" And then my mother stood up and making a curious noise in her throat like the strangulation of a sob, she put Fanny's letter into the fire and took the poker to thrust it into the glow and make it burn. We all stared in silence as the letter curled up and darkened, burst into a swift flame and became in an instant a writhing, agonised, crackling, black cinder. Then she sat down again, remained still for a moment, and then after a fierce struggle with her skirt-pocket dragged out a poor, old, dirty pocket-handkerchief and began to weep—at first quietly and then with a gathering passion. The rest of us sat aghast at this explosion.

" ' You mustn't go near Fanny, 'Arry ; not if mother forbids,' said Ernest at last, gently but firmly.

" Matilda looked at me in grim enquiry.

" ' I *shall*,' I said, and was in a terror lest the unmanly tears behind my eyes should overflow.

" ' 'Arry ! ' cried my mother amidst her sobs. ' You'll break—you'll break my heart ! First Fanny ! Then you.'

" ' You see ! ' said Ernest.

" The storm of her weeping paused as though she waited to hear my answer. My silly little face must have been very red by this time and there was something wrong and uncontrollable about my voice, but I said what I meant to say. ' I shall go to Fanny,' I said, ' and I shall just ask her straight out whether she's leading a bad life.'

" ' And suppose she is ? ' asked Matilda.

" ' I shall reason with her,' I said. ' I shall do all I can to save her. Yes—even if I have to find some work that will keep her. . . . She's my sister.' . . .

" I wept for a moment or so. ' I can't help it, mother,' I sobbed. ' I got to see Fanny ! '

" I recovered my composure with an effort.

" ' *So*,' said Matilda, regarding me, I thought, with rather more irony and rather less admiration than I deserved. Then she turned to my mother. ' I don't see that Harry can say fairer than that,' she said. ' I think you'll have to let him see her after that. He'll do all he can to save her, he says. Who knows ? He might bring her to repentance.'

" ' More likely the other way about,' said my mother, wiping her eyes, her brief storm of tears now over.

" ' I can't 'elp feeling it's a mistake,' said Ernest, ' for 'Arry to go and see 'er.'

" ' Well, anyhow don't give it up because you've forgotten the address, Harry,' said Matilda, ' or else you *are* done. Let it be your own free-will and not forgetfulness, if you throw her over. One hundred and two Brantismore Gardens, Earl's Court. You'd better write it down.'

" ' One hundred and two—Brantismore Gardens.'

" I went over to my books on the corner table to do as she advised sternly and resolutely in a fair round hand on the fly-leaf of Smith's *Principia Latina*."

§ 6

" My first visit to Fanny's flat was quite unlike any of the moving scenes I acted in my mind before-hand. I went round about half-past eight when shop was done on the evening next but one after Ernest's revelation. The house seemed to me a very dignified one and I went up a carpeted stair-case to her flat. I rang the bell and she opened the door herself.

" It was quite evident at once that the smiling young woman in the doorway had expected to see someone else instead of the gawky youth who stood before her, and that for some moments she had not the slightest idea who I was. Her expression of radiant welcome changed to a defensive coldness. ' What do you want, please ? ' she said to my silent stare.

" She had altered very much. She had grown, though now I was taller than she was, and her wavy brown hair was tied by a band of black velvet with a brooch on one side of it, adorned with clear-cut

stones of some sort that shone and twinkled. Her
face and lips had a warmer colour than I remembered. And she was wearing a light soft greenish-
blue robe with loose sleeves ; it gave glimpses of
her pretty neck and throat and revealed her white
arms. She seemed a magically delightful being,
soft and luminous and sweet-scented and altogether
wonderful to a young barbarian out of the London
streets. Her delicacy overawed me. I cleared my
throat. ' Fanny ! ' I said hoarsely, ' don't you
know me ? '

" She knitted her pretty brows and then came
her old delightful smile. ' Why ! It's Harry ! '
she cried and drew me into the little hall and hugged
and kissed me. ' My little brother Harry, grown
as big as I am ! How wonderful ! '

" Then she went by me and shut the door and
looked at me doubtfully. ' But why didn't you
write to me first to say you were coming ? Here
am I dying for a talk with you and here's a visitor
who's coming to see me. May come in at any
moment. Now what am I to do ? Let me see ! '

" The little hall in which we stood was bright
with white paint and pretty Japanese pictures. It
had cupboards to hide away coats and hats and an
old oak chest. Several doors opened into it and
two were ajar. Through one I had a glimpse of
a sofa and things set out for coffee, and through the
other I saw a long mirror and a chintz-covered arm-
chair. She seemed to hesitate between these two
rooms and then pushed me into the former one
and shut the door behind us.

" ' You should have written to tell me you were

coming,' she said. ' I'm dying to talk to you and
here's someone coming who's dying to talk to *me*.
But never mind ! let's talk all we can. How are
you ? *Well*—I can see that. But are you getting
educated ? And mother, how's mother ? What's
happened to Prue ? And is Ernest as hot-tempered
as ever ? '

" I attemped to tell her. I tried to give her an
impression of Matilda Good and to hint not too
harshly at my mother's white implacability. I began
to tell her of my chemist's shop and how much
Latin and Chemistry I knew, and in the midst of
it she darted away from me and stood listening.

" It was the sound of a latch-key at the door.

" ' My other visitor,' she said, hesitated a moment
and was out of the room, leaving me to study her
furniture and the coffee machine that bubbled on
the table. She had left the door a little ajar and
I heard all too plainly the sound of a kiss and then
a man's voice. I thought it was rather a jolly voice.

" ' I'm tired, little Fanny ; oh ! I'm tired to death.
This new paper is the devil. We've started all
wrong. But I shall pull it off. Gods ! if I hadn't
this sweet pool of rest to plunge into, I'd go off
my head ! I'd have nothing left to me but head-
lines. Take my coat ; there's a dear. I smell
coffee.'

" I heard a movement as though Fanny had checked
her visitor almost at the door of the room I was
in. I heard her say something very quickly about
a brother.

" ' Oh, *Damn !* ' said the man very heartily. ' Not
another of 'em ! How many brothers have you

got, Fanny? Send him away. I've only got an hour altogether, my dear——'

" Then the door closed sharply—Fanny must have discovered it was ajar—and the rest of the talk was inaudible.

" Fanny reappeared, a little flushed and bright-eyed and withal demure. She had evidently been kissed again.

" ' Harry,' she said, ' I hate to ask you to go and come again, but that other visitor—I'd promised him first. Do you mind, Harry? I'm longing for a good time with you, a good long talk. You get your Sundays, Harry? Well, why not come here at three on Sunday when I'll be quite alone and we'll have a regular good old tea? Do you mind, Harry?'

" I said I didn't. In that flat ethical values seemed quite different to what they were outside.

" ' After all, you did ought to have written first,' said Fanny, ' instead of just jumping out on me out of the dark.'

" There was no one in the hall when she showed me out and not even a hat or coat visible. ' Give me a kiss, Harry,' she said and I kissed her very readily. ' Quite sure you don't mind?' she said at her door.

" ' Not a bit,' I said. ' I ought to have written.'

" ' Sunday at three,' she said, as I went down the carpeted staircase.

" ' Sunday at three,' I replied at the bend of the stairs.

" Downstairs there was a sort of entrance hall to all the flats with a fire burning in a fire-place and a man ready to call a cab or taxi for anyone who wanted one. The prosperity and comfort of it all impressed me greatly, and I was quite proud to be walking out of such a fine place. It was only when I had gone some way along the street that I began to realise how widely my plans for the evening had miscarried.

" I had not asked her whether she was living a bad life or not and I had reasoned with her not at all. The scenes I had rehearsed in my mind before-hand, of a strong and simple and resolute younger brother saving his frail but lovable sister from terrible degradations, had indeed vanished altogether from my mind when her door had opened and she had appeared. And here I was with the evening all before me and nothing to report to my family but the profound difference that lies between romance and reality. I decided not to report to my family at all yet, but to go for a very long walk and think this Fanny business over thoroughly, returning home when it would be too late for my mother to cross-examine me and ' draw me out ' at any length.

" I made for the Thames Embankment, for that afforded uncrowded pavements and the solemnity and incidental beauty appropriate to a meditative promenade.

" It is curious to recall now the phases of my mind that night. At first the bright realities I came from dominated me : Fanny pretty and prosperous, kindly and self-assured, in her well-lit, well-furnished flat, and the friendly and confident voice I had heard speaking in the hall, asserted themselves as facts to be accepted and respected. It was delightful

after more than two years of ugly imaginations to
have the glimpse of my dear sister again so undefeated
and loved and cared for and to look forward to a
long time with her on Sunday and a long confabulation upon all I had done in the meantime and all
I meant to do. Very probably these two people
were married after all, but unable for some obscure
reason to reveal the fact to the world. Perhaps
Fanny would tell me as much in the strictest confidence on Sunday and I could go home and astonish
and quell my mother with the whispered secret.
And even as I developed and cuddled this idea it
grew clear and cold and important in my mind that
they were not married at all, and the shades of a
long-accumulated disapproval dimmed that first
bright impression of Fanny's little nest. I felt a
growing dissatisfaction with the part I had played
in our encounter. I had let myself be handled and
thrust out as though I had been a mere boy instead
of a brother full of help and moral superiority. Surely
I ought to have said something, however brief, to
indicate our relative moral positions ! I ought to
have faced that man too, the Bad Man, lurking no
doubt in the room with the mirror and the chintz-
covered chair. He had avoided seeing me—because
he could not face me ! And from these new aspects
of the case I began to develop a whole new dream
of reproach and rescue. What should I have said
to the Bad Man ? ' And so, Sir, at last we meet——'

" Something like that.

" My imagination began to leap and bound and
soar with me. I pictured the Bad Man, dressed
in that ' immaculate evening dress ' which my novels

told me marked the deeper and colder depths of male depravity, cowering under my stream of simple eloquence. 'You took her,' I would say, 'from our homely but pure and simple home. You broke her father's heart'—yes, I imagined myself saying that!—'And what have you made of her?' I asked. 'Your doll, your plaything! to be pampered while the whim lasts and then to be cast aside!' Or— 'tossed aside'?

"I decided 'tossed aside' was better.

"I found myself walking along the Embankment, gesticulating and uttering such things as that."

"But you knew better?" said Firefly. "Even then."

"I knew better. But that was the way our minds worked in the ancient days."

§ 7

"But," said Sarnac, "my second visit to Fanny, like my first, was full of unexpected experiences and unrehearsed effects. The carpet on the pleasant staircase seemed to deaden down my moral tramplings, and when the door opened and I saw my dear Fanny again, friendly and glad, I forgot altogether the stern interrogations with which that second interview was to have opened. She pulled my hair and kissed me, took my hat and coat, said I had grown tremendously and measured herself against me, pushed me into her bright little sitting-room, where she had prepared such a tea as I had never seen before, little ham sandwiches, sandwiches of a delightful stuff called Gentleman's Relish, strawberry jam, two sorts

of cake, and little biscuits to fill in any odd corners.
'You are a dear to come and see me, Harry. But
I had a sort of feeling that whatever happened you
would come along.'

"'We two always sort of hung together,' I said.

"'Always,' she agreed. 'I think mother and
Ernie might have written me a line. Perhaps they
will later. Ever seen an electric kettle, Harry?
This is one. And you put that plug in there.'

"'I know,' I said, and did as I was told. 'There's
resistances embedded in the coating. I've been
doing some electricity and chemistry. Council classes.
Six'r seven subjects altogether. And there's a shop-
window in Tothill Street full of such things.'

"'I expect you know all about them,' she said.
'I expect you've learnt all sorts of sciences,' and
so we came to the great topic of what I was learning
and what I was going to do.

"It was delightful to talk to someone who really
understood the thirst for knowledge that possessed
me. I talked of myself and my dreams and ambitions,
and meanwhile, being a growing youth, my arm swept
like a swarm of locusts over Fanny's wonderful tea.
Fanny watched me with a smile on her face and steered
me with questions towards the things she most wanted
to know. And when we had talked enough for a
time she showed me how to play her pianola and I
got a roll of Schumann that Mr. Plaice had long ago
made familiar to me and had the exquisite delight of
playing it over for myself. These pianolas were
quite easy things to manage, I found ; in a little
while I was already playing with conscious expression.

"Fanny praised me for my quickness, cleared

her tea-things away while I played, and then came and sat beside me and listened and talked and we found we had learnt quite a lot about music since our parting. We both thought great things of Bach,— whom I found I was calling quite incorrectly Batch —and Mozart, who also had to be pronounced a little differently. And then Fanny began to question me about the work I wanted to do in the world. ' You mustn't stay with that old chemist much longer,' she declared. How would I like to do some sort of work that had to do with books, bookselling or helping in a library or printing and publishing books and magazines ? ' You've never thought of writing things ? ' asked Fanny. ' People do.'

" ' I made some verses once or twice,' I confessed, ' and wrote a letter to the *Daily News* about temperance. But they didn't put it in.'

" ' Have you ever wanted to write ? '

" ' What, books ? Like Arnold Bennett ? *Rather !* '

" ' But you didn't quite know how to set about it.'

" ' It's difficult to begin,' I said, as though that was the only barrier.

" ' You ought to leave that old chemist's shop,' she repeated. ' If I were to ask people I know and found out some better sort of job for you, Harry, would you take it ? '

" ' *Rather !* ' said I."

" Why not altogether ? " interrupted Firefly.

" Oh ! we used to say *Rather*," said Sarnac. " It was artistic understatement. But you realise how dreadfully I lapsed from all my preconceived notions about Fanny and myself. We talked the whole evening away. We had a delightful cold picnic supper in a pretty little dining-room with a dresser, and Fanny showed me how to make a wonderful salad with onions very finely chopped and white wine and sugar in the dressing. And afterwards came some more of that marvel, the pianola, and then very reluctantly I took my leave. And when I found myself in the streets again I had once more my former sense of having dropped abruptly from one world into another, colder, bleaker, harder, and with entirely different moral values. Again I felt the same reluctance to go straight home and have my evening dimmed and destroyed by a score of pitiless questions. And when at last I did go home I told a lie. 'Fanny's got a pretty place and she's as happy as can be,' I said. 'I'm not quite sure, but from what she said, I believe that man's going to marry her before very long.'

" My cheeks and ears grew hot under my mother's hostile stare.

" ' Did she tell you that ? '

" ' Practically,' I lied. ' I kind of got it out of her.'

" But 'e's married already ! ' said my mother.

" ' I believe there is something,' I said.

" ' *Something* ! ' said my mother scornfully. ' She's stolen another woman's man. 'e belongs to 'er —for ever. No matter what there is against 'er. "Whomsoever God Hath Joined, Let No Man Put Asunder " !—that's what I was taught and what I believe. 'E may be older ; 'e may have led her astray, but while she and 'e harbour together the sin is 'ers smutch as 'is. Did you see 'im ? '

" ' He wasn't there.'

" ' 'Adn't the face. That's so much to their credit. And are you going there again ? '

" ' I've kind of promised——'

" ' It's against my wishes, 'Arry. Every time you go near Fanny, 'Arry, you disobey me. Mark that. Let's be plain about that, once and for all.'

" I felt mulish. ' She's my sister,' I said.

" ' And I'm your mother. Though nowadays mothers are no more than dirt under their children's feet. Marry 'er indeed ! Why *should* 'e ? Likely. 'E'll marry the next one. Come, Prue, take that bit of coal off the fire and we'll go up to bed.' "

§ 8

" And now," said Sarnac, " I must tell you of the queer business organisation of Thunderstone House and the great firm of Crane & Newberry, for whom, at Fanny's instance, I abandoned Mr. Humberg and his gold-labelled bottles of nothingness. Crane & Newberry were publishers of newspapers, magazines and books, and Thunderstone House was a sort of fountain of printed paper, spouting an unending wash of reading matter into the lives of the English people.

" I am talking of the world two thousand years ago," said Sarnac. " No doubt you have all been good children and have read your histories duly, but at this distance in time things appear very much foreshortened, and changes that occupied lifetimes and went on amidst dense clouds of doubt, misunderstanding and opposition seem to be the easiest and most natural of transitions. We were all taught that the scientific method came into human affairs first of all in the world of material things, and later on in the matters of psychology and human relationship, so that the large-scale handling of steel, and railways, automobiles, telegraphs, flying machines and all the broad material foundations of the new age were in existence two or three generations before social, political and educational ideas and methods were modified in correspondence with the new necessities these things had created. There was a great unanticipated increase in the trade and population of the world and much confusion and conflict, violent social stresses and revolutions and great wars, before even the need of a scientific adjustment of human relationships was recognised. It is easy enough to learn of such things in general terms but hard to explain just what these processes of blind readjustment meant in anxiety, suffering and distress to the countless millions who found themselves born into the swirl of this phase of change. As I look back to that time in which I lived my other life I am reminded of a crowd of people in one of my old Pimlico fogs. No one had any vision of things as a whole ; everybody was feeling his way slowly and clumsily from one just perceptible thing to another. And nearly everybody was uneasy and disposed to be angry.

" It is clear beyond question to us now, that the days of illiterate drudges were already past in the distant nineteenth century, for power-machinery had superseded them. The new world, so much more complicated and dangerous, so much richer and ampler, was a world insisting upon an educated population, educated intellectually and morally. But in those days these things were not at all clear, and it was grudgingly and insufficiently that access to knowledge and enlightenment was given by the learned and prosperous classes to the rapidly accumulating masses of the population. They insisted that it should be done by special channels and in a new and different class of school. I have told you of what passed for my education, reading and writing, rudimentary computations, 'jogfry' and so forth. That sort of process, truncated by employment at thirteen or fourteen, when curiosity and interest were just beginning to awaken, was as far as education had gone for the bulk of the common men and women in the opening years of the twentieth century. It had produced a vast multitude of people, just able to read, credulous and uncritical and pitifully curious to learn about life and things, pitifully wanting to see and know. As a whole the community did nothing to satisfy the vague aspirations of those half-awakened swarms ; it was left to ' private enterprise ' to find what profits it could in their dim desires. A number of great publishing businesses arose to trade upon the new reading public that this ' elementary ' education, as we called it, had accumulated.

"In all ages people have wanted stories about life. The young have always wanted to be told about the stage on which they are beginning to play their parts, to be shown the chances and possibilities of existence, vividly and dramatically, so that they may imagine and anticipate their own reactions. And even those who are no longer youthful have always been eager to supplement their experiences and widen their judgement by tales and histories and discussions. There has been literature since there has been writing, since indeed there was enough language for story-telling and reciting. And always literature has told people what their minds were prepared to receive, searching for what it should tell rather in the mind and expectation of the hearer or reader—who was the person who paid—than in the unendowed wildernesses of reality. So that the greater part of the literature of every age has been a vulgar and ephemeral thing interesting only to the historian and psychologist of later times because of the light it threw upon the desires and imaginative limitations of its generation. But the popular literature of the age in which Harry Mortimer Smith was living was more abundant, more cynically insincere, lazy, cheap and empty than anything that the world had ever seen before.

"You would accuse me of burlesque if I were to tell you the stories of the various people who built up immense fortunes by catering for the vague needs of the new reading crowds that filled the hypertrophied cities of the Atlantic world. There was a certain Newnes of whom legend related that one day after reading aloud some item of interest to his family he remarked, 'I call that a regular tit-bit.' From that feat of nomenclature he went on to the idea of a weekly periodical full of scraps of interest, cuttings from books and newspapers and the like. A hungry multitude, eager and curious, was ready to feed greedily on such *hors d'œuvre*. So *Tit-Bits* came into existence, whittled from a thousand sources

by an industrious and not too expensive staff, and
Newnes became a man of wealth and a baronet.   His
first experiment upon the new public encouraged
him to make a number of others.   He gave it a
monthly magazine full of short stories drawn from
foreign sources.   At first its success was uncertain,
and then a certain Dr. Conan Doyle rose to fame
in it and carried it to success with stories about crime
and the detection of crime.   Every intelligent person
in those days, everyone indeed intelligent or not,
was curious about the murders and such-like crimes
which still abounded.   Indeed, there could have been
no more fascinating and desirable subject for us ;
properly treated such cases illuminated the prob-
lems of law, training and control in our social welter
as nothing else could have done.   The poorest people
bought at least a weekly paper in order to quicken
their wits over murder mysteries and divorces, driven
by an almost instinctive need to probe motives and
judge restraints. But Conan Doyle's stories had
little of psychology in them ; he tangled a skein
of clues in order to disentangle it again, and his
readers forgot the interest of the problem in the
interest of the puzzle.

" Hard upon the heels of Newnes came a host
of other competitors, among others a certain Arthur
Pearson and a group of brothers Harmsworth who
rose to great power and wealth from the beginning
of a small weekly paper called *Answers*, inspired
originally by the notion that people liked to read
other people's letters.   You will find in the histories
how two of these Harmsworths, men of great thrust
and energy, became Lords of England and prominent

figures in politics, but I have to tell of them now simply to tell you of the multitude of papers and magazines they created to win the errand-boy's guffaw, the heart of the factory girl, the respect of the aristocracy and the confidence of the *nouveau riche*. It was a roaring factory of hasty printing. Our own firm at Thunderstone House was of an older standing than these Newnes, Pearson, Harmsworth concerns. As early as the eighteenth century the hunger for knowledge had been apparent, and a certain footman turned publisher, named Dodsley, had produced a book of wisdom called the *Young Man's Companion*. Our founder, Crane, had done the same sort of thing in Early Victorian times. He had won his way to considerable success with a *Home Teacher* in monthly parts and with Crane's *Circle of the Sciences* and a weekly magazine and so forth. His chief rivals had been two firms called Cassell's and Routledge's, and for years, though he worked upon a smaller capital, he kept well abreast of them. For a time the onrush of the newer popular publishers had thrust Crane's and his contemporaries into the background and then, reconstructed and reinvigorated by a certain Sir Peter Newberry, the old business had won its way back to prosperity, publishing a shoal of novelette magazines and cheap domestic newspapers for women, young girls and children, reviving the *Home Teacher* on modern lines with a memory training system and a *Guide to Success* by Sir Peter Newberry thrown in, and even launching out into scientific handbooks of a not too onerous sort.

"It is difficult for you to realise," said Sarnac,

" what a frightful lot of printed stuff there was in that old world. It was choked with printed rubbish just as it was choked with human rubbish and a rubbish of furniture and clothing and every sort of rubbish ; there was too much of the inferior grades of everything. And good things incredibly rare ! You cannot imagine how delightful it is for me to sit here again, naked and simple, talking plainly and nakedly in a clear and beautiful room. The sense of escape, of being cleansed of unnecessary adhesions of any sort, is exquisite. We read a book now and then and talk and make love naturally and honestly and do our work and thought and research with well-aired well-fed brains, and we live with all our senses and abilities taking a firm and easy grip upon life. But stress was in the air of the twentieth century. Those who had enough courage fought hard for knowledge and existence, and to them we sold our not very lucid or helpful *Home Teacher* and our entirely base *Guide to Success* ; but great multitudes relaxed their hold upon life in a way that is known now only to our morbid psychologists. They averted their attention from reality and gave themselves up to reverie. They went about the world distraught in a day-dream, a day-dream that they were not really themselves, but beings far nobler and more romantic, or that presently things would change about them into a dramatic scene centering about themselves. These novelette magazines and popular novels that supplied the chief part of the income of Crane & Newberry, were really helps to reverie—mental drugs. Sunray, have you ever read any twentieth-century novelettes ? "

"One or two," said Sunray. "It's as you say. I suppose I have a dozen or so. Some day you shall see my little collection."

"Very likely *ours*—half of them,—Crane & Newberry's I mean. It will be amusing to see them again. The great bulk of this reverie material was written for Crane & Newberry by girls and women and by a type of slack imaginative men. These 'authors,' as we called them, lived scattered about London or in houses on the country-side, and they sent their writings by post to Thunderstone House, where we edited them in various ways and put the stuff into our magazines and books. Thunderstone House was a great rambling warren of a place opening out of Tottenham Court Road, with a yard into which huge lorries brought rolls of paper and from which vans departed with our finished products. It was all a-quiver with the roar and thudding of the printing machinery. I remember very vividly to this day how I went there first, down a narrow roadway out of the main thoroughfare, past a dingy public-house and the stage door of a theatre."

"What were you going to do—pack up books? Or run errands?" asked Radiant.

"I was to do what I could. Very soon I was on the general editorial staff."

"Editing popular knowledge?"

"Yes."

"But why did they want an illiterate youngster like yourself at Thunderstone House?" asked Radiant. "I can understand that this work of instructing and answering the first crude questions of the new reading classes was necessarily a wholesale improvised affair, but surely there were enough learned men at the ancient universities to do all the editing and instructing that was needed ! "

Sarnac shook his head. " The amazing thing is that there weren't," he said. " They produced men enough of a sort but they weren't the right sort."

His auditors looked puzzled.

" The rank-and-file of the men they sent out labelled M.A. and so forth from Oxford and Cambridge were exactly like those gilt-lettered jars in Mr. Humberg's shop, that had nothing in them but stale water. The pseudo-educated man of the older order couldn't teach, couldn't write, couldn't explain. He was pompous and patronising and prosy ; timid and indistinct in statement, with no sense of the common need or the common quality. The promoted office-boy, these new magazine and newspaper people discovered, was brighter and better at the job, comparatively modest and industrious, eager to know things and impart things. The editors of our periodicals, the managers of our part publications and so forth were nearly all of the office-boy class, hardly any of them, in the academic sense, educated. But many of them had a sort of educational enthusiasm and all of them a boldness that the men of the old learning lacked. . . ."

Sarnac reflected. " In Britain at the time I am speaking about—and in America also—there were practically two educational worlds and two traditions of intellectual culture side by side. There was all this vast fermenting hullabaloo of the new publishing, the new press, the cinema theatres and so forth, a crude mental uproar arising out of the new ele-

mentary schools of the nineteenth century, and
there was the old aristocratic education of the seventeenth and eighteenth centuries, which had picked
up its tradition from the Augustan age of Rome.
They didn't mix. On the one hand were these
office-boy fellows with the intellectual courage and
vigour—oh ! of Aristotle and Plato, whatever the
quality of their intellectual equipment might be ;
on the other the academic man, affectedly Grecian,
like the bought and sold learned man of the days
of Roman slavery. He had the gentility of the
household slave ; he had the same abject respect for
patron, prince and patrician ; he had the same meti-
culous care in minor matters, and the same fear of
uncharted reality. He criticised like a slave, sneering
and hinting, he quarrelled like a slave, despised all
he dared despise with the eagerness of a slave. He
was incapable of serving the multitude. The new
reading-crowd, the working masses, the ' democracy '
as we used to call it, had to get its knowledge and
its wisdom without him.

" Crane, our founder, had had in his day some
inkling of the educational function such businesses
as his were bound to serve in the world, but Sir
Peter Newberry had been a hard tradesman, intent
only on recovering the prosperity that the newer
popular publishers had filched away from our firm.
He was a hard driving man ; he drove hard, he
paid in niggardly fashion and he succeeded. He
had been dead now for some years and the chief
shareholder and director of the firm was his son
Richard. He was nicknamed the Sun ; I think
because someone had quoted Shakespeare about the

winter of our discontent being made summer by this Sun of York. He was by contrast a very genial and warming person. He was acutely alive to the moral responsibility that lay behind the practical irresponsibility of a popular publisher. If anything, he drove harder than his father, but he paid generously ; he tried to keep a little ahead of the new public instead of a little behind ; the times moved in his favour and he succeeded even more than his father had done. I had been employed by Crane & Newberry for many weeks before I saw him, but in the first office I entered in Thunderstone House I saw the evidences of his personality in certain notices upon the wall. They were printed in clear black letters on cards and hung up. It was his device for giving the house a tone of its own.

"I remember 'We lead ; the others imitate,' and 'If you are in any doubt about its being too good put it in.' A third was : 'If a man doesn't know what you know that's no reason for writing as if he was an all-round fool. Rest assured there is something he knows better than you do.'"

§ 9

"It took me some time to get from the yard of Thunderstone House to the office in which these inscriptions were displayed. Fanny had told me to ask for Mr. Cheeseman, and when I had discovered and entered the doorway up a flight of steps, which had at first been masked by two large vans, I made this demand of an extremely small young lady enclosed in a kind of glass cage. She had a round face and

a bright red button of a nose. She was engaged, I
realised slowly, in removing a foreign stamp from
a fragment of envelope by licking the back of the
paper. She did not desist from this occupation but
mutely asked my business with her eyes.

" ' Oran-amoiment ? ' she asked, still licking.

" ' Pardon ? '

" ' Oran-amoiment ? '

" ' I'm sorry,' I said, ' I don't get it quite.'

" ' Mus' be deaf,' she said, putting down the
stamp and taking a sufficient breath for slow loud
speech. ' 'Ave you *gottonappointment* ? '

" ' Oh ! ' I said. ' Yes. I was told to come here
to-day and see Mr. Cheeseman between ten and twelve.'

She resumed her struggle with the stamp for a
time. ' S'pose you don't c'lect stamps ? ' she asked.
' 'Sintresting 'obby. Mr. Cheeseman's written a
little 'andbook about it. Looking for a job, I suppose ? May 'ave to wait a bit. Will you fill up
that bit of paper there ? Formality we 'ave to insist
on. Pencil. . . .'

" The paper demanded my name and my business
and I wrote that the latter was ' literary employment.'

" ' Lordy,' said the young lady when she read
it. ' I thought you was in for the ware'ouse. I say,
Florence,' she said to another considerably larger
girl who had appeared on the staircase, ' look at 'im.
'E's after litry emplyment.'

" ' Cheek ! ' said the second young lady after
one glance at me, and sat down inside the glass box
with a piece of chewing gum and a novelette just
published by the firm. The young lady with the
button nose resumed her stamp damping. They

kept me ten minutes before the smaller one remarked :
' Spose I better take this up to Mr. Cheeseman,
Flo,' and departed with my form.

" She returned after five minutes or so. ' Mr.
Cheeseman says 'e can see you now for *one* minute,'
she said, and led the way up a staircase and along a
passage that looked with glass windows into a printer's
shop and down a staircase and along a dark passage
to a small apartment with an office table, one or two
chairs, and bookshelves covered with paper-covered
publications. Out of this opened another room, and
the door was open. ' You better sit down here,'
said the young lady with the button nose.

" ' That Smith ? ' asked a voice. ' Come right in.'

" I went in, and the young lady with the button
nose vanished from my world.

" I discovered a gentleman sunken deeply in
an arm-chair before a writing-table, and lost in con-
templation of a row of vivid drawings which were
standing up on a shelf against the wall of the room.
He had an intensely earnest, frowning, red face, a
large broad mouth intensely compressed, and stiff
black hair that stood out from his head in many
directions. His head was slightly on one side and
he was chewing the end of a lead pencil. ' Don't
see it,' he whispered. ' Don't see it.' I stood awaiting
his attention. ' Smith,' he murmured, still not looking at me, ' Harry Mortimer Smith. Smith, were
you by any chance educated at a Board School ? '

" ' Yessir,' I said.

" ' I hear you have literary tastes.'

" ' Yessir.'

" ' Then come here and stand by me and look

at these damned pictures there. Did you ever see such stuff?'

"I stood by his side but remained judiciously silent. The drawings I now perceived were designs for a magazine cover. Upon all of them appeared the words 'The New World' in very conspicuous lettering. One design was all flying machines and steamships and automobiles; two others insisted upon a flying machine; one showed a kneeling loin-clothed man saluting the rising sun—which however rose behind him. Another showed a planet earth half illuminated, and another was simply a workman going to his work in the dawn.

"'Smith,' said Mr. Cheeseman; 'it's you've got to buy this magazine, not me. Which of these covers do you prefer? It's your decision. *Fiat experimentum in corpore vile.*'

"'Meaning me, Sir?' I said brightly.

"His bristle eyebrows displayed a momentary surprise. 'I suppose we're all fitted with the same tags nowadays,' he remarked. 'Which do you find most attractive?'

"'Those aeroplane things, Sir, seem to me to be shoving it a bit too hard,' I said.

"'H'm,' said Mr. Cheeseman. 'That's what the Sun says. You wouldn't buy on that?'

"'I don't think so, Sir. It's been done too much.'

"'How about that globe?'

"'Too like an Atlas, Sir.'

"'Aren't geography and travel interesting?'

"'They are, Sir, but somehow they aren't attractive.'

"'Interesting but not attractive. H'm. Out of

the mouths of babes and sucklings. . . . So it's
going to be that labour chap there in the dawn.
You'd buy that, eh ? '

" ' Is this going to be a magazine about inventions
and discoveries and progress, Sir ? '

" ' Exactly.'

" Well, the Dawn's good, Sir, but I don't think
that sort of Labour Day Cartoon man is going to be
very attractive. Looks rheumatic and heavy, Sir.
Why not cut him out and keep the dawn ? '

" ' Bit too like a slice of ham, Smith—thin pink
streaks.'

" I was struck by an idea. ' Suppose, Sir, you
kept that dawn scene and made it a bit earlier in the
year. Buds on the trees, Sir. And perhaps snowy
mountains, rather cold and far off. And then you
put a hand right across it—just a big hand—pointing,
Sir.'

" ' Pointing up ? ' said Mr. Cheeseman.

" ' No, Sir, pointing forward and just a little up.
It would sort of make one curious.'

" ' It would. A woman's hand.'

" ' Just a hand I think, Sir.'

" ' You'd buy that ? '

" ' I'd jump at it, Sir, if I had the money.'

" Mr. Cheeseman reflected for some moments,
chewing his pencil serenely. Then he spat out
small bits of pencil over his desk and spoke. ' What
you say, Smith, is exactly what I've been thinking.
Exactly. It's very curious.' He pressed a bell-
push on his desk and a messenger girl appeared.
' Ask Mr. Prelude to come here. . . . So you
think you'd like to come into Thunderstone House,

Smith. I'm told you know a little about science already. Learn more. Our public's moving up to science. I've got some books over there I want you to read and pick out anything you find interesting.'

" ' You'll be able to find me a job, Sir ? ' I said.

" ' I've got to find you a job all right. Orders is orders. You'll be able to sit in that room there. . . .'

" We were interrupted by the arrival of Mr. Prelude. He was a tall, thin, cadaverous man with a melancholy expression.

" ' Mr. Prelude,' said Mr. Cheeseman, waving his arm at the cover sketches ; ' this stuff won't do. It's—it's too banal. We want something fresher, something with a touch of imagination. What I want to see on the cover is—well, say a dawn—a very calm and simple scene, mostly colour, mountain range far away just flushed with sunrise, valley blue and still, high streamer clouds touched with pink. See ? Trees perhaps in the foreground— just budding—spring *motif* and morning *motif*. See ? All a little faint and backgroundy. Then a big hand and wrist across the page pointing at something, something high and far away. See ? '

" He surveyed Mr. Prelude with the glow of creative enthusiasm on his face. Mr. Prelude looked disapproval. ' The Sun will like that,' he said.

" ' It's the goods,' said Mr. Cheeseman.

" ' Why not those flying machines ? '

" ' Why not midges ? ' asked Mr. Cheeseman.

" Mr. Prelude shrugged his shoulders. ' I've got no use for a magazine on progress without a flying machine or a Zeppelin,' he said. ' Still—it's your affair.'

" Mr. Cheeseman looked a little dashed by his colleague's doubt, but he held to his idea. ' We'll get a sketch made,' he said. ' How about Wilkinson ? '

" They discussed some unknown Wilkinson as a possible cover designer. Then Mr. Cheeseman turned to me. ' By the by, here's a youngster we've got to make use of, Prelude. We don't know what he can do, but he seems intelligent. I thought we'd use him to sift some of those scientific books. What he likes, *they*'ll like. *I* can't read that stuff. I'm too busy.'

" Mr. Prelude surveyed me. ' You never know what you can do till you try,' he said. ' Do you know anything of science ? '

" ' Not very much,' I said. ' But I've done some physiography and chemistry and a little geology. And read a lot.'

" ' You don't want to know very much,' said Mr. Prelude. ' You're better without it here. Makes you High-Brow. High-Brow goes to tens of thousands, but Crane & Newberry go to hundreds of thousands. Not that our brows aren't rising some in this establishment. Educational and improving, we're going to be. So far as is consistent with our profits. See that notice,—*We lead* ? All the same, Cheeseman,' said Mr. Prelude, ' the thing that has sold, the thing that sells and the thing that's going to sell, is the magazine with a pretty girl on the cover—and the less costume the better. Consistent with decency. Now here's—what your name ? '

" ' Smith, Sir.'

" ' Smith. And here's all these covers on the bookstall. And then I produce *this*. Which does he buy ? '

" *This* was the cover of the summer number of Newberry's Story Magazine, on which two young ladies in skin-tight bathing dresses disported themselves on a sandy beach.

" 'Smith goes for this,' said Mr. Prelude triumphantly.

" I shook my head.

" 'You mean to say that isn't attractive ?' said Mr. Cheeseman, turning in his chair and pointing with his well-chewed pencil.

" I reflected.

" 'There's never anything about them inside,' I said.

" 'Got you there, Prelude !' said Mr. Cheeseman.

" 'Not a bit. He bought six or seven before he found that out. And most of 'em forgot about it when they read inside.' "

§ 10

" I found my introduction to Thunderstone House far less terrifying than I had anticipated. It was gratifying to have come so near to what Mr. Cheeseman had thought about the magazine cover, and there were presently other very reassuring coincidences of the same sort. I was immediately interested in the editorial and publishing work that was going on about me, and my mind took one of those forward strides that are characteristic of adolescence. I was still a boy when I left Mr. Humberg ; I had not been with Crane & Newberry six weeks before I perceived that I was a capable and responsible young man. I began to form opinions rapidly, to write with confidence ; even my handwriting suddenly grew up from a careless or over-careful boyish scrawl to a consistent and characteristic script. I began to think about the clothes I was wearing and of the impression I made upon other people.

"In quite a little time I was writing short contributions to some of our minor weeklies and monthlies and suggesting articles and ' features ' as we called them to Mr. Cheeseman. The eighteen shillings a week at which I started went up in a series of jerks to three pounds, which was quite a big salary in those days for a youngster not yet eighteen. Fanny took the keenest interest in my work and displayed an extraordinary understanding of its conditions. She seemed to know all about Mr. Cheeseman and Mr. Prelude and the rest of my colleagues directly I mentioned them.

"One day I was working in the room next to Mr. Cheeseman's with another youngster called Wilkins at a rather odd little job. One of the authors our firm employed had written a long story for the *Story Reader's Paradise*, and it had been set up by the printers and passed for press before it was discovered that in a careless moment she had given her chief villain the name of a very prominent lawyer who unhappily also had a country house in a village almost identical in name with the corresponding village in the story. The prominent lawyer might see fit to consider this use of his name as libellous and make trouble for us. So Wilkins and I were going through two sets of proofs, one to check the other, and we were changing the name of the prominent lawyer to an entirely different one whenever it occurred.

To brighten the task we had made a game of it. Each one raced down his galley proof and called the name of ' Reginald Flake ' whenever he found it and scored a point for every name he called first. I was some points up when I heard a voice in the passage that seemed oddly familiar to me. ' They're all spread out on my desk, sir, if you like to come into my room,' I heard Mr. Cheeseman say.

" ' Fay-nits,' said Wilkins. ' It's the Sun.'

" I turned round as the door opened and saw Mr. Cheeseman holding the door open for a good-looking youngish man, with rather handsome regular features and a sort of bang of brown hair over his forehead. He wore a pair of very round large spectacles with glasses tinted a faint yellow colour. He met my eyes and an expression of partial recognition came into his and faded again. Either he recognised me or he recognised a resemblance in me. He followed Mr. Cheeseman across the room. Then he turned sharply.

" ' Of course,' he said smiling and returning a step or two toward me. ' You must be young Smith. How are you getting on here ? '

" ' I'm working for Mr. Cheeseman mostly,' I said standing up.

" He turned to Mr. Cheeseman.

" ' Very satisfactory, sir. Quick, interested ; he'll do well here.'

" ' I'm glad to hear it—very glad. Everyone has a chance here and there's no favours. No favours. The best man does the job. Glad to see you among the directors whenever you care to come up to us, Smith.'

" ' I'll do my best, Sir.'

" He hesitated, smiled again in a very friendly way and went into Mr. Cheeseman's room. . . .

" ' Where are we ? ' I said. ' Middle of galley 32 ? Score, 22–29.'

" ' How d'you know *'im* ? ' asked Wilkins in a fierce undertone.

" ' I don't know him,' I said, suddenly hot and flushed. ' I've never seen him before.'

" ' Well, he knew you.'

" ' He's heard about me.'

" ' Who from ? '

" ' How the deuce should *I* know ? ' I asked with needless heat.

' " Oh ! ' said Wilkins and reflected. ' But——'

" He glanced at my troubled face and said no more.

" But at the game of ' Reginald Flake ' he over-hauled me and beat me at the end of the book, 67–42."

§ 11

" I concealed altogether from my mother the share that Fanny had had in getting me my new job and all the opportunities it carried with it in Thunderstone House, and so it was possible for her to find some pride and satisfaction in my in-creasing prosperity. I was presently able to double and then still further to increase my contribution to the household expenses, and I exchanged my attic, which was handed over to Prue for her very own, for the room which had once sheltered the old Moggeridges. It was rearranged as a bed-sitting room for me, and soon I had first one and then several shelves full of books and a writing-desk of my own.

"And also I concealed from my mother, for there was no use in distressing her, the frequency of my visits to Fanny. We began to make little excursions together, for Fanny, I discovered, was often very lonely. Newberry was a very busy man, and often he could not come near her for ten days or a fortnight, and although she had some women friends, and classes and lectures, there were gaps often of several days when she would have had no one to speak to but the servant who came in daily to her, if it had not been for me. But all this companioning of Fanny I tried to hide from my mother, though now and then her suspicions stabbed my falsehoods. Ernie and Prue, however, were able to follow the calls of love unhampered by the family shame, and presently they were both engaged and his young lady and her young man were brought to a Sunday tea-party in the drawing-room—through the kind permission of Mr. and Mrs. Milton who were as usual, 'away.' Ernie's Young Lady—I've completely forgotten her name—proved to be a well-dressed self-possessed young woman with a vast knowledge of people in what we used to call 'society'; she talked freely and fashionably, taking the larger share of the conversation, of Ascot and Monte Carlo and the Court. Prue's Mr. Pettigrew was of a more serious quality, and of the things he said I remember now only that he expressed a firm conviction that Messages from the Dead were Bound to Come in a few years' time. He was a chiropodist and very well thought of in chiropodological circles."

"Stop!" cried Radiant. "What is this? You are talking nonsense, Sarnac. What is chiropodological—hand—foot—scientific?"

"I thought you'd ask me that," said Sarnac, smiling. "Chiropody was—corn-cutting."

"Corn-cutting—harvesting," said Starlight. "But where do the hands and feet come in? There were machines then, were there not?"

"No, this was a different sort of corn. Mr. Humberg's shop was full of corn-salves and corn-cures. Corns were painful and tiresome callosities produced on people's feet by the pressure of ill-fitting boots. We don't know of such things nowadays, but they darkened scores of lives in Pimlico."

"But why did they wear ill-fitting boots?" demanded Radiant. "Oh!—never mind. Never mind. I know. A mad world which made boots at hazard without looking at the feet that had to wear them! And wore boots that hurt it when no sane people would dream of wearing boots! Go on with your story."

"Let me see," said Sarnac. "I was talking of a tea-party, a family tea-party in the drawing-room —in which we talked of everything in the world but my sister Fanny. And quite a little while after that tea-party my mother fell ill and died.

"It was a swift and sudden illness. She caught a cold and would not go to bed. When she did go to bed, she got up after one day of it, because she couldn't bear to think of all that Prue might be doing or not doing in the house-work downstairs. And her cold turned to pneumonia, the same sort of inflammation that had carried off the Moggeridges, and she died in three days.

"Now when the fever came upon her she changed suddenly from something white and hard and unapproachable to something flushed and pitiful. Her face grew smaller and younger looking, her eyes bright, and something came into them that reminded me of Fanny when Fanny was distressed. And all my habit of sullen resistance to my mother melted when I saw her struggling for breath on her tumbled pillow and realised that she might be near the end of all her hates and drudgeries. Matilda Good became again the old friend who had known her since she was a young woman, and they called each other 'Tilda' and 'Marty' instead of Matilda and Martha. Matilda for all her varicose veins was up and down stairs fifty times a day; and there was much sending out for expensive things, the more expensive the better, that Matilda thought my mother might 'fancy.' They stood appealingly untouched upon the table by her bedside. Once or twice towards the end my mother asked for me, and when I came in the evening and bent over her she whispered hoarsely, ''Arry boy—promise me ! . . . Promise me ! . . .'

"I sat down and took the hand she held out to me, and so holding to me, she dozed.

"What she wanted me to promise she never said ; and whether it was some last vow she wanted to extract from me that would separate me from Fanny for ever, or whether her thoughts about Fanny had changed under the shadow of death and she had some new message for her, I cannot imagine to this day. Perhaps she herself did not know what I had to promise ; a dying desire for predominance moved her. Will stirred in her and faded again to nothing. 'Promise me !' Fanny she never mentioned by name and we did not dare to bring my sister in to her. Ernest came and kissed her and knelt down by the bedside and suddenly, dreadfully wept aloud like the child he was and set us all weeping ; he was her firstborn and her dearest, he had known her before her final embitterment, he had always been a dutiful son to her.

"Presently she was lying there very straight and still, as hushed and still as my father's shop on Sundays, and the traffics and struggles and angers of life had done with her for ever. Her face was now neither young nor old, a marble face of peace. All her peevish resentment was smoothed and wiped away. It had never occurred to me before that she had or had not good looks, but now I saw that Fanny's fine regularity of feature came from her. She was like Fanny, like an immobile, unhumorous Fanny.

"I stood beside her still body oppressed by a grief too wide and deep for tears, an immense grief that was not so much for her as for all that distress of life she had embodied. For now I saw that there was not and there never had been anything hateful in her ; I saw for the first time the devotion of her, the misguided passion for right, the mute, blundering, tormented and tormenting love in her heart. Even her love of Fanny was a love capsized and inverted ; her fallen daughter had been to her a detested changeling for the pretty clever little girl who was to have been a paragon of feminine

virtue. Except for Ernest how bitterly and repeatedly
had we children offended her rigid and implacable
standards, Fanny and I openly and rebelliously and
Prue by discovery ! For Prue—I will not tell you
the details of Matilda's exposure—pilfered.

" Long before we children began to thwart my
mother there must have been a still more monstrous
disappointment for her. What sort of dreams of
manly piety and decorum had she wrapped about
my poor, maundering, ramshackle, loose-limbed father
when he and she walked out together in their Sunday
clothes, making the best and more than the best
of themselves ? He must have been a tall, good-
looking, young man then, and reassuringly apt with
pious reflections. What shocks had he, gross, clumsy,
wayward, ignorant and incompetent as the dear man
was, inflicted upon her set and limited expectations?

" And then think of my Uncle John Julip again,
that wonderful and adored elder brother with the
manners of a sporting baronet, who had slowly
shrivelled down to the figure of a drunken thief !
Everything had shrivelled for her,—poor soul ! In
our streets in those old days men were permitted
to sell brightly coloured distended bladders to children,
the most apt instruments for acute disappointment
you can imagine ; and the life God had given my
mother was very like one of these bladders. It
had burst and shrivelled down to a limp and empty
residue that nothing could ever restore. She had
faced her declining days, prematurely wrinkled,
weary, laborious and unloved except by one dutiful
son. . . .

" Yes, the thought of Ernest was a consolation to

me. Surely his loyalty had meant happiness for her."

Sarnac paused. "I find it impossible," he said, "to disentangle my thoughts as I stood by my mother's death-bed from a thousand things that have come to me since about her. I have had to tell of her as an antagonist, as a hard uncharitable soul. That was her rôle in my story. But she was indeed just the creature and victim of that disordered age which had turned her natural tenacity to a blind intolerance and wasted her moral passion upon ugly and barren ends. If Fanny and Ernest and I had shown any stoutness against the disadvantages of our start in life, if we had won for ourselves any knowledge or respect, we inherited that much steadfastness from her ; such honesty as we had was hers. If her moral harshness had overshadowed and embittered our adolescence, her passionate mothering had sheltered our childhood. Our father would have loved us, wondered at us and left us about. But early in her life, that fear, that terror-stricken hatred of sex that overshadowed the Christian centuries, that frantic resort to the suppressions, subjugations and disciplines of a stereotyped marriage in its harshest form, a marriage as easy to step into and as hard to leave as a steel trap with its teeth hidden by the most elaborate secrecies and misrepresentations, had set its pitiless grip upon my mother's imagination and blackened all the happier impulses in life for her. She was ready, if necessary, to pass all her children through the fires of that Moloch, if by so doing their souls might be saved. She did it the more bitterly because she was doing it against the deeper undeveloped things in her own nature.

"Such things, more dimly appreciated perhaps, passed through the mind of Harry Mortimer Smith, my former self, as he stood beside his dead mother. He was torn—I was torn—by a sense of irrational separation and by the haunting persuasion of lost opportunities. There were things I felt that I might have said, propitious moments I might have seized to make things better between us. I had differed from her so harshly ; I might have been so much kinder to her and still have held my way. She lay there a feeble, little, old woman, thin, worn and prematurely aged. How often had I struck at her with all my rebel strength, blind to the fact that I could wound her as only a child can wound the mother who bore it. She had been darkened and I also had been darkened, and now—now it was all too late. The door had closed between us. And was closed for ever. For ever. . . ."

§ 12

"The year and a half that intervened between my mother's death and the beginning of the First World War—the War that came before the Poison Gas War and the Great Desolation—were years of rapid growth for me, mental and physical alike. I remained with Matilda Good because I had come to love that clumsy, wise, friendly creature almost as if she was my second mother, but now I was prosperous enough to occupy the whole of the second floor and to have a sitting-room separate from my bedroom. I still came down to the underground breakfast-room for breakfast or supper or high tea because I liked talking with Matilda. Prue had married Mr. Pettigrew by that time, and in her stead two grey and sedulous women came in—they were sisters, one a spinster and the other the wife of a broken-down prize-fighter—to do the drudgeries Prue and my mother had done.

" My chief companion in those days was my sister Fanny. Our childhood's alliance was renewed and strengthened. We had a need for each other ; we were able to help each other as no one else could help us. I found out very soon that Fanny's life was divided into two very unequal parts ; that she had hours and sometimes days of excitement and happiness with Newberry, who loved her greatly and gave her all the time he could steal away for her and introduced her to such friends as he could trust to respect her and keep their secret, and also she had long stretches of uneventful solitude in which she was terribly left to herself. My sister Fanny was plucky and loyal and devoted, but before we two got together again I think she found those grey intervals of suspended animation dreary and dangerous and sometimes almost intolerable. Often she had nothing to live for at all, nothing bright and vital, but the almost daily note, a hasty word or so he scribbled to her. And the better he was, the worse it was for her. The fact that he was pleasant and delightful and deeply in love with her, the very brightness of being with him, made those great intervals seem darker and duller."

" Hadn't she work ? " asked Sunray.

" And fellow workers, and other women ? " asked Firefly.

"Not in her position. Not as an unmarried woman—of lowly origins—with a lover."

"But there were others in the same position? Surely there were many!"

"A scattered class, a class made to be ashamed of itself. Newberry and Fanny were lovers, such lovers as we are to-day ; they got through with it and at last, I believe, they married according to the custom of the time. But they were the exceptional ones, they knew what they wanted and had stout hearts. Most of these irregular unions succumbed to the boredom in-between and to the temptations of separation. Forgetfulness and jealousy played havoc with these insecure couples. The girls in their phases of loneliness picked up with other men and the first lover suspected their infidelities and strayed away. I have a lot to tell you yet about jealousy in the old world ; it was not regarded as an ugly thing but as a rather high-spirited thing. People let it go and were proud of it. And the majority of these irregular unions were not even love unions in the first place, they were vice unions, dishonest on either side. Drugs and drink crept very easily into lives divided between over-excitement and tedium and darkened by a general disapproval. The defiant pose was the easiest pose. The unmarried lover was made a social outcast and driven towards other sorts of social outcasts, more evil and unhappy. . . . You see perhaps now why my sister Fanny was rather alone and aloof, for all that she belonged to a numerous class.

"I suppose," said Sarnac, "that the object of

that rigid legal marriage of the old world was to keep lovers together. In countless cases it kept the wrong people together and lovers apart. But then you must remember that in those days children were supposed to be providential accidents ; they were indeed accidents of cohabitation and that altered all the conditions of the question. There were no proper schools for children, no sort of refuge if the parents parted and tore the home asunder. We are so secure ; it is hard to imagine now the chancy insecurity of the ancient days. It is hard to imagine the dangers that hung about an unprotected child. In our world nowadays we all seem to get paired ; sooner or later each finds a mate and marriage is a natural and necessary relationship instead of a compulsory device. All the priests of all the religions that have ever been in the world could not bind me to Sunray more firmly than I am bound to-day. Does one get a book and an altar to marry the axe to its handle ? . . .

" None of which does in the least degree affect the fact that my sister Fanny suffered dreadfully from loneliness before she rediscovered me.

" She was full of curiosities and enterprise, and she took possession of my leisure to explore all sorts of shows and resorts in and about old London, museums, picture-galleries, parks, gardens and heaths, that I should otherwise never have visited. Indeed she might not have visited them either if I had not been available as her escort, because in that world of crazy suppressions, most of these places were haunted by furtive love-hunters and feeble-minded folk who might have been irritating

and tiresome to a solitary girl so pretty as Fanny.
They would have followed her about and accosted her
when they got her alone, and thrust their disagreeable
cravings between her and the beauty and sunshine.

" But together we went gaily to all sorts of interesting things. This old London I am describing to
you had a large share of parks and gardens ; there
was a pleasing quaintness about all of them and
much unpremeditated loveliness. There was a certain Richmond Park, to which we often resorted,
with many fine old trees and grassy spaces and
wildernesses of bracken, that got very yellow and
gay in autumn, and a quantity of deer. You might
have been transported from this age to Richmond
Park two thousand years ago, and still fancied yourself in the northland parks of to-day. The great
trees, like nearly all trees in those days, were, it is
true, infested with fungus and partly decayed, but
Fanny and I never noticed that. They seemed
great healthy trees to us. And there was a view
from a hill-crest of the winding Thames, a very
delightful view. And then there were the oddest
old gardens and flower spaces at Kew. I remember
a quite good rock-garden and glass-houses of flowers ;
the brightest flowers the old world imagined possible.
And there were paths through a jungle of rhododendra, primitive small rhododendra, but bright
coloured and a great delight to Fanny and me. There
was a place where we had tea at little tables in the
open air. In that frowsty old germ-saturated world
with its dread of draughts and colds and coughs
it gave one a bright sense of adventure to eat food
in the open air.

" We went to museums and picture-galleries and talked about what the pictures meant and we talked of a thousand things together. There comes back to me one conversation we had at a place called Hampton Court, a queer, old, red-brick palace with a great grape-vine under glass and an ancient garden beside the Thames. There were flower-beds full of half-wild herbaceous flowers, and we walked beside them under trees until we came to a low wall that looked upon the river, and we sat down on a seat and there, after a silence, suddenly Fanny, like one who has been pent up beyond endurance, began talking of love.

" She began by asking questions about the girls I had met and the girls at Thunderstone House. I described one or two of them to her. My chief friend among them was Milly Kimpton from the counting-house ; we had got to the pitch of taking teas together and such-like friendly acts. ' That's not love,' said Fanny the wise, ' lending each other books. You don't begin to know what love is yet, Harry.

" ' But you will, Harry—you will.

" ' Don't you be too late about it, Harry. There's nothing in life like loving someone, Harry. People don't talk to you about it and lots of people don't know what they are missing. It's all the difference between being nothing or something. It's all the difference between being dead or alive. When you are really loving someone you're all right and nothing can harm you. And when you aren't, nothing is right, everything is wrong. But love is a queer thing, Harry, and about as dreadful as it is dear. It gets wrong. Sometimes it all goes wrong and

it's awful ; it slips from you somehow ; it goes
and you're left mean and little—ever so mean !—
and you can't get back and it seems you hardly want
to get back. You're dead and you're damned and
done for, and then again it all comes back again
like the sunrise—like being born afresh.'

" And then with a desperate shamelessness she
began to talk of Newberry and how much she loved
him. She told little irrelevant things about his
'ways.' 'He comes to me whenever he can,' she
said, and repeated this presently. 'He's all my life,'
she said. 'You don't know what he is to me. . . .'

" Then her constant dread of a separation crept
up to the surface of her thoughts.

" ' Perhaps,' she said, ' it will always go on like
this. . . . I don't care if it does, I don't care if
I never marry him. I wouldn't care—not if at last
I'm thrown aside. I'd go through it all again and
count myself lucky even if I knew for certain I was
to be dropped and cast aside.'

"Queer Fanny ! Her face was flushed and her
eyes shining with tears. I asked myself what had
been happening.

" ' He'll never throw me aside, Harry. He'll
never throw me aside. He can't. He can't. He's
half as old again as I am and yet he comes to me
in his trouble. Once—— Once he cried to me.
Men, all of you, are so strong, and yet so helpless. . . .

" ' You've got to have a woman to come to . . .

" ' Just a little while ago—— Well—— He
was ill. He was very ill. He has pain in his eyes
and sometimes he's afraid about them. This time,
suddenly, he had frightful pains. And he thought

he couldn't see. He came straight to me, Harry. He called a cab and came to me, and he came feeling his way upstairs to me and fumbling at the door ; and I nursed him in my darkened room until the pain had gone. He didn't go home, Harry, where there were servants and nurses to be got and attendants and everything ; he came to me. It was me he came to. Me ! He's my man. He knows I'd give my life for him. I would, Harry. I'd cut my body to pieces bit by bit, if it would make him happy.

" ' It wasn't so much the pain he had, Harry, as the fear. He's not the one to mind a bit of pain or be afraid of many things. But he was afraid and scared. He'd never been afraid before, but he was afraid of going blind—he was too afraid to go to the specialist. It was like a little child, Harry, and him so big and strong—afraid of the dark. He thought they'd get hold of him so that perhaps he'd not be able to come to me. He thought he wouldn't be able to see his beloved magazines and papers any more. And the pain just turned the screw on him. He clung to me.

" ' It was me made him go. I took him there. He wouldn't have gone if it hadn't been for me. He'd have just let things drift on and not a soul in the world, for all his money and power, to mother him. And then he might really have gone blind if it hadn't been taken in time. I pretended to be his secretary and I took him and waited in the waiting-room for him. I dreaded they'd hurt him. I was listening for something to happen all the time. I had to look at their old *Graphics* as if I didn't care a rap what they were doing to him. And

then he came out smiling with a green shade on
and I had to stand up stiff and cool and wait to hear
what he had to say. I *was* scared by that shade,
Harry. Scared! I held my breath. I thought it
had come. "It isn't so bad as we fancied, Miss
Smith," he says—offhand like. "You kept the taxi?
You'll have to take my arm I'm afraid." "Certainly,
sir," I said, mimpsy-like. I was careful to be kind
of awkward taking his arm. There were people
there in the waiting-room and you never know.
Acted respectful. Me!—that has had him in my
arms a thousand times.

"'But when we were in the taxi and safe he
pushed up the shade and took me into his arms and
he hugged me and he cried—he cried wet tears.
And held me. Because he'd got me still and his
sight still and the work he loves to do. Things
would have to be done to his eyes but he'd keep
his sight—and he has. There's been no trouble
now. Not for months.'

"She sat looking away from me over the shining river.

"'How could he ever leave me?' she said.
'After a time like that?'

"Stoutly she spoke, but even to my youthful eyes
she seemed little and lonely, sitting there on the
old red wall.

"I thought of the busy bustling man with the
big tortoise-shell glasses away from her, and of one
or two things I had heard whispered about him.
It seemed to me then that no men were good enough
for the women in the world.

"'When he's tired or in trouble,' said Fanny,
sure and still, 'he'll always come back to me.'"

231

CHAPTER THE SIXTH
Marriage in War Time
§ 1

"AND now," said Sarnac, "comes a change of costume. You have been thinking of me, I suppose, as a gawky youth of seventeen or eighteen, dressed in those ill-fitting wholesale clothes we used to call 'ready-mades.' That youth wore a white collar round his neck and a black jacket and dark grey trousers of a confused furtive patterning and his hat was a black hemisphere with a little brim, called a Bowler. Now he changes into another sort of 'ready-mades,' even more ill-fitting,—the khaki uniform of a young British soldier in the Great World War against Germany. In 1914 Anno Domini, a magic wand, the wand of political catastrophe, waved to and fro over Europe, and the aspect of that world changed, accumulation gave place to destruction and all the generation of young men I have described as being put together from such shops as those one saw in Cheapside, presently went into khaki and fell into ranks and tramped off to the lines of ditches and desolation that had extended themselves across Europe. It was a war of holes and barbed wire and bombs and big guns like no war that had ever happened before. It was a change of phase in the world muddle. It was like some liquid which has been growing hotter and hotter, suddenly beginning to boil and very swiftly boiling over. Or it was like a toboggan track in the mountains, when after a long easy, almost level run, one comes to a swift drop and a wild zig-zag of downward curves. It was the same old downward run at a dramatic point.

" Change of costume there was and change of atmosphere. I can still recall the scared excitements of the August days when the war began and how incredulous we English were when we heard that our own little army was being driven back before the German hosts like a spluttering kitten pushed by a broom, and that the French lines were collapsing. Then came the rally of September. At the beginning we British youngsters had been excited spectators, but as the tale of our army's efforts and losses came home to us we crowded to the recruiting offices, by thousands and scores of thousands, until at last our volunteers could be counted by the million. I went with the crowd.

" It may seem a curious thing to you that I lived through all the Great World War against Germany, that I was a soldier in it and fought and was wounded and went back and took part in the final offensive, that my brother Ernest became a sergeant and won a medal for gallantry and was killed within a few weeks of the concluding Armistice, that all the circumstances of my life were revolutionised by the war and that nevertheless it does not come into the story of my life as a thing of importance in itself to that story. As I think of it now, I think of the Great World War as a sort of geographical or atmospheric fact, like living ten miles from your working place or being married in an April shower. One would have to travel the ten miles every day or put up an umbrella as one came out of church, but it wouldn't touch what one was intimately or alter in any essential the living substance of one's life. Of course the World War killed and tortured millions of us, impoverished us all and dislocated the whole world. But that only meant that so many millions went out of life and that there was a fractional increase in everyone's anxiety and disorder ; it didn't change the nature and passions, the ignorances and bad habits of thought of the millions who remained. The World War arose out of these ignorances and misconceptions and it did nothing to alter them. After it was all over the world was a good deal rattled and much shabbier than before, but it was still the same old mean and haphazard world, acquisitive, divided, cantingly patriotic, idiotically prolific, dirty, diseased, spiteful and conceited. It has taken two score centuries of research and teaching, training, thought and work to make any great alteration in that.

" I admit the outbreak of the World War had a really tremendous air of being an end and a beginning. There were great days in it at first, and for us British as much as for any people. We apprehended the thing in splendid terms. We thought quite honestly—I speak of the common people—that the Imperialisms of Central Europe were wholly wrong and that we were wholly right ; hundreds of thousands of us gave ourselves gladly in the sincere belief that a new world was to be won by victory. That spirit was not confined to Britain, nor to either side in this war. I am convinced that the years 1914, 1915 and 1916 saw finer crops of brave and generous deeds and noble sacrifices, of heroic toil and heroic patience, than any years that ever came

before in the whole history of mankind or than
any of the years that followed for many centuries.
The young people were wonderful ; death and
honour reaped gloriously among them. And then
the inherent unsoundness of the issue began to wear
through and that false dawn faded out of men's
hearts. By the end of 1917 the whole world was
a disillusioned world, with but one hope left, the
idealism of the United States of America and the
still untested greatness of President Wilson. But
of that and what it came to, you read about in the
history books and I will not talk about it now. A
God in that man's position might have unified the
world in the twentieth century and saved it centuries
of tragic struggle. President Wilson was not a
God. . . .

" And I do not think I need tell you very much
of the war itself as I saw it. It was a strange phase
in human experience and it was described and painted
and photographed and put on record very completely. Most of us have read quite a lot about
it—except of course Firefly. You know how human
life concentrated for four whole years upon the
trenches that stretched across Europe on either
front of Germany. You know how thousands of
miles of land were turned into wildernesses of mud-
holes and wire. Nowadays of course nobody reads
the books of the generals and admirals and politicians
of that time, and all the official war histories sleep
the eternal sleep in the vaults of the great libraries,
but probably you have all read one or two such
human books as Enid Bagnold's *Diary without Dates*
or Cogswell's *Ermytage and the Curate* or Barbusse's

THE DREAM

Le Feu or Arthur Green's *Story of a Prisoner of War* or that curious anthology, *The War Stories of Private Thomas Atkins*, and probably you have seen photographs and films and also pictures painted by such men as Nevinson and Orpen and Muirhead Bone and Will Rothenstein. All of them, I can certify now, are very true books and pictures. They tell of desolation passing like the shadow of an eclipse across the human scene.

" But the mind has the power of reducing and effacing every sort of impression that drags pain with it. I spent great parts out of two years in that noxious, gun-pocked land of haste and hiding, and that time now seems less than many days of my peace-time life. I killed two men with the bayonet in a trench, and it remains as though it was done by someone else and had no significance for me at all. I remember much more clearly that I felt very sick when afterwards I found my sleeve saturated with blood and blood on my hand, and how I tried to get it off by rubbing my arm in the sand because there was no water to be got. In the trenches life was hideously uncomfortable and tedious and while it lasted I was, I know, interminably bored by the drag of the hours, but all those hours are concentrated now into a record of the fact. I remember the shock of the first shell that burst near me and how slowly the smoke and dust unfolded, and how there was a redness in the smoke and how for a time it blotted out the light. That shell burst in a field of yellow-flowering weeds and stubble against the sun, but I do not recall what preceded it nor what followed it ; shell-bursts rattled me more

and more as the war went on, but they left weaker
and weaker pictures.

"One of my most vivid memories of that time
is the excitement of my first leave from the front,
and how my party arrived at Victoria Station and
were guided in a clattering throng to a sort of trans-
port drain called the Underground Railway by
elderly volunteers wearing brassards. I was still
muddy from the trenches ; there had been no time
for a wash and a brush-up, and I was carrying my
rifle and other gear ; we crowded into a brightly
lit first-class carriage in which were a number of
people in evening dress who were going out to
dinner and to the theatre. There could not have
been a more vivid contrast if I had seen Firefly there
in all her loveliness. There was one young man
not much older than myself between two gorgeously
dressed women. He had a little white bow under
his pink chin and a silk neck-wrap, he had a black
cloak with a cape and an opera hat. I suppose he
was an invalid but he looked as fit as I. I felt a
momentary impulse to say something humiliating
to him. I don't think I did. I do not remember
that I did. But I looked at him and then at the
brown stain on my sleeve and the wonder of life
possessed me.

"No—I said nothing. I was in a state of intense
exhilaration. The other fellows were gay and inclined to be noisy, one or two were a little drunk
but I was quietly exalted. I seemed to be hearing
and seeing and perceiving with such an acuteness
as I had never known before. Fanny I should see
on the morrow, but that evening I hoped to see

Hetty Marcus with whom I was in love. I was in love with her with an intensity that only soldier-boys who had been living in the mud of Flanders for half a year could understand."

§ 2

"How," asked Sarnac, "can I make you see Hetty Marcus, dark-eyed, warm-skinned, wayward and fragile, who brought me to love and death two thousand years ago?

"In a way, she was like Sunray here. She was of her type. She had the same darkness in her eyes, the same still bearing. She was like Sunray's hungry sister. With a touch of fire in her blood.

"Yes—and she had those same stumpy little fingers. . . . *Look* at them!

"I met her on those very Downs I used to walk over with my father when I was a boy, to steal the produce from Lord Bramble's gardens. I had a short leave before I was drafted to France and I did not spend it in London with Matilda Good and Fanny as you may think I should have done, but I went with three other youngsters who had enough money to do so, to Cliffstone. I don't know whether I can make it clear to you why I went to Cliffstone. I was excited at the thought of going into the actual warfare, I meant to do brave and wonderful things over there, but also I was terribly overshadowed by the thought that I might be killed. I did not think of wounds or suffering, I do not think I feared those things at all, but I had a profound dread and hatred of extinction before ever I had fully lived,

before I had ever tasted many of the most alluring
things in life. I had always promised myself love
and great adventures with women, and I was
passionately distressed at the possibility of being
cheated of those intensities. All of us young inno-
cents were in the same case. It was I who had
thought of Cliffstone, near to our training camp,
with its band and promenade and its flitting glancing
girls. There if anywhere, it seemed to me, we
must snatch something from life before the great
shells splashed us to pieces and the clay of Flanders
devoured us. We sneaked off from our families
with those fires of protesting romance in our brains
and veins.

"You cannot imagine how many millions of lads
there were in Europe then, pitifully eager not to
miss altogether the secret and magic experiences of
love before they died. I cannot tell you of the
pothouses and prostitutes that lay in wait for us
or of the gaunt moonlight on the beach. I cannot
tell you of temptation and ignorance and disease.
It is too ugly to tell you ; such things are passed
and done with, and men suffer them no more. We
groped in darkness where now men walk in the
light. One of my mates had an ugly misadventure ;
all had ugly experiences and I escaped by chance
rather than any merit of my own from those slovenly
snares. I was for a moment fastidious and I recoiled.
And I had not drunken as the others had, because
some streak of pride in me had made me habitually
wary with drink.

"But I was in a storm of excitements and distresses. I was slipping into the pit though I hated

it, and to escape it I set myself to revive my memories
of the days when I was a boy. I went to Cherry
Gardens to see the old home and then to my father's
grave—it was neat and pretty with Fanny's money—
and then I determined. to walk over the Downs
to recall, if I could, something of the wonder that
I had felt when first I went over them to Chessing
Hanger. And also, if you understand me, I felt
love and romance would be there. I hadn't abandoned the quest that had brought me to Cliffstone ;
I had only jumped a foul ditch on my way. When
I was a child I had supposed Heaven was over the
Downs, and certainly the golden summer sunsets
were. It seemed natural to turn my back on Cliffstone and go up into the only really lovely country
I had ever known, if I wanted to find romance.

" And I found it.

" I was thrilled but not a bit surprised when I
saw Hetty appear over the skyline of the hill and
come right over the brow and stand with her hands
behind her back and the sun shining on her hair,
looking out across the woods and cornfields to Blythe
and the distant marches and the sea. She had taken
her hat off and was holding it behind her. She
wore an ivory-coloured silk blouse very open at
the neck and it was just as though you could see
her body through the flimsy stuff.

" She dropped into a sitting position, now looking
at her world and now plucking at the little dwarfish
flowers in the Downland turf.

" I stood for a time agape at her. Then my
whole being was filled with a tremulous resolve to
talk to her. My path curved up the slope and

carried me over the shoulder of the hill not very far from her. I followed it, stopping ever and again as if to look at the land and sea below, until it brought me as near to her as it could, and then I left it and with a clumsy affectation of carelessness strolled up to the summit until I stood beside her and about six yards away. I pretended not to observe her. I clenched my hands to keep my self-control. She had become aware of me and she was quite motionless now, sitting up and looking at me, but she did not seem in the least dismayed. Your fine face she had, Sunray, and your dark eyes, and I have never known anyone, not even you, who could keep a face so still. Not rigid or hard or staring it was, but quietly, profoundly, still, like a face in some beautiful picture.

" I was all a-tremble, my heart was beating fast but I kept my wits about me.

" ' Was there ever a lovelier view ? ' I said. ' I suppose that bit of blue there that looks like a raft where the water shines, I suppose that is Denge Ness ? '

" She did not answer for what seemed a long time. She surveyed me with an unfathomable expression. Then she spoke and as she spoke she smiled. ' You know that is Denge Ness as well as I do.'

" I smiled at her smile. Shy pretences were not for her. I came a step or so nearer with a conversational air. ' I have known this view,' I said, ' since I was a boy of ten. But I did not know anyone else set any value upon it.'

" ' Nor I,' she said. ' I came to look at it perhaps for the last time,' she vouchsafed. ' I'm going away.'

" ' I'm going away too.'

" ' Over there ? ' she asked, and nodded her head to where the land of France hung like a cloud in the sky.

" ' In a week or so.'

" ' I'll get to France too. But not so soon as a week or two. But I am going into the Women's Auxiliary Army Corps and I know I shall get over there at last. I join up to-morrow. How can one stay at home with all you boys out there, getting ———'

" She was going to say getting ' *killed.*' But she caught the word back and finished it with, 'Getting into all sorts of danger and trouble.'

" ' One has to go,' I said.

" She looked at me with her head a little on one side. ' Tell me,' she said. ' Do you *want* to go ? '

" ' Not a bit. I hate the whole monstrous business. But there's no way out. The Germans have put it on us and we have to go through with it.'

" That was how we all saw it in England during the War. But I won't stop now to argue what really caused a war that ended two thousand years ago. ' The Germans put it on us. I hate going. I wanted to go on with the work I was doing. Now everything is upset.'

" ' Everything,' she said and thought for some moments. ' I hate going too,' she said.

" ' It drags on week after week, month after month,' I complained. ' The boredom of it ! The drills, the salutes, the silly little officers ! If only they would take us and raffle us and kill us and have done with it so that we could either die or go home and do something sensible ! My life is being wasted. I have been in the machine a year—and I've only got thus far on my way to France ! When I see a German soldier at last I shall want to kiss him I shall be so glad. But either I shall kill him or he will kill me—and that will be the end of the story.'

"'And yet one can't keep out of it,' she said.

"'And there is something tremendous about it,' she went on. 'Once or twice I have been up here when there were air-raids. I live quite close here. These air-raids get more and more frequent nowadays. I don't know what they are coming to. You see the searchlights now, every night, waving about like the arms of a drunken man. All over the sky. But before that you hear the pheasants in the woods, clucking and crying. They always hear it first. Other birds take it up. They cry and twitter. And then far away the guns begin rumbling. At first a little sound—"*pud-pud*," then like the whoof of a hoarse dog. And then one gun after another picks it up as the raid comes nearer. Sometimes you can catch the whirr of the engines of the Gothas. There's a great gun behind the farm-house away there and you wait for that and when it fires it hits you on the chest. Hardly anything is to be seen except the search-lights. There's a little flicker in the sky—and star shells. But the guns—riot. It's mad but it's immense. It takes you. Either you are wild with fright or you are wild with excitement. I can't sleep. I walk about my room and long to be out. Twice I've gone out into the night, into the moon-light—with everything a-quiver. Gone for long walks. Once shrapnel fell in our orchard with a hiss like rain. It ripped the bark of the apple trees and tore off twigs and branches and killed a hedgehog. I found the little wretch in the morning, nearly cut in two. Death haphazard! I don't mind the death and the danger so much. But it's the quiver in the world I can't endure. Even in the daytime sometimes, you can't quite hear them, but you can *feel* the guns, over beyond there. . . .

" ' Our old servant,' she said, ' believes it is the end of the world.'

" ' For us it may be,' I said.

" She made no answer.

" I looked at her face and my imagination rioted.

" I began to talk with a bare simplicity such as we rarely attained in that shy and entangled age. But my heart was beating fast. ' For years,' I said, ' I have dreamt of the love of a girl. It was to have been the crown of life. I have saved myself up for it. I have had a friend or so, but it wasn't love. And now I am near to going. Out there. It is only a few days before I go over there—to whatever is waiting for me. And when it seems beyond hope I come upon someone. . . . Don't think me mad, please. Don't think I'm lying. I am in love with you. Indeed I am. You seem altogether beautiful to me. Your voice, your eyes —everything. I could worship you. . . .

" I couldn't say a word more for a moment or so. I rolled over on the turf and looked her in the face. ' I'm sorry,' I said. ' I'm a silly young Tommy suddenly in love—oh ! desperately in love.'

" Her grave face regarded me. She did not

look frightened or disconcerted. Perhaps her heart beat faster than I thought. But her voice when she spoke was constrained.

" 'Why are you talking like that? You've just met me. . . . How can you love me? It isn't possible people should love like this.'

" ' I've seen you long enough——'

" I could not talk. I met her eyes. Hers dropped before mine. The warm colour mounted to her cheeks. She bit her lips.

" ' You,' she said in a low voice, ' are just in love with love.'

" ' Anyhow, I am in love,' I said.

" She plucked a spray of minute flowers and forgot it in her hand.

" ' This is your last day? ' she asked, and made my heart beat faster.

" ' It may be my last altogether for this sort of thing. Who can tell? . . . For a long time anyhow. Why should it hurt you to let me love you to-day? Why shouldn't you be kind to me? Civil to me—anyhow. I don't ask for so very much. If—suppose—we went for a walk together? Just a long walk. If we spent most of the day together? Somewhere we might get something to eat.' . . .

" She sat considering me gravely.

" ' Suppose I did,' she said as if to herself. ' Suppose I did.'

" ' What harm could it do you? '

" ' What harm could it do? ' she repeated with her eyes on mine.

" If I had been older and more experienced I might have known from her warm flushed face and her dark eyes that she too was in love with love that day, and that our encounter was as exciting for her as for me. Suddenly she smiled ; she showed herself for an instant as ready as myself. Her constraint had vanished.

"'I'll come,' she decided, and rose with an effortless ease to her feet, and then at my eager movement as I sprang up before her : 'But you'll have to be good, you know. It's just a walk—and a talk. . . . Why shouldn't we ? . . . If we keep away from the village.'"

§ 3

"It would seem the queerest story in the world if I told you how we two youngsters spent that day, we who were such strangers that we did not know each other's names and yet who were already drawn so closely together. It was a day of kindly beauty and warmth and we rambled westward until we came to a ridge that dropped steeply to a silvery, tree-bordered canal, and along that ridge we went until we reached a village and a friendly inn, where there were biscuits and cheese and some apples to make a lunch upon. For a time a mood of shyness followed our first avowals, then Hetty talked of her home and of her place in the world. It was only after we had eaten together that we became easy and familiar with each other. It was only as the sun was sinking in the west and our day drew to its golden end that we embraced suddenly as we sat together on a felled tree in a wood, and that I learnt from her what a sweet and wonderful delight the kiss of love may be."

§ 4

Sarnac paused.

"It happened two thousand years ago but it seems to me that it happened just six years from now. Once more I am back in that wood among the long warm shadows of the evening and all my dreams and imaginations awake to reality with Hetty's body in my arms and her lips to mine. I have been able to tell you my story hitherto with a sort of wonder and detachment, as though I showed it you through a telescope. But I have been telling you overmuch perhaps of Fanny and Matilda Good because I have had a sort of reluctance about Hetty. She is still so fresh in my mind that she seems as I name her to come even here and to be living still, a perplexity between Sunray, who is so like her and so unlike her, and myself. I love her again and hate her again as though I was still that assistant editor, that writer of rubbish, in lost and forgotten Thunderstone House in dead old London. . . .

"And I can't describe things now," said Sarnac, "as I have described them up to this. I seem no longer to look back into past things. My memories are living and suffering ; they inflame and hurt. I loved Hetty ; she was all the delight of love to me. I married her, I divorced her, I repented of the divorce and I was killed for her sake.

"And it seems as if I was killed not a day ago. . . .

"I married while I was in England before I was passed for active service again after my wound. I was wounded in the arm——"

Sarnac stopped and felt his arm. Sunray looked

sharply at it and ran her hand down it from shoulder to elbow as if to reassure herself. The others burst into laughter at her manifest anxiety and her expression of relief, the guest-master being particularly delighted.

"I *was* wounded nevertheless. I was a sitting-up case in the ambulance. I could tell you stories about the nurses and the hospital and how we had a panic about a submarine as we crossed to England. . . . I married Hetty before I went back because we were now altogether lovers and it was just possible she might have a child. And moreover there was a business about allowances if I got killed that was an added inducement to marry. In those days of haphazard death for the young there was a world-wide fever of love-making and countless such snatched marriages.

"She had never got to France as she had said she hoped to do. For most of the time she was driving a car for the Ministry of Supplies in London. We spent two days of wild endearment, the only honeymoon we could get, at her mother's farm at Payton Links, a little hamlet near Chessing Hanger. (I do not think I have told you that she was the only daughter of a farmer and that Mrs. Marcus, her mother, was a widow.) Hetty had been a clever girl, an elementary school teacher and bookish and enterprising for a country place. She had never mentioned me to her mother until she had written to tell of her approaching marriage.

"When her mother had driven us from the station to the farm and I had helped her to put away the pony, the old lady's non-committal manner relaxed

and she said, ' Well, it might have been worse.
You've looks and fairish shoulders for one who's
town-bred. You can kiss me, my boy, though
Smith is a poor exchange for Marcus, and I can't see
how anyone can ever expect to get a living for man
and wife at a fancy trade like publishing. I'd hoped
at first she meant a publican. But publishing she
says it is. Whether you're properly old enough
for Hetty, Time will show.'

" Time did show very rapidly that I was not
properly old enough for Hetty, though I resisted
the demonstration with passionate vigour.

" In this world of ours we are by comparison
very simple and direct. In that old world we should
have seemed shockingly simple and direct. It's
not only that they wrapped up and hid their bodies
in all sorts of queer garments and wrappings but
also that they wrapped up and distorted and hid
their minds. And while we to-day have the same
simple and clean ideas all over the world about sexual
restraints and sexual freedoms, people in those days
had the most various and complicated codes, half-
hidden and half-confessed. And not merely half-
hidden but imperfectly realised, subconscious rather
than thought out and settled. Few of these codes
respected the freedom of other people or set any
bounds to the most extravagant developments of
jealousy. And while Hetty's thoughts about love
and marriage had been nourished on a diet of country-
side folk and then of novels and poetry devoured
with avidity and had had tremendous releases in the
lax atmosphere of war-time London, I, in spite of
my love for and faith in Fanny, had almost unwit-

tingly adopted the rigid standards of my mother. As we used to say in those days, Hetty's was a much more artistic temperament than mine. For my part I did not so much think as assume that the worship of a man for a woman gave place to mastery as soon as her love was won, that the problem of absolute fidelity for both lovers was to be facilitated on his side by an absolute submissiveness on hers. And about her, wherever she went, invisible but real, there had to be a sort of cloistered quality. It was implicit, moreover, that she had never thought of love before she met her predestined and triumphant lover. Ridiculous and impossible you will say ! But Sunray here has read the old novels and she can witness that that was the code."

Sunray nodded. "That is the spirit of them," she said.

"Well, in fact, Hetty was not only half a year older than I but ages beyond me in the business of love. She was my teacher. While I had been reading about atoms and Darwin and exploration and socialism, she had been sucking the honey of sensuous passion from hints and half-hints in old romances and poems from Shakespeare and the old playwrights. And not only, I realise now, from books. She took me as one captures and tames an animal and made my senses and my imagination hers. Our honeymoon was magical and wonderful. She delighted in me and made me drunken with delights. And then we parted wonderfully with the taste of her salt tears on my lips, and I went off to the last five months of the War.

"I can see her now, slender as a tall boy in her

khaki breeches and driver's uniform, waving to my train as it drew out of Chessing Hanger station.

" She wrote adorable and whimsical love-letters that made me ache to be with her again, and just when we were forcing the great German barrier of the Hindenberg line, came one to tell me we were to have a child. She had not told me of it before, she said, because she had not been quite sure of it. Now she was sure. Would I love her still, now that she would be no longer slim and gracious ? Love her still ! I was filled with monstrous pride.

" I wrote back to tell her how my job at Thunderstone House was being saved for me, how we would certainly get a little house, a ' dear little house,' in some London suburb, how I would worship and cherish her. Her answer was at once tender and unusual. She said I was too good to her, far too good ; she repeated with extraordinary passion that she loved me, had never loved and could never love anyone but me, that she hated my absence more than she could tell, and that I was to do everything I could, move heaven and earth to get my discharge and come home to her and be with her and never, never, *never* leave her again. She had never wanted my arms about her as she wanted them now. I read nothing between the lines of that outbreak. It seemed just a new mood amidst the variety of her moods.

" Thunderstone House wanted me back as soon as possible, and the War had done much to increase the power and influence of all magazine publishers and newspaper proprietors. I got out of the army within three months of the Armistice and came back to a very soft and tender and submissive Hetty, a new Hetty more wonderful even than the old. She was evidently more passionately in love with me than ever. We took some furnished rooms in a part of London called Richmond, near the Thames and a great park, and we sought vainly for that bright little house in which our child was to be born. But there were no bright little houses available.

"And slowly a dark shadow fell across the first brightness of our reunion. The seasonable days passed but Hetty's child was not born. It was not born indeed until it was nearly two months too late for it to be my child."

§ 5

"We are trained from earliest childhood in the world to be tolerant and understanding of others and to be wary and disciplined with our own wayward impulses, we are given from the first a clear knowledge of our entangled nature. It will be hard for you to understand how harsh and how disingenuous the old world was. You live in a world that is as we used to say 'better bred.' You will find it difficult to imagine the sudden storm of temptation and excitement and forgetfulness in Hetty's newly aroused being that had betrayed her into disloyalty, and still more difficult will you find the tangle of fear and desperate dishonesty that held her silent from any plain speech with me after my return. But had she spoken instead of leaving it to me to suspect, discover and accuse, I doubt if she would have found any more mercy in me for her pitiful and abominable lapse.

"I see now that from the day I returned to Hetty she was trying to tell me of her disaster and failing to find a possible way of doing so. But the vague intimations in her words and manner dropped like seeds into my mind and germinated there. She was passionately excited and made happy by my coming back ; our first week together was the happiest week of my old-world life. Fanny came to see us once and we went and had a dinner at her flat, and something had happened to her too, I knew not what, to make her very happy. Fanny liked Hetty. When she kissed me good night after her dinner, she held me and whispered : 'She's a dear. I thought I'd be jealous of your wife, Harry, but I love her.'

"Yes, we were very happy for that week. We walked along together back to our rooms instead of taking a taxi, for it was better for Hetty to walk. A happy week it was that stretched almost to a happy fortnight. And then the shadows of suspicion gathered and deepened.

"It was in bed in the darkness of the night that I was at last moved to speak plainly to Hetty. I woke up and lay awake for a long time, very still and staring at my bleak realization of what had happened to us. Then I turned over, sat up in bed and said, 'Hetty. This child is not mine.'

"She answered at once. It was plain she too had been awake. She answered in a muffled voice as though her face lay against the pillow. 'No.'

"'You said, no?'

"She stirred, and her voice came clearer.

"'I said no. Oh Husbind-boy I wish I was dead ! I wish to God I was dead.'

" I sat still and she said no more. We remained like two fear-stricken creatures in the jungle, motionless, in an immense silence and darkness.

" At last she moved. Her hand crept out towards me, seeking me, and at that advance I recoiled. I seemed to hang for a moment between two courses of action, and then I gave myself over to rage. ' You'd *touch* me ! ' I cried, and got out of bed and began to walk about the room.

" ' I knew it ! ' I shouted. ' I knew it! I felt it ! And I have loved you ! You cheat ! You foul thing ! You lying cheat ! ' "

§ 6

" I think I described to you earlier in the story how my family behaved when Fanny left us, how we all seemed to be acting and keeping up a noise of indignation as if we were afraid of some different and disturbing realisations coming through to us should that barrage of make-believe morality fail. And just as my father and my mother behaved in that downstairs kitchen in Cherry Gardens so now I behaved in that desolating crisis between myself and Hetty. I stormed about the room, I hurled insults at her. I would not let the facts that she was a beaten and weeping thing, that she certainly loved me, and that her pain tortured me, prevail against my hard duty to my outraged pride.

" I lit the gas, I don't remember when, and the scene went on in that watery Victorian light. I began dressing, for never more was I to lie in bed with Hetty. I meant to dress and, having said my

say, to go out of the house. So I had to be scornful
and loudly indignant, but also I had to find my various
garments, pull my shirt over my head and lace up
my boots. So that there were interludes in the
storm, when Hetty could say something that I had
to hear.

"'It all happened in an evening,' she said. 'It
isn't as though I had planned to betray you. It
was his last day before he left and he was wretched.
It was the thought of you made me go with him.
It was just kindness. There were two of our girls
going to have dinner with their boys and they asked
me to come and that was how I met him. Officers
they were all three, and schoolfellows. Londoners.
Three boys who were going over—just as you were.
It seemed rotten not to make a party for them.'

"I was struggling with my collar and stud but
I tried to achieve sarcasm. 'I see,' I said, 'under
the circumstances mere politeness dictated—what
you did. . . . Oh, my God!'

"'Listen how it happened, Harry. Don't shout
at me again for a minute. Afterwards he asked
me to come to his rooms. He said the others were
coming on. He seemed such a harmless sort!'

"'Very!'

"'He seemed the sort who'd surely get killed.
And I was sorry for him. He was fair like you.
Fairer. And it seemed all different that night.
And then he got hold of me and kissed me and I
struggled, but I didn't seem to have the strength
to resist. I didn't realise somehow.'

"'That's pretty evident. That I *can* believe.'

"'You've got no pity, Harry. Perhaps it's just.

THE DREAM

I suppose I ought to have seen the risk. But we aren't all strong like you. Some of us are pulled this way and that. Some of us do the thing we hate. I did what I could. It was like waking-up to realise what had happened. He wanted me to stay with him. I ran out from his rooms. I've never seen him since. He's written but I haven't answered.'

" ' He knew you were a soldier's wife.'

" ' He's rotten. He knew it. He planned it while we were at dinner. He prayed and promised and lied. He said he wanted just a kiss, just one kiss for kindness. He began with that kiss. I'd been drinking wine, and I'm not used to wine. Oh, Harry ! Husbind-boy, if I could have died ! But I'd kissed and played about with boys before I met you. It seemed so little—until it was too late.'

" ' And here we are ! ' said I.

" I came and sat down on the bed and stared at Hetty's dishevelled distress. She was suddenly pitiful and pretty. 'I suppose I ought to go and kill this swine,' I said. ' I feel more like killing you.'

" ' Kill me,' she said. ' I wish you would.'

" ' What's his name ? Where is he now ? '

" ' *He* doesn't matter a rap,' said Hetty. ' You may hang for me if you like, but you shan't hang for a thing like that. I tell you he doesn't matter. He's a dirty accident. He happened.'

" ' You're shielding him.'

" ' *Him !* ' she said. ' I'm shielding you.'

" I stared at her. Again came a moment when I seemed to hang undecided at the parting of two courses, and again I decided to explode into rage.

256

My *God* ! ' I cried, and then louder and standing up, ' My *God* ! ' Then I ranted at her. ' I suppose I've only got myself to blame for all this. What did I know of what you were before I met you ? I guess I wasn't the first and I guess *he* won't be the last. What do names matter ? I guess you thanked Heaven for a green dud when you met me.' And so on. I paced about the room as I raved.

" She sat up on the bed, her hair disordered and her eyes tearful, regarding me with a still and mournful face. ' Oh, Harry ! ' she would say ever and again, or ' Oh, Boy ! ' while I let my clumsy fancy rove through a wilderness of coarse reproaches. Ever and again I would come up to her and stand over her. ' Tell me his name,' I would shout and she would shake her head.

" At last I was dressed. I looked at my watch. ' Five.'

" ' What are you going to do ? ' she asked.

" I don't know. Go, I suppose. I can't stay here. I should be sick. I shall get most of my things together and go. I'll find a lodging somewhere. It's nearly dawn. I'll go before you need get up. Meanwhile I'll sit in the other room. I can lie on the sofa for a bit.

" ' But the fire's not lit ! ' she said, ' and it's cold. It's not even laid. And you'll need some coffee ! '

" She stared at me with eyes full of solicitude.

" And forthwith she shuffled out of bed and slipped her feet into her bedroom slippers and put on a gay dressing-gown that had been a great delight to us —ten days ago. She went meekly by me, moving her poor heavy body rather wearily, and found some fire-lighters in a cupboard and knelt by the fire-place and began to rake out the ashes of the overnight fire. I made no movement to prevent her. I began to collect together various books and small possessions I intended to take with me.

" She was only apprehending the situation very slowly. She turned to me in the middle of her fire-lighting. ' I suppose you'll leave me a little money to go on with ? ' she said.

" That gave me a base opportunity. ' I'll leave you money all right,' I sneered. ' I suppose I've got to keep you until we're free. Then it will be *his* job. Or the next man's.'

" She occupied herself with the fire. She filled a kettle and put it ready. Then she sat down in an arm-chair by the hearth. Her face was white and drawn but she shed no tears. I went to the window and pulled up the blind and stared at the street outside with its street lamps still alight; every-thing was gaunt and bleak in the colourless cold horror of the earliest dawn.

" ' I shall go to mother,' she said, shivering and pulling her dressing-gown about her shoulders. ' It will be dreadful for her to know what has happened. But she's kind. She'll be kinder than anyone. . . . I shall go to her.'

" ' You can do what you like,' I said.

" ' Harry ! ' she said. ' I've never loved any man but you. If I could kill this child—— If it would please you if I killed this child——'

" She spoke with white lips. ' Yes. I tried all I knew. Some things I couldn't bring myself to do. And now it's a thing that's alive. . . .'

" We stared at one another in silence for some moments.

" ' No ! ' I said at last. ' I can't stand it. I can't endure it. Nothing can alter it now. You tell a tale. How do I know ? You've cheated once and you can cheat again. You gave yourself to that swine. If I live to a hundred I'll never forgive that. You gave yourself. How do I know you didn't tempt him ? You gave. You can go. Go where you gave yourself ! They're things no decent man can forgive. Things that are dirty to forgive. He stole you and you let him steal you and he can have you. I wish—— If you'd had the beginnings of a sense of honour you'd never have let me come back to you. To think of these last days here. And you—you with this secret next your heart ! The filthiness of it ! You—you, whom I've loved.'

" I was weeping.

Sarnac paused and stared into the fire. " Yes," he said, " I was weeping. And the tears I shed— it is wonderful—the tears I shed were tears of the purest self-pity.

" And all the time I saw the thing from my own standpoint alone, blind to the answering tragedy in Hetty's heart. And the most grotesque thing is that all the time she was getting me coffee and that when it was ready I drank her coffee ! At the end she wanted to kiss me, to kiss me ' good-bye ' she said, and I rebuffed her and struck her when she came near me. I meant only to thrust her back but my hand clenched at the opportunity. ' *Harry !* ' she whispered. She stood like a stunned thing watching me go, and then turned suddenly and swiftly and ran back to the bedroom.

"I slammed the outer door and went downstairs into the empty morning Richmond streets; altogether empty of traffic they were, under the flush of dawn.

"I carried my bag towards the railway-station that would take me to London; my bag was heavy with the things I had brought away, and it dragged upon my arm, and I felt myself a tragically ill-used but honourably self-vindicated young man."

§ 7

"Oh, poor little things!" cried Starlight. "Oh! poor, little, pitiful pitiless creatures! This story hurts me. I couldn't endure it, if it were anything more than a dream. Why were they all so hard upon each other and so deaf to the sorrow in each other?"

"We knew no better. This world now has a tempered air. In this world we breathe mercy with our first fluttering gasp. We are so taught and trained to think of others that their pain is ours. But two thousand years ago men and women were half-way back to crude Nature. Our motives took us unawares. We breathed infections. Our food was poisoned. Our passions were fevers. We were only beginning to learn the art of being human."

"But didn't Fanny——?" began Firefly.

"Yes," said Willow; "didn't Fanny, who was naturally so wise about love, didn't she take you in hand and send you back to forgive and help your wretched Hetty?"

"Fanny heard my version of our story first," said Sarnac. "She never realised the true values of the business until it was too late to stop the divorce.

When I told her that Hetty had lived a life of depravity in London while I was in the trenches, she heard me with amazement but never doubted my word.

"'And she seemed such a dear,' said Fanny. 'She seemed so in love with you. It's wonderful how different women are! There's women who seem to change into something else directly they get out of sight of you round a corner. I *liked* your Hetty, Harry. There was something sweet about her, be what she may. I never dreamt she'd deceive you and let you down. Fancy!—going about London picking up men! It's just as though she'd done it to me.'

"Matilda Good too was wonderfully sympathetic. 'No woman goes wrong only just once,' said Matilda. 'You're right to end it.' The Miltons were giving up her drawing-room floor, I could have it, if I cared to take it. I was only too glad to take it and return to my old home.

"Hetty, I suppose, packed up her own belongings as well as she could. She went down from Richmond to her mother's farm at Payton Links, and there it was her child was born.

"Now I want to tell you," said Sarnac, "what is, I believe, the most remarkable thing in all this story I am telling you. I do not remember in all that time right up to and including our divorce, that I felt any impulse of pity or kindliness, much less of love, towards Hetty. And yet in my dream I was very much the same sort of man as I am to-day. I was a man of the same type. But I was driven by a storm of amazed and outraged pride and sexual jealousy of the most frantic sort towards acts of spite that are almost inconceivable here and now. I was doing all I could to divorce Hetty in such a way as to force her into marriage with Sumner— for that was the man's name—because I had learnt that he was a hopelessly bad character and because I believed he would make her miserable and mar her life altogether. I wanted to do that to punish her, to fill her with bitter regrets for her treatment of me. But at the same time it drove me to the verge of madness to think that he should ever possess her again. If my wishes could have been given creative force, Hetty would have gone to Sumner disfigured and diseased. They would have come together again amidst circumstances of horrible cruelty ! "

" Sarnac ! " cried Sunray, " that you should even *dream* such things ! "

" Dream ! It is as men were. It is as they are, except for the education and the free happiness that release us. For we are not fourscore generations from the Age of Confusion, and that was but a few thousands more from the hairy ape-men who bayed the moon in the primeval forests of Europe. Then it was the Old Man in lust and anger ruled his herd of women and children and begot us all. And in the Age of Confusion after the Great Wars man was, and he still is, the child of that hairy Old Ape-Man. Don't I shave myself daily ? And don't we educate and legislate with our utmost skill and science to keep the old beast within bonds ? But our schools in the days of Harry Mortimer Smith were still half-way back to the cave ; our science was only beginning. We had no sexual education at all, only concealments and repressions. Our code was still the code of jealousy—thinly disguised. The pride and self-respect of a man was still bound up with the animal possession of women—the pride and self-respect of most women was by a sort of reflection bound up with the animal possession of a man. We felt that this possession was the keystone of life. Any failure in this central business involved a monstrous abasement, and against that our poor souls sought blindly for the most extravagant consolations. We hid things, we perverted and misrepresented things, we evaded the issue. Man is a creature which under nearly every sort of stress releases hate and malign action, and we were then still subjected to the extremest stresses.

"But I will not go on apologising for Harry Mortimer Smith. He was what the world made him and so are we. And in my dream I went about that old world, doing my work, controlling my outward behaviour and spending all the force of my wounded love for Hetty in scheming for her misery.

"And one thing in particular was of immense importance to my tormented being. It was that I should get another lover quickly, that I should dispel the magic of Hetty's embraces, lay the haunting ghost of my desire for her. I had to persuade myself that I had never really loved her and replace her in my heart by someone I could persuade myself was my own true love.

"So I sought the company of Milly Kimpton again. We had been close companions before the War, and it was not difficult to persuade myself that I had always been a little in love with her. Always

she had been more than a little in love with me. I
told her my story of my marriage and she was hurt
for my sake and indignant beyond means with the
Hetty I presented to her.

"She married me within a week of the completion
of my divorce."

§ 8

"Milly was faithful and Milly was kind , she
was a cooling refuge from the heat and distresses
of my passion. She had a broad, candid face that
never looked either angry or miserable ; she held
her countenance high, smiling towards heaven with
a pleasant confidence and self-satisfaction; she was
very fair and she was broad shouldered for a woman.
She was tender but not passionate ; she was intelligently interested in things but without much whim
or humour. She was nearly a year and a half older
than I. She had, as people used to say, 'taken a
great fancy' to me when first I came into the firm,
a crude and inexperienced youngster. She had
seen me rise very rapidly to Mr. Cheeseman's position
on the editorial staff—he had been transferred to
the printing side—and at times she had helped me
greatly. We were both popular in Thunderstone
House, and when we married there was a farewell
dinner to Milly, who gave up her position then in
the counting-house; there were speeches and a wonderful wedding-present of dinner-knives and silver forks
and spoons in a brass-bound chest of oak with a
flattering inscription on a silver plate. There had
been a good deal of sympathy with Milly in Thunder-

stone House, especially among the girls, and a good deal of indignation at me when my first marriage occurred, and my belated recognition of my true destiny was considered a very romantic and satisfactory end to the story.

" We secured a convenient little house in a row of stucco houses all built together to have one architectural effect, called Chester Terrace, close to one of the inner parks of London known as Regent's Park. Milly, I discovered, had a little fortune of nearly two thousand pounds, and so she was able to furnish this house very prettily according to current taste, and in this house in due course she bore me a son. I rejoiced very greatly and conspicuously over this youngster's arrival. I think you will understand how essential it was to my obsession for defeating and obliterating Hetty that Milly should bear me a child.

" I worked very hard during that first year of married life and on the whole I was happy. But it was not a very rich nor a very deep sort of happiness. It was a happiness made up of rather hard and rather superficial satisfactions. In a sense I loved Milly very dearly; her value was above rubies, she was honest and sweet and complaisant. She liked me enormously, she was made happy by my attentions; she helped me, watched for my comfort, rejoiced at the freshness and vigour of my work. Yet we did not talk very freely and easily together. I could not let my mind run on before her ; I had to shape what I said to her feelings and standards, and they were very different feelings and standards from my own. She was everything a wife should be except

in one matter ; she was not for me that particular
dear companion for whom the heart of every human
being craves, that dear companion with whom you
are happy and free and safe. That dear companionship I had met—and I had thrust it from me. Does
it come twice in a life to anyone ? "

"How should I know ? " said Sunray.

"We know better than to reject it," said Radiant.

"Perhaps after many years," said Willow, answering Sarnac's question, "after one has healed and grown
and changed."

"Milly and I were close friends indeed, but we
were never dear companions. I had told Hetty
about my sister Fanny on the evening of our first
day together when we walked over the hills, she was
instantly sure that she would love Fanny, Fanny had
seemed very brave and romantic to Hetty's imagination ; but I did not tell Milly of Fanny until
close upon our marriage. You will say that it was
not Milly's fault that I was shy with her on Fanny's
account, but assuredly it was a fault in our relationship. And it was clear that Milly accepted Fanny
on my account and refrained from too searching a
commentary because of me. Milly believed profoundly in the institution of marriage and in the
obligation of an unlimited chastity upon women.
'It is a pity she cannot marry this man,' said Milly,
anticipating perplexities. 'It must make everything
so inconvenient for her—and everyone who knows
her. It must be so difficult to introduce her to
people.'

"'You needn't do that,' I said.

"'My people are old-fashioned.'

" ' They needn't know,' I said.

" ' That would be the easier way for me, Harry.'

" I found my own declarations of affection for Fanny considerably chilled by the effort Milly made to be generous in the matter.

" I found it still more difficult to tell her that Fanny's lover was Newberry.

" ' Then is that how you got into Thunderstone House ? ' asked Milly when at last I got to that revelation.

" ' It's how I got my chance there,' I admitted.

" ' I didn't think it was like that. I thought you'd made your way in.'

" ' I've made my way up. I've never been favoured.'

" ' Yes—but——— Do you think people know, Harry ? They'd say all sorts of things.'

" You perceive that Milly was not a very clever woman and also that she was very jealous of my honour. ' I don't think anyone knows who matters,' I said. ' Neither I nor Fanny advertise.'

" But it was clear Milly did not like the situation. She would have much preferred a world without sister Fanny. She had no curiosity to see this sister that I loved so dearly or to find any good in her. On various small but quite valid scores she put off going to see her for a whole week. And always I had to remind her of Fanny and speak of Fanny first before Fanny could be talked about. In all other matters Milly was charming and delightful to me, but as far as she could contrive it she banished Fanny from our world. She could not see how much of my affection went also into banishment.

" Their meeting when at last it came about was bright rather than warm. An invisible athermanous screen had fallen not only between Milly and Fanny but between Fanny and myself. Milly had come, resolved to be generous and agreeable in spite of Fanny's disadvantageous status, and I think she was a little disconcerted by Fanny's dress and furniture, for Milly was always very sensitive to furniture and her sensitiveness had been enhanced by our own efforts to equip a delightful home on a sufficient but not too extravagant expenditure. I had always thought Fanny's furnishings very pretty, but it had never occurred to me that they were as Milly put it, ' dreadfully good.' But there was a red lacquer cabinet that Milly said afterwards might be worth as much as a hundred pounds, and she added one of those sentences that came upon one like an unexpected thread of gossamer upon the face : ' It doesn't seem right somehow.'

" Fanny's simple dress I gathered was far too good also. Simple dresses were the costliest in those days of abundant material and insufficient skill.

" But these were subsequent revelations, and at the time I did not understand why there should be an obscure undertone of resentment in Milly's manner, nor why Fanny was displaying a sort of stiff sweetness quite foreign to my impression of her.

" ' It's wonderful to meet you at last,' said Fanny. ' He's talked about you for years. I can remember once long before—long before the War—and everything—at Hampton Court. I can remember sitting on those seats by the river and his talking about you.'

"'I remember that,' I said, though it wasn't the part about Milly that had stuck in my memory.

"'We used to go about together no end in those days,' said Fanny. 'He was the dearest of brothers.'

"'I hope he'll still be,' said Milly very kindly.

"'A son's a son till he gets a wife,' said Fanny, quoting an old-woman's proverb.

"'You mustn't say that,' said Milly. 'I hope you'll come to see us—quite often.'

"'I'd love to come,' said Fanny. 'You're lucky to get a house so easily, these days.'

"'It isn't quite ready yet,' said Milly. 'But as soon as ever it is we must find some day when you are free.'

"'I'm often free,' said Fanny.

"'We'll fix a day,' said Milly, obviously quite resolute to ensure that we had no unexpected calls from Fanny when other people might be about.

"'It's nice you having been in the counting-house and understanding all about his work,' said Fanny.

"'My people didn't like my going into business at all,' said Milly. 'But it's lucky I did.'

"'Lucky for Harry,' said Fanny. 'Are your—people London people?'

"'Dorset,' said Milly. 'They didn't like my coming to London. They're just a little bit churchy and old-fashioned, you know. But it's college or business, I said, and you don't find me staying at home to dust and put out the flowers. One has to take a firm line with one's people at times. Didn't you find that so? There was a convenient aunt in Bedford Park to secure the proprieties and head off the otherwise inevitable latch-key, and it was business instead of college because my best uncle, Uncle Hereward—he's the Vicar of Peddlebourne—objects to the higher education of women. And there was also a question of finance.'

"'It must be interesting for Harry to meet your people,' said Fanny.

"'He's completely conquered Aunt Rachel,' said Milly. 'Though she started hostile. Naturally, as I'm about the only Kimpton of three generations they pitched their expectations high. They'd like me to have a husband with a pedigree a yard long.'

"I felt Milly was rather over-emphasising the county family side of the Kimptons—her father was a veterinary surgeon near Wimborne—but I did not appreciate the qualities in Fanny's bearing and furniture that were putting Milly into this self-assertive mood.

"They went on to talk with a certain flavour of unreality of the hygienic and social advantages of Regent's Park. 'It's easy to get to for one's friends,' said Milly. 'And quite a lot of interesting people, actors and critics and writers and all that sort of people, live round and about there. Of course Harry will want to know more and more of the artistic and literary world now. I expect we'll have to have a Day for them and give them tea and sandwiches. It's a bore, but it's necessary, you know. Harry's got to know people.'

"She smiled at me between pride and patronage.

"'Harry's going up in the world,' said my sister.

"'That's what makes it all so wonderful,' said Milly. 'He's a wonderful brother for you.'

" She began to praise the beauty of Fanny's flat, and Fanny offered to show her all over it. They were away some time and I went to the window, wishing stupidly after the manner of a man that they could somehow contrive to be a little different and a little warmer with each other. Didn't they both love me and shouldn't that be a bond of sisterhood between them ?

" Then came tea, one of Fanny's wonderful teas, but I was no longer the indiscriminate devourer of teas that I had been. Milly praised it all like a visiting duchess.

" ' Well,' said Milly at last with the air of one who has many appointments, ' it's time to go I'm afraid.' . . .

" I had been watching Fanny very closely throughout this visit and contrasting her guarded and polished civilities with the natural warmth of her reception of Hetty, half a year before. I felt I could not wait for another occasion before I had a word or two with her. So I kissed her good-bye—even her kiss had changed—and she and Milly hesitated and kissed, and I went down past the landing with Milly and heard the door close above. ' I've left my gloves,' I said suddenly. ' You go on down. I won't be a moment.' And I darted back upstairs.

" Fanny did not come to the door immediately.

" ' What is it, Harry ? ' she said, when she appeared.

" ' Gloves ! ' said I. ' No ! Here they are in my pocket. Silly of me ! . . . You *do* like her, Fanny ? You think she's all right, don't you ? She's a little shy with you, but she's a dear.'

" Fanny looked at me. I thought her eyes were

hard. 'She's all right,' she said. 'Quite all right. You'll never have to divorce *her*, Harry.'

"I didn't know. I want you to—like her. I thought—you didn't seem quite warm.'

"'Silly old Harry!' said Fanny, with a sudden return to her old manner. And she took me and kissed me like a loving sister again.

"I went down two steps from the door and turned.

'"I'd hate it,' I said, 'if you didn't think she was all right.'

"'She's all right,' said Fanny. 'And it's Good Luck to you, Harry. It's—— You see it's about Good-Bye for me. I shan't be seeing very much of you now with that clever wife of yours to take you about. Who's so *well*-connected. But Good Luck, old Brudder! Oh! *always* Good Luck!'

"Her eyes were brimming with tears.

"'God send you are happy, Harry dear—after your fashion. It's—it's different.' . . .

"She stopped short. She was weeping.

"She banged her door upon me, and I stood puzzled for a moment and then went down to Milly."

Love and Death

§ 1

"IN the two years that followed I learnt to love and trust my stiff-spirited wife more and more. She was very brave in a conscious and deliberate way, very clear-headed, very honest. I saw her fight, and it was not an easy fight, to bring our son into the world, and that sort of crisis was a seal between man and woman in those days even as it is to-day. If she never got to any just intuitions about my thoughts and feelings I did presently arrive at a fairly clear sense of hers. I could feel for her ambitions and humiliations. She worked hard to make our home bright and efficient. She had a taste for sound and 'solid' things and temperate harmonies. In that old world, encumbered with possessions and with an extreme household autonomy, servants were a very important matter indeed and she managed ours with just that measured kindliness and just that avoidance of intimacy that was needed by the social traditions of the time. She had always been intelligently interested in the internal politics of Thunderstone House and she showed the keenest desire for my success there. 'I'll see you a director before ten years,' she said. And I worked very hard indeed and not merely for ambition's sake. I really understood and believed in the educational importance of that great slovenly business. Newberry came to recognise in me a response to his own ideas. He would consult me about new schemes and the modification of old procedure. He relied

on me more and more and talked with me more
and more frequently. And it is a queer thing to
recall that by a sort of convention between us we
never mentioned or alluded to my sister Fanny in
any of our discussions.

"I changed a good deal during my first two and
a half years of married life. I matured and hardened.
I became a man of the world. I was put up for
and elected a member of a good club, and developed
my gift for talk. I met a widening variety of
people, and some of them were quite distinguished
people, and I found they did not overawe me.
I possessed a gift for caustic commentary that
gained me some reputation as a wit, and I felt a
growing interest in the showy and sterile game
of party politics. My ambitions grew. I was
active ; I was self-satisfied. I had largely forgotten
my intense sexual humiliation. But I was not a
very happy man. My life was like a handsome,
well-appointed room with a north light ; the bowls
were full of cut flowers but the sunlight never came
in."

§ 2

"For two years and a half I saw nothing of Hetty
and it was not my fault that I ever saw her again.
I did everything I could to eradicate her from my
existence. I destroyed her photographs and every
little vestige of her that might distress me by its
memories. If I caught myself in a reverie in which
she figured I forced my attention to other things.
Sometimes when I made a new success I had a flash

of desire that she should witness it. Ugly, I agree,
but is it not what we still are—except for civilisation ?
She came back sometimes in dreams, but they were
anger-soaked dreams. And I cultivated my pride
and love for Milly. With increasing prosperity
Milly's skill in dressing herself developed ; she
became a very handsome effective woman ; she gave
herself to me with a smiling sense of temperate and
acceptable giving.

"In those days we had not learnt to analyse our
motives. We were much less observant of ourselves
than men and women are to-day. I had set my
mind upon loving Milly and I did not realize that
the essential thing in loving is a thing beyond our
wills. Fanny and Hetty I loved by nature and
necessity, but my days were now far too completely
apportioned between work and Milly for much
companionship with Fanny to survive, and Hetty in
my heart was like one of those poor shrivelled corpses
of offending monks they walled up in the monasteries
during the Age of Christendom in Europe. But
I found now a curious liveliness in my interest in
women in general. I did not ask what these wander-
ings of attention signified ; I was ashamed of them
but I gave way to them. Even when I was in Milly's
company I would look at other women and find a
vague excitement if the intent of my glances was
returned.

"And I began to read novels in a new spirit,
though I did not know why I was taking to novels ;
I was reading them, I see now, for the sake of the
women I found in them. I do not know, Sunray,
whether you realise how much the novels and plays

of those days served to give men and women love-phantoms with whom they made imaginative excursions. We successful and respectable ones went our dignified and satisfied ways, assuaging the thin protests of our starved possibilities with such unsubstantial refreshment.

"But it was because of that wandering eye for women that I encountered Hetty again. It was in the springtime that I came upon her, either in March or very early April, in some public gardens quite near to Chester Terrace. These gardens were not in my direct way from the underground railway station, which took me to and fro between home and business and my house, but I was in no hurry for Milly's tea-party and the warmth and sunlight drew me to this place of blossom and budding green. They were what we should call spring gardens nowadays, small but cleverly laid out for display with an abundant use of daffodil, narcissus, hyacinth, almond-blossom and the like, with hard paths and seats placed to command happy patches of colour. On one of these seats a woman was sitting alone with her back to me looking at a patch of scyllas. I was struck by the loveliness of her careless pose. Such discoveries of the dear beauty that hides in the world would stir me like a challenge and then stab me with pain. She was dressed very poorly and simply, but her dingy clothing was no more than the smoked glass one uses to see the brightness of the sun.

"I slackened my pace as I went past and glanced back to see her face. And I saw the still face of Hetty, very grave and sorrowful, Hetty, no longer a girl but a woman, looking at the flowers and quite unheedful of my regard.

" Something greater than pride or jealousy seized me then. I went a few steps farther and stopped and turned, as though no other thing was possible.

" At that she became aware of me. She looked up, doubted, and recognised me.

" She watched me with that motionless face of hers as I came and sat down beside her. I spoke in a voice of astonishment on the edge of a storm of emotion. 'Hetty,' I said, 'I couldn't go past you !'

" She did not answer immediately. 'Are you —— ?' she began and stopped. 'I suppose we were bound to meet again,' she said, 'sooner or later. You look as if you had grown, Harry. You look well and prosperous.'

" ' Do you live in this part of London ?' I asked.

" ' Camden Town just now,' she said. ' We move about.'

" ' You married—Sumner ?'

" ' What did you expect me to do ? What else was there to do. I've drunk my cup to the dregs, Harry.'

" ' But—— You had the child ?'

" ' It died—it died all right. Poor little mite. And my mother died a year ago.'

" ' Well, you've got Sumner.'

" ' I've got Sumner.'

" At any time before that meeting I should have exulted over the death of Sumner's child, but in the presence of Hetty's misery that old hatred would not come back for its gratification. I was looking at her face which was so familiar and so changed, and it was as if I woke up again to love for her after two years and a half of insensibility. What a beaten and unhappy thing she was—she whom I had loved and hated so bitterly?

" ' It seems a long way back now to Kent, Harry —and mother's farm,' she said.

" ' You've parted with it ? '

" ' Farm and furniture—and mostly it's gone. Sumner bets. He's betted most of it away. It's hard, you see, to find a job but easy to fancy a winner. Which doesn't win. . . .'

" ' My father used to do that,' I said. ' I'd like to shoot every race-horse in England.'

" ' I hated selling the farm,' she said. ' I sold the farm and came into this dingy old London. Sumner dragged me here and he's dragging me down. It's not his fault ; it's how he's made. But when a spring day comes like this—— ! I think of Kent and the wind on the downs and the blackthorn in the hedges and the little yellow noses of the primroses and the first elder leaves coming out, until I want to cry and scream. But there's no getting out of it. Here I am. I've come to look at these flowers here. What's the good ? They just hurt me.'

" She stared at the flowers.

" ' My God ! ' I said, ' but this hurts me too. I didn't expect——'

" ' What did you expect ? ' she asked, and turned that still face of hers to me and silenced me.

" ' I don't see that it should hurt you,' she said. ' I brought it on myself. You didn't do it. It happened to me. It was my fault. Though why God made me love beautiful things—and then set a trap for me and made me fool enough to fall into it—— ! '

" Silence fell between us.

" ' Meeting you like this,' I began presently, ' makes me see things—so differently. You see— in those old days—in some ways you seemed so much stronger than I was. I didn't understand. . . . I see—— This makes me feel—— I ought to have taken better care of you.'

" ' Or shown me mercy. I was dirty and shameful—yes. All that. But you were merciless, Harry. Men are merciless to women. I did—all through —I loved you, Harry. In a way I've always loved you and I love you now. When I looked up and saw it was you coming back to me—— For a minute you were just like the old Harry. For a moment—— It was like Spring coming real. . . . But it's no good talking like that now, Harry. It's too late.'

" ' Yes,' I agreed. ' Too late. . . .'

" She watched my face through a long pause. I weighed my words when I spoke. ' Up to now,' I said, ' I've never forgiven. Now—— Now I see you here I wish—I wish to God—I had forgiven you. And made a fight for it with you. We might —— Suppose Hetty, suppose I had forgiven you—— ? '

" ' Harry dear,' she said softly, ' you don't want to be seen here making a woman cry. We won't talk of that. Tell me about yourself. I've heard you married again. A beautiful woman. Sumner saw that I heard of that. Are you happy, Harry? You look prosperous, and everyone isn't prosperous these post-war times.'

"'That's all so-and-so, Hetty. I work hard. I've got ambitions. I'm still a publisher's assistant at the old place but I'm near to being a director. I'm high up. My wife—— She's a dear and a great help to me. . . . Somehow meeting you . . . My God! Hetty, what a mess we made of things! It's all very well, but the second time of marrying isn't like the first. You and I—— I'm a sort of blood brother to you and nothing can change it. The wood—that little wood where you kissed me! Why did we smash it up, Hetty? Why did we do it? Two fools who'd got so precious a thing! That's all past. But hate is dead between us. That's past too. If there was anything I could do for you now I would do it.'

"A gleam of the old humour came. 'If you could kill Sumner,' she said, 'and smash the world and destroy the memories of three years . . . It's no good, Harry. I ought to have kept myself clean. And you—you might have been gentler with me.'

"'I couldn't, Hetty.'

"'I knew you couldn't. And I couldn't foresee that my blood would betray me one evening. And here we are! Like meeting after we are dead. Spring comes now but it comes for other people. All these little crocus trumpets—like a brass band it is—they are trumpeting up the next lot of lovers. Better luck to them!'

"We sat still for a time. In the background

of my mind Milly and her assembled tea-cups became evident as a faint urgency. 'You're late,' she'd say.

"'Where are you living, Hetty?' I asked. 'What is your address?'

"She shook her head after a moment's thought. 'Better you shouldn't know.'

"'But somehow I might help.'

"'It would only disturb us all. I've got my cup—of dirty water—to drink. I've got to stand what I'm in for. What could you do to help me?'

"'Well,' said I, 'my address anyhow is easy to keep in mind. It's just what it was when we—— In the days when we lived—— Thunderstone House it is. Someday there might be something——'

"'It's good of you.'

"We stood up face to face, and as we stood there a thousand circumstances vanished and nothing remained but our hurt and injured selves. 'Good-bye, Hetty,' I said. 'Good luck.'

"Our hands met. 'Good luck to you, Harry. It's no good, but I'm glad we met like this. And to find you forgive me a little at last.'"

§ 3

"That meeting had a profound effect upon me. It banished much aimless reverie from my mind; it unlocked the prison in which a whole multitude of forbidden thoughts had been confined. I thought enormously of Hetty. They were vague and impossible thoughts; they came in the night, on the way to business, even during slack moments in business hours; rehearsals of dramatised encounters, explanations, magic turns of circumstances that suddenly restored our lost world to us. I tried to suppress these cloudy imaginations but with little avail ; they overspread my mental skies in spite of me. I can't tell you how many times I walked through those gardens in Regent's Park ; that detour became my normal route from the station to my home. And I would even go out of my customary way along some side-path because I had caught a glimpse far off, between the tree-branches and the flower-beds, of a solitary woman. But Hetty never came back there.

"In my brooding over Hetty a jealousy and hatred of Sumner developed steadily. I do not think I had any desire for Hetty myself but I wanted intensely to get her away from him. This hostility to Sumner was the ugly undertow of my remorse and re-awakened love of Hetty. He was the evil thing that had deprived me of Hetty. I did not reflect for a moment that it was I with my relentless insistence upon divorce that had forced her back to him.

"And all this dreaming and brooding and futile planning, all this body of desire for something more to happen between Hetty and myself, went on without my breathing a word of it to any living soul. It was on my conscience that it was disloyal to Milly, and I even made a half-hearted attempt to tell Milly that I had met Hetty and been shocked at her poverty and unhappiness. I wanted to bring her into my own state of mind and have her feel as I did. I threw out a remark one day—we had gone to Hampstead Heath for a walk one afternoon—that I had

once walked along that ridge by the Round Pond
with Hetty during my last leave. ' I wonder how
she is living now,' I said.

" Milly did not answer immediately, and when
I looked at her her face was flushed and hard. ' I
hoped you had forgotten her,' she said in a suffocated
voice.

" ' This brought it back to me.'

" ' I try never to think of her. You don't know
what that woman meant to me—the humiliation.

" ' It was not only for myself,' she added. ' It
was for you.'

" She said no more but it was manifest how terribly
the mere name of Hetty had disturbed her."

" Poor little things ! " cried Firefly. " How
insanely jealous you all were ! "

" And I did not go to Fanny and tell her about
Hetty for a time. I had misrepresented Hetty to
her as a figure of common depravity and I found it
difficult to put that right. Nowadays I did not see
so much of Fanny as I had formerly done. She
was living half-way across London from me. Her
relations with Newberry were now much more public
than they had been and she had developed a circle
of acquaintances who cared for her. But this pub-
licity made Milly more stiff towards her because
she feared that a scandal would be made about Fanny
in relation to my position in the firm of Crane &
Newberry. Near Pangbourne, Newberry had taken
a bungalow and there Fanny would spend whole
weeks at a time, quite out of our range.

" But presently a situation developed which sent
me post-haste to Fanny for help and advice."

§ 4

"Suddenly in July when I was beginning to think I should never hear from her again, Hetty appealed to me for help. Would I meet her one evening, she asked, by the fountain in the Park near the Zoological Gardens, and then we could get chairs and she would tell me what she had in mind. She did not want me to write her a letter, Sumner had become very jealous of her, and so would I put an advertisement in the *Daily Express* with the letters A B C D and giving the hour and date. I made an appointment for the earliest possible evening.

"Instead of the despondent and spiritless Hetty I had met in the spring I found a Hetty high strung and excited. 'I want some place where we shan't be seen,' she said as I came up to her. She took my arm to turn me about, and led the way towards two green chairs standing apart a little away from the main walk that here traversed the park. I noted that she was still wearing the same shabby dress she had had on our previous encounter. Her manner with me was quite different from the manner of our former meeting. There was something familiar and confident about her as though in between she had met me in imagination a multitude of times —as no doubt she had.

"'You meant all you said, Harry, when we talked before?' she began.

"'Everything.'

"'You will help me if you can?'

"'Everything I can.'

"'Suppose I asked you for some money?'

" ' Naturally.'

" ' I want to get away from Sumner. I have a chance. I could do it.'

" ' Tell me about it, Hetty. All I can do, I will.'

" ' Things have changed, Harry, since that day we met. I'd got into a sort of despairing state. I took whatever came. Seeing you changed me. I don't know why but it did. Perhaps I was going to change anyhow. But I can't stand being with Sumner any longer. And there's a chance now. I shall want a lot of money—sixty or seventy pounds.'

" I thought. ' That's quite possible, Hetty. If you can wait a week or so. Ten days say.'

" ' You see I have a friend, a girl who married a Canadian. She stayed here to have her child when he went home and now she goes out to him. She's been ill ; she's not very strong and she doesn't want to face the voyage alone. It would be easy for me to get out there with her as her cousin and companion. If I had an outfit—— We've discussed it all. She knows someone who could manage about a passport for me. In my maiden name. That's the scheme. I could have my outfit sent to her place. I could slip away.'

" ' You'd take another name ? Begin again over there ? '

" ' Yes. . . .'

" I sat considering this project. It pleased me. ' There need be no trouble about the money,' I said.

" ' I can't go on living with Sumner. You never saw him. You don't know what he's like.'

" ' I've heard he was good looking.'

" ' Don't I know that face—flushed and weak !
He's a liar and a cheat. He has a conceit he can
best everyone. And he's begun drinking. God
knows why I married him. It seemed the natural
thing somehow since you had divorced me. The
child had to have a father. . . . But he disgusts
me, Harry. He disgusts me. I can't go on. I
can't endure it. You can't imagine it—in those
little lodgings—in the hot weather. To keep a
maudlin drunken man away from one. . . . If I
hadn't seen this way out something worse might
have happened.'

" ' Can't you come away from him at once ? ' I
asked. ' Why should you ever go back to him ? '

" ' No. I must get clear away or there will be
mischief. And you mustn't be in it. He'd think
of you at once. If he had a hint it was you. That's
what you have to do about the money and everything, letters or anything—get it to me without
your being mixed up with it. You must get me
money, not cheques. We mustn't be seen to meet.
Even about here it's risky. He's got into a gang.
He's been getting deeper and deeper into a rotten
set. They blackmail the bookies. They go about
with revolvers. They pass on things to one another.
It grew out of betting and now they call it getting
a bit of their own back. . . . If they spot you in
it, they'll come for you.'

" ' Trench warfare in London. I'll risk it.'

" ' You needn't risk anything—if we are discreet.
If there was some one I could see—who'd hand
things on.'

" I thought at once of my sister Fanny.

" ' That would be safe,' said Hetty. ' As safe as could be. And I'd love to see her again. I loved her when I met her. . . . But all this is awful good of you, Harry. I don't deserve a moment's kindness.'

" ' Nonsense ! I pushed you into the dirt, Hetty.'

" ' I jumped into it.'

" ' Fell into it. It's nothing very much, Hetty, to give you a hand to get out of it again.'

§ 5

" I went the next day to my sister Fanny to prepare her for Hetty's call. Fanny sat in an arm-chair and listened and watched my face as I told my story, confessed how I had exaggerated Hetty's offence and asked for help. ' I ought to have seen her, Harry, before I took your word for it,' she said. ' Of course, even now, I can't imagine how a girl who loves one man could ever stand the kiss of another as she did, but then, as you say, she'd been drinking. We women aren't all made alike. There's all sorts make a world. Some girls—the backbone goes out of them when they feel a man's kisses. You and me, Harry, we aren't made like that. I've been thinking while you sat talking there, how like we both are to poor mother really—for all she quarrelled with me. We'll grow hard presently if we aren't careful. And your Hetty was young and she didn't know. Only once it was. And all her life's been spoilt by it ! . . . I didn't know it was like that, Harry.'

" ' And my sister Fanny began to recall her

impressions of Hetty. She recalled her fine animation and the living interest of her talk. 'When
she left I said to myself, she's got wit ; that's the
first witty woman I've ever met. She's got poetry
in her. Everything she says comes out a little
different from the things most people say. She
says things that come like flowers in a hedgerow.
So she did. Does she still ? '

" ' I never thought of it like that before,' I said.
' I suppose she has a sort of poetry. Only the other
day—when I met her first. What was it she said ?
Something.'

" ' It's no good quoting, Harry. Witty things
should bloom where they grow. They're no good
as cut-flowers. But you and I are fairly quick and
fairly clever, Harry, but we've never had any of that.'

" ' I've always loved her talk,' I said.

" I began to explain the situation to Fanny more
fully and to show how she could help in it. I was
not to see Hetty again ; Fanny was to see her, pay
her the hundred pounds we could put together for
her, communicate with the friends she was to accompany and get her away. Fanny listened gravely
and agreed.

"Then she reflected.

" ' Why don't you take her to Canada yourself,
Harry ? ' she asked abruptly."

§ 6

" I did not answer Fanny for some moments.
Then I said, ' I don't want to.'

" ' I can see you love Hetty still.'

"'Love. But I don't want that.'

"'You don't want to be with her?'

"'It's out of the question. Why ask a painful thing like that? All that is dead.'

"'Isn't a resurrection possible? Why is it out of the question? Pride?'

"'No.'

"'Why then?'

"'Milly.'

"'You don't love Milly.'

"'I won't have you discuss that, Fanny. I do love her.'

"'Not as you love Hetty.'

"'Quite differently. But Milly trusts me. She keeps faith with me. I'd as soon steal money —from a child's money-box — as go back on Milly.'

"'It's wonderful how fine men can be to the wives they don't love,' said Fanny bitterly.

"'Newberry's different,' I said. 'I've got my little son. I've got my work. And though you will never have it, I love Milly.'

"'In a way. Is she company for you? Is she fun?'

"'I trust and love her. And as for Hetty, you don't understand about Hetty. I love her. I love her enormously. But it's like two ghosts meeting by moonlight. We two are dead to each other and —sorrowful. It isn't as though it was anything like your case over again. I see Hetty in hell and I'd do nearly anything in life to get her out. I don't even want to meet her. I want to get her away out of this filth and stupidity to where she can begin again. That's all I want and that's all she wants. How could she and I ever come together again ? How could we kiss again as lovers kiss ? Poor defiled things we are ! And all my cruelty. You're thinking of something else, Fanny. You're not thinking of Hetty and me.'

" ' Maybe I am,' said Fanny. ' Yes, I think I am. And so she is to go to Canada and begin again—till her health comes back and her courage comes back. It isn't natural for a woman of her temperament to live without a man to love her, Harry.'

" ' Let her live and love,' said I. ' She'll have changed her name. Her friends will stand by her. They won't give her away. Let her forget. Let her begin again.'

" ' With another man ? '

" ' It may be.'

" ' You don't mind the thought of that ? '

" I was stung but I kept my temper. ' Have I any right to mind the thought of that now ? '

" ' But you will. And you will go on living with this wife you trust and respect. Who's dull spirited—dull as ditchwater.'

" ' No. Who's my son's mother. Who is trustworthy. Whom I'm pledged to. And I've got my work. It may seem nothing to you. It's good enough for me to give myself to it. Can't I love Hetty, can't I help her out of the net she's in, and yet not want to go back to impossible things ? '

" ' Grey Monday mornings,' said Fanny.

" ' As if all life wasn't grey,' I said.

" And then," said Sarnac, " I remember that I

made a prophecy. I made it—when did I make it? Two thousand years ago? Or two weeks ago? I sat in Fanny's little sitting-room, an old-world creature amidst her old-world furnishings, and I said that men and women would not always suffer as we were suffering then. I said that we were still poor savages, living only in the bleak dawn of civilisation, and that we suffered because we were under-bred, under-trained and darkly ignorant of ourselves, that the mere fact that we knew our own unhappiness was the promise of better things and that a day would come when charity and understanding would light the world so that men and women would no longer hurt themselves and one another as they were doing now everywhere, universally, in law and in restriction and in jealousy and in hate, all round and about the earth.

" ' It is still too dark for us,' I said, ' to see clearly where we are going, and everyone of us blunders and stumbles and does wrong. Everyone. It is idle for me to ask now what is the right thing for me to do? Whatever I do now will be wrong. I ought to go with Hetty and be her lover again—easily I could do that and why should I deny it?—and I ought to stick to Milly and the work I have found in the world. Right road or left road, both lead to sorrow and remorse, but there is scarcely a soul in all this dark world, Fanny, who has not had to make or who will not presently have to make a choice as hard. I will not pull the skies down upon Milly, I *cannot* because she has put her faith in me. You are my dear sister Fanny and I love you and we have loved each other. Do you remember how you used to take me round to school and hold my hand at the crossings ? Don't make things too hard for me now. Just help me to help Hetty. Don't tear me to pieces. She is still alive and young and—Hetty. Out there—she at least can begin again.' "

§ 7

" Nevertheless, I did see Hetty again before she left England. There came a letter for me at Thunderstone House in which she proposed a meeting.

" ' You have been so kind to me,' she wrote. ' It is the next best thing to your never having left me. You have been a generous dear. You've given back happiness to me. I feel excited already at the thought of the great liner and the ocean and full of hope. We've got a sort of picture of the ship ; it is like a great hotel ; with our cabin marked in it exactly where it is. Canada will be wonderful ; Our Lady of the Snows; and we are going by way of New York, New York like nothing else on earth, cliffs and crags of windows, towering up to the sky. And it's wonderful to have new things again. I sneak off to Fanny's just to finger them over. I'm excited—yes, and grateful—yes, and full of hope—yes. And Harry, Harry, my heart aches and aches. I want to see you again. I don't deserve to but I want to see you again. We began with a walk and why shouldn't we end with a walk ? Thursday and Friday all the gang will be at Leeds. I could get away the whole day either day and it would be a miracle if anyone knew. I wish we could have that same old walk again. I suppose it's too far and impossible. We'll save that, Harry, until we're both quite dead and then we'll be two little swirls of breeze in the grass or two bits of thistledown going side by side. But there was that other walk we had when we went to Shere and right over the North Downs to Leatherhead. We looked across the Weald and saw our own South Downs far, far away. Pinewood and heather there was ; hills beyond hills. And the smoke of rubbish-burning.'

"I was to write to Fanny's address.

"Of course we had that walk, we two half-resuscitated lovers. We did not make love at all though we kissed when we met and meant to kiss when we parted. We talked as I suppose dead souls might talk of the world that had once been real. We talked of a hundred different things—even of Sumner. Now that she was so near escape from him her dread and hatred had evaporated. She said Sumner had a passionate desire for her and a real need of her and that it was not fair to him and very bad for him that she despised him. It wounded his self-respect. It made him violent and defiant. A woman who cared for him, who would take the pains to watch him and care for him as a woman should do for a man, might have made something of him. ' But I've never cared for him, Harry ; though I've tried. But I can see where things hurt him. I can see they hurt him frightfully at times. It doesn't hurt him any the less because he does ugly things.' He was vain, too, and ashamed of his incapacity to get a sufficient living. He was drifting very rapidly to a criminal life and she had no power over him to hold him back.

THE DREAM

"I can still see Hetty and hear her voice, as we walked along a broad bridle-path between great rhododendron bushes, and she talked, grave and balanced and kind she was, of this rogue who had cheated her and outraged her and beaten her. It was a new aspect of Hetty and yet at the same time it was the old dear Hetty I had loved and wasted and lost, clear minded and swift, with an understanding better than her will.

"We sat for a long time on the crest of the Downs above Shere where the view was at its widest and best, and we recalled the old days of happiness in Kent and talked of the distances before us and of crossing the sea and of France and so of the whole wide world. 'I feel,' she said, 'as I used to when I was a child, at the end of the school quarter. I'm going away to new things. Put on your frock, put on your hat; the big ship is waiting. I am a little frightened about it and rather happy. . . . I wish —— But never mind that.'

"'You wish—— ?'

"'What else could I wish?'

"'You mean——?'

"'It's no good wishing.'

"'I've got to stick the job I've taken. I've got to see it through. But if you care to know it, Hetty, I wish so too. My God !—if wishes could release one !'

"'You've got your job here. I wouldn't take you away, Harry, if I could. Sturdy you are, Harry, and you'll go through with it and do the work you're made to do—and I'll take what comes to me. Over there I guess I'll forget a lot about Sumner and the things that have happened in between—and think a lot about you and the South Downs and this—how we sat side by side here.

"'Perhaps,' said Hetty, 'heaven is a place like this. A great hillside to which you come at last, after all the tugging and pushing and the hoping and the disappointments and the spurring and the hungers and the cruel jealousies are done with and finished for ever. Then here you sit down and rest. And you aren't alone. Your lover is here and he sits beside you and you just touch shoulder to shoulder, very close and very still, and your sins are forgiven you ; your blunders and misunderstandings they matter no longer ; and the beauty takes you and you dissolve into it, you dissolve into it side by side and together you forget and fade until at last nothing remains of all the distresses and anger and sorrow, nothing remains of you at all but the breeze upon the great hillside and sunshine and everlasting peace. . . .'

"'All of which,' said Hetty, rising abruptly to her feet and standing over me, ' is just empty nothingness. Oh Harry ! Harry ! One feels things and when one tries to say them it is just words and nonsense. We've hardly started on our way to Leatherhead and you'll have to be back by seven. So get up, old Harry. Get up and come on. You are the dearest person alive and it has been sweet of you to come with me to-day. I was half-afraid you'd think it wasn't wise. . . .'

"In the late afternoon we got to a place called Little Bookham and there we had tea. About a mile farther on was a railway station and we found a train for London ; it came in as we got on to the platform.

"Everything had gone well so far and then came the first gleam of disaster. At Leatherhead we sat looking out on the station platform and a little ruddy man came trotting along to get into the compartment next to us, a little common fellow like an ostler with a cigar under his Hebrew nose, and as he was about to get in he glanced up at us. Doubt and then recognition came into his eyes and at the sight of him Hetty recoiled.

"'Get in,' said the guard, blowing his whistle, and the little man was hustled out of sight.

"Hetty was very white. 'I know that man,' she said, 'and he knows me. He's named Barnado. What shall I do ? '

"'Nothing. Does he know you very well ? '

"'He's been to our rooms—thiee or four times.'

"'He may not have been sure it was you.'

"'I think he did. Suppose he were to come to the window at the next station to make certain. Could I pretend not to be myself ? Refuse to recognize him or answer to my name ? '

"'But if he was convinced it was you in spite of your bluff that would instantly make him suspicious and off he'd go to your husband ! If on the other hand you took it all quite casually—said I was your cousin or your brother-in-law—he might think nothing of it and never even mention it to Sumner. But making him suspicious would send him off to Sumner right away. Anyhow, you go to Liverpool to-morrow. I don't see that his recognition of you matters.'

" ' I'm thinking of you,' she said.

" ' But he doesn't know who I am. So far as I know none of that lot has seen me. . . .'

" The train slowed down at the next station. Mr. Barnado appeared, cigar and all, bright eyed and curious.

" ' Blest if I didn't say to myself that's Hetty Sumner ! ' said Mr. Barnado. ' Wonderful 'ow one meets people ! '

" ' My brother-in-law, Mr. Dyson,' said Hetty, introducing me. ' We've been down to see his little daughter.'

" ' I didn't know you 'ad a sister, Mrs. Sumner.'

" ' I haven't,' said Hetty, with a note of pain in her voice. ' Mr. Dyson is a widower.'

" ' Sorry,' said Mr. Barnado. ' Stupid of me. And what age might the little girl be, Mr. Dyson ? '

" I found myself under the necessity of creating, explaining and discussing an orphan daughter. Mr. Barnado had three and was uncomfortably expert about children and their phases of development. He was evidently a model father. I did as well as I could, I drew out Mr. Barnado's family pride rather than indulged my own, but I was immensely relieved when Mr. Barnado exclaimed, ' Gawd ! 'Ere's Epsom already ! Glad to 'ave met you, Mr.——.'

" ' Damn ! ' I said to myself. I had forgotten.

" ' Dixon,' said Hetty hastily, and Mr. Barnado, after effusive farewells, proceeded to remove himself from the carriage.

" ' Thank Heaven ! ' said Hetty, ' he didn't come

on to London. You're the poorest liar, Harry, I've ever known. As it is—no harm's been done.'

" ' No harm's been done,' said I, but two or three times before we reached the London station where we were to part for ever, we recurred to the encounter and repeated the reassuring formula that no harm had been done.

" We parted at Victoria Station with very little emotion. Mr. Barnado had brought us back, as it were, to an everyday and incidental atmosphere. We did not kiss each other again. The world about us had become full now of observant eyes. My last words to Hetty were ' Everything's all right ! ' in a business-like, reassuring tone, and the next day she slipped off to join her friends at Liverpool and passed out of my life for ever."

§ 8

" For three or four days I did not feel this second separation from Hetty very greatly. My mind was still busy with the details of her departure. On the third day she sent me a wireless message, as we used to call it, to Thunderstone House. ' Well away,' she said. ' Fine weather. Endless love and gratitude.' Then slowly as the days passed my sense of loss grew upon me, the intimations of an immense loneliness gathered and spread until they became a cloud that darkened all my mental sky. I was persuaded now that there was no human being who could make me altogether happy but Hetty, and that for the second time I was rejecting the possibility of companionship with her. I had wanted love, I perceived, without sacrifice, and in that old world, it seems to me now, love was only possible at an exorbitant price, sacrifice of honour, sacrifice of one's proper work in the world, humiliations and distresses. I had shirked the price of Hetty and she was going from me, taking out of my life for ever all those sweet untellable things that were the essence of love, the little names, the trivial careless caresses, the exquisite gestures of mind and body, the moments of laughter and pride and perfect understanding. Day by day love went westward from me. Day and night I was haunted by a more and more vivid realization of a great steamship, throbbing and heaving its way across the crests and swelling waves of the Atlantic welter. The rolling black coal-smoke from its towering funnels poured before the wind. Now I would see that big ocean-going fabric in the daylight ; now lit brightly from stem to stern, under the stars.

" I was full of unappeasable regret, I indulged in endless reveries of a flight across the Atlantic in pursuit of Hetty, of a sudden dramatic appearance before her ;—' Hetty, I can't stand it. I've come ' —and all the time I stuck steadfastly to the course I had chosen. I worked hard and late at Thunderstone House ; I did my best to shunt my imagination into new channels by planning two new quasi-educational publications, and I set myself to take Milly out to restaurants to dinner and to the theatre and to interesting shows. And in the midst of some picture-show perhaps I would find my rebel mind speculating what sort of thing Hetty would have said of it, had she been there. There was a little show of landscapes at the Alpine Gallery and several were pictures of Downland scenery and one showed a sunlit hillside under drowsy white clouds. It was almost like seeing Hetty.

"It was exactly a week after Hetty's landing in New York that I first encountered Sumner. It was my usual time of arrival and I was just turning out of Tottenham Court Road into the side street that led to the yard of Thunderstone House. There was a small public-house in this byway and two men were standing outside it in attitudes of expectation. One of them stepped out to accost me. He was a little flushed Jewish man, and for the moment I did not recognize him at all.

"'Mr. Smith?' said he, and scrutinised me queerly.

"'At your service,' said I.

"'Not by any chance Mr. Dyson or Dixon, eh?' he asked with a leer.

"'Barnado!' cried my memory and placed him. My instant recognition must have betrayed itself in my face. Our eyes met and there were no secrets between them. 'No, Mr. Barnado,' I said with incredible stupidity; 'my name's just plain Smith.'

"'Don't mention it, Mr. Smith, don't mention it,' said Mr. Barnado with extreme politeness. 'I had a sort of fancy I might have met you before.' And turning to his companion and raising his voice a little, he said, 'That's him all right, Sumner—sure as eggs are eggs.'

"Sumner! I glanced at this man who had given my life so disastrous a turn. He was very much my own height and build, fair with a blotched complexion and wearing a checked grey suit and an experienced-looking grey felt hat. He might have been my unsuccessful half-brother. Our eyes met in curiosity and antagonism. 'I'm afraid I'm not the man you want,' I said to Barnado and went on my way. I didn't see any advantage in an immediate discussion in that place. I perceived that an encounter was inevitable, but I meant it to happen amidst circumstances of my own choice and after I had had time to consider the situation properly. I heard something happen behind me and Barnado said : 'Shut up, you fool ! You've found out what you want to know.' I went through the passages and rooms of Thunderstone House to my office and there, when I was alone, I sat down in my arm-chair and swore very heartily. Every day since the departure of Hetty I had been feeling more and more sure that this at least was not going to happen. I had thought that Sumner was very easily and safely and completely out of the story.

" I took my writing-pad and began to sketch out the situation. '*Ends to be secured,*' I wrote.

" '*No.* 1. *Hetty must not be traced.*

" '*No.* 2. *Milly must hear nothing of this.*

" '*No.* 3. *No blackmailing.*'

" I considered. '*But if a lump payment,*' I began. This I scratched out again.

" I had to scheme out the essential facts. '*What does S. know ? What evidence exists ? Of what ? No clue to lead to Fanny ? There is nothing but that journey in the train. He will have a moral certainty but will it convince anyone else ?*'

" I wrote a new heading : '*How to handle them ?*'

" I began to sketch grotesques and arabesques

over my paper as I plotted. Finally I tore it up into very small fragments and dropped it into my wastepaper basket. A messenger-girl rapped and came in with a paper slip, bearing the names of Fred Sumner and Arthur Barnado.

'They've not put the business they want to talk about,' I remarked.

" 'They said you'd know, Sir.'

" 'No excuse. I want everybody to fill in that,' I said. 'Just say I'm too busy to see strangers who don't state their business. And ask them to complete the form.'

" Back came the form : 'Enquiry about Mr. Sumner's missing wife.'

" I considered it calmly. 'I don't believe we ever had the manuscript. Say I'm engaged up to half-past twelve. Then I could have a talk of ten minutes with Mr. Sumner alone. Make that clear. I don't see where Mr. Barnado comes in. Make it clear it's a privilege to see me.'

" My messenger did not reappear. I resumed my meditations on the situation. There was time for a lot of aggressive energy to evaporate before half-past twelve. Probably both of the men had come in from the outskirts and would have nowhere to wait but the streets or a public-house. Mr. Barnado might want to be back upon his own business at Epsom. He'd played his part in identifying me. Anyhow, I didn't intend to have any talk with Sumner before a witness. If he reappeared with Barnado I should refuse to see them. For Barnado alone I had a plan and for Sumner I had a plan, but not for the two of them together.

" My delaying policy was a good one. At half-past twelve Sumner came alone and was shown up to me.

" ' Sit down there,' I said abruptly and leant back in my chair and stared at his face and waited in silence for him to begin.

" For some moments he did not speak. He had evidently expected me to open with some sort of question and he had come ready loaded with a reply. To be plumped into a chair and looked at, put him off his game. He tried to glare at me and I looked at his face as if I was looking at a map. As I did so I found my hatred for him shrinking and changing. It wasn't a case for hatred. He had such a poor, mean, silly face, a weak arrangement of plausibly handsome features. Every now and then it was convulsed by a nervous twitch. His straw-coloured moustache was clipped back more on one side than the other, and his rather frayed necktie had slipped down to display his collar stud and the grubbiness of his collar. He had pulled his mouth a little askew and thrust his face forward in an attempt at fierceness, and his rather watery blue eyes were as open and as protruded as he could manage.

" ' Where's my wife, Smith ? ' he said at last.

" ' Out of my reach, Mr. Sumner, and out of yours.'

" ' Where've you hid her ? '

" ' She's gone,' I said. ' It's no work of mine.'

" ' She's come back to you.'

" I shook my head.

" ' You know where she is ? '

" ' She's gone clear, Sumner. You let her go.'

THE DREAM

"'Let her go! *You* let her go, but I'm not going to. I'm not that sort. Here's this girl you marry and mess about with and when she comes across a man who's a bit more of a man than you are and handles her as a woman ought to be handled, you go and chuck her out and divorce her, divorce her with her child coming, and then start planning and plotting to get her away from the man she's given her love to——'

"He stopped for want of words or breath. He wanted to exasperate me and start a shouting match. I said nothing.

"'I want Hetty back,' he said. 'She's my wife and I want her back. She's mine and the sooner this foolery stops the better.'

"I sat up to the desk and put my elbows on it.

"'You won't get her back,' I said very quietly. 'What are you going to do about it?'

"'By God! I'll have her back—if I swing for it.'

"'Exactly. And what are you going to do?'

"'What *can't* I do? I'm her husband.'

"'Well?'

"'You've got her.'

"'Not a scrap of her.'

"'She's missing. I can go to the police.'

"'Go to them. What will they do?'

"'I can put them on to you.'

"'Not a bit of it. They won't bother about me. If your wife's missing and you go to the police, they'll clear up all your gang with their enquiries. They'll be only too glad of the chance. Trouble *me*! They'll dig up the cellars in *your* house and

304

in your previous house to find the body. They'll search you and ransack you. And what they don't do to you, your pals will.'

"Sumner leaned forward and grimaced like a gargoyle to give his words greater emphasis. ' *Yew* were the last man seen with her,' he said.

" ' Not a scrap of evidence.'

"Sumner cursed vigorously. ' He *saw* you.'

" ' I can deny that absolutely. Frowsty little witness your friend Barnado. Don't be too sure he'll stick it. Nasty business if a woman disappears and you find yourself trying to fix something that won't hold water on to someone her husband dislikes. If I were you, Sumner, I wouldn't take that line. Even if he backs you up, what does it prove ? You know of nobody else who pretends to have seen me with Hetty. You won't be able to find anybody.' . . .

"Mr. Sumner extended his hand towards my table. He was too far away to bang it properly so he pulled his chair up closer. The bang when it came was ineffective. ' Look 'ere,' he said and moistened his lips. ' I want my Hetty back and I'm going to have her back. You're precious cool and cucumberish and all that just now, but by God ! I'll warm you up before I've done with you. You think you can get her away and bluff me off. Never made such a mistake in your life. Suppose I *don't* go to the police. Suppose I go for direct action. Suppose I come round to your place, and make a fuss with your wife.'

" ' That will be a nuisance,' I said.

"He followed up his advantage. ' A masterpiece of a nuisance.'

"I considered the forced fierceness of his face.

"'I shall say I know nothing about your wife's disappearance and that you are a blackmailing liar. People will believe me. My wife will certainly believe me. She'd make herself do so if your story was ten times as possible. Your friend Barnado and you will make a pretty couple of accusers. I shall say you are a crazy jealous fool, and if you keep the game up I shall have you run in. I'd not be altogether sorry to have you run in. There's one or two little things I don't like you for. I'd not be so very sorry to get quits.'

"I had the better of him. He was baffled and angry but I saw now plainly that he had no real fight in him.

"'And you know where she is?' he said.

"I was too full of the spirit of conflict now to be discreet. 'I know where she is. And you don't get her—whatever you do. And as I said before, What can you do about it?'

"'My God!' he said. 'My own wife.'

"I leant back with the air of a man who had finished an interview. I looked at my wrist-watch.

"He stood up.

"I looked up at him brightly. 'Well?' I said.

"'Look here!' he spluttered. 'I don't stand this. By God! I tell you I want Hetty. I want her. I want her and I'll do what I like with her. D'you think I'll take *this*? Me? She's mine, you dirty thief!'

"I took up a drawing for an illustration and held it in my hand, regarding him with an expression of mild patience that maddened him.

"'Didn't I marry her—when I needn't have? If you wanted her, why the devil didn't you keep her when you had her? I tell you I won't stand it.'

"'My dear Sumner, as I said before, What can you do about it?'

"He leant over the desk, shook a finger as though it was a pistol barrel in my face. 'I'll let daylight through you,' he said. 'I'll let daylight through you.'

"'I'll take my chance of that,' I said.

"He expressed his opinion of me for a bit.

"'I won't argue your points,' I said. 'I guess we're about through with this interview. Don't shock my clerk, please, when she comes in.' And I rang the bell on my desk.

"His parting shot was feeble. 'You've not heard the last of me. I mean what I told you.'

"'Mind the step,' said I.

"The door closed and left me strung up and trembling with excitement but triumphant. I felt I had beaten him and that I could go on beating him. It might be he would shoot. He'd probably got a revolver. But it was ten to one he'd take the trouble to get a fair chance at me and screw himself up to shooting pitch. And with his loose twitching face and shaky hand it was ten to one against his hitting me. He'd aim anyhow. He'd shoot too soon. And if he shot me it was ten to one he only wounded me slightly. Then I'd carry through my story against him. Milly might be shaken for a time, but I'd get the thing right again with her.

"I sat for a long time turning over the possibilities

of the case. The more I considered it the more satisfied I was with my position. It was two o'clock and long past my usual lunch time when I went off to my club. I treated myself to the unusual luxury of a half-bottle of champagne."

§ 9

" I never believed Sumner would shoot me until I was actually shot.

" He waylaid me in the passage-way to the yard of Thunderstone House as I was returning from lunch just a week after our first encounter and when I was beginning to hope he had accepted his defeat. He had been drinking, and as soon as I saw his flushed face, half-angry and half-scared, I had an intimation of what might befall. I remember that I thought then that if anything happened he must get away because otherwise he might be left to tell his tale after I was dead. But I didn't really believe he was man enough to shoot and even now I do not believe that. He fired through sheer lack of nervous and muscular co-ordination.

" He did not produce his pistol until I was close up to him. ' Now then,' said he, ' you're for it. Where's my wife ? ' and out came the pistol a yard from me.

" I forget my answer. I probably said, ' Put that away ' or something of that sort. And then I may have seemed about to snatch it. The report of the pistol, which sounded very loud to me, came at once, and a feeling as though I'd been kicked in the small of the back. The pistol was one of those that go

on firing automatically as long as the trigger is gripped.
It fired two other shots, and one got my knee and
smashed it. 'Damn the thing !' he screamed and
threw it down as though it had stung him. 'Get
out, you fool. Run !' I said as I lurched towards
him, and then as I fell I came within a foot of his
terrified face as he dashed past me towards the main
thoroughfare. He thrust me back with his hand
as I reeled upon him.

"I think I rolled over on to my back into a sitting
position after I fell, because I have a clear impression
of him vanishing like the tail of a bolting rabbit into
Tottenham Court Road. I saw a van and an omnibus
pass across the space at the end of the street, heedless
altogether of the pistol shots that had sounded so
terrible in my ears. A girl and a man passed with
equal indifference. He was clear. Poor little beast !
I'd stolen his Hetty. And now——

"I was very clear-headed. A little numbed where
I had been hit but not in pain. I was chiefly aware
of my smashed knee, which looked very silly with
its mixture of torn trouser and red stuff and a little
splintered pink thing that I supposed was an end of
bone.

"People from nowhere were standing about me
and saying things to me. They had come out of
the yard or from the public-house. I made a swift
decision. 'Pistol went off in my hand,' I said, and
shut my eyes.

"Then a fear of a hospital came upon me. 'My
home quite handy,' I said. 'Eight Chester Terrace,
Regent's Park. Get me there, please.'

"I heard them repeating the address and I recognized the voice of Crane & Newberry's door porter. ' That's right,' he was saying. ' It's Mr. Mortimer Smith. Anything I can do for you, Mr. Smith ? '

" I do not remember much of the details of what followed. When they moved me there was pain. I seem to have been holding on to what I meant to say and do, and my memory does not seem to have recorded anything else properly. I may have fainted once or twice. Newberry was in it somehow. I think he took me home in his car. ' How did it happen ? ' he asked. That I remember quite clearly.

" ' The thing went off in my hand,' I said.

" One thing I was very certain about. Whatever happened they were not going to hang that poor, silly, hunted cheat Sumner. Whatever happened, the story of Hetty must not come out. If it did, Milly would think only one thing : that I had been unfaithful to her and that Sumner had killed me on that account. Hetty was all right now. I needn't bother about Hetty any more. I had to think of Milly—and Sumner. It is queer, but I seem to have known I was mortally wounded from the very instant I was shot.

" Milly appeared, full of solicitude.

" ' Accident,' I said to her with all my strength. ' Went off in my hand.'

" My own bed.

" Clothes being cut away. Round my knee the cloth had stuck. The new grey suit which I'd meant should last the whole summer.

" Then two strangers became conspicuous, doctors, I suppose, whispering, and one of them had his sleeves up and showed a pair of fat pink arms. Sponges and a tinkle of water dripping into a basin. They prodded me about. Damn! That *hurt!* Then stinging stuff. What was the good of it? I was in the body they were prodding, and I knew all about it and I was sure that I was a dead man.

"Milly again.

"'My dear,' I whispered. 'Dear!' and her poor, tearful face beamed love upon me.

"Valiant Milly! Things had never been fair to her.

"Fanny? Had Newberry gone to fetch her? Anyhow he had vanished.

"She'd say nothing about Hetty. She was as safe as—safe as what?—what did one say?—anything safe.

"Poor dears! What a fuss they were all in. It seemed almost shameful of me to be glad that I was going out of it all. But I was glad. This pistol shot had come like the smashing of a window in a stuffy room. My chief desire was to leave kind and comforting impressions on those poor survivors who might still have to stay on in the world of muddle for years and years. Life! What a muddle and a blundering it had been! I'd never have to grow old now anyhow. . . .

"There was an irruption. People coming in from the dressing-room. One was a police inspector in uniform. The other showed policeman through his plain clothes. Now was the time for it! I was quite clear-headed—quite. I must be careful what I said. If I didn't want to say anything I could just close my eyes.

"'Bleeding internally,' said someone.

"Then the police inspector sat down on the bed. What a whale he was !—and asked me questions. I wondered if anyone had caught a glimpse of Sumner. Sumner, bolting like a rabbit. I must risk that.

"'It went off in my hand,' I said.

"'What was he saying? How long had I had that revolver?

"'Bought it this lunch time,' I said.

"Did he ask why? He did. 'Keep up my shooting.'

"Where? He wanted to know where. 'Highbury.'

"'What part of Highbury?' They wanted to trace the pistol. That wouldn't do. Give Mr. Inspector a paper chase. '*Near* Highbury.'

"'Not in Highbury?'

"I decided to be faint and stupid. 'That way,' I said faintly.

"'A pawnshop?'

"Best not to answer. Then as if by an effort, 'Lil' shop.'

"'Unredeemed pledges?'

"I said nothing to that. I was thinking of another touch to the picture I was painting.

"I spoke with weak indignation. 'I didn't think it was loaded. How was I to know it was loaded? It ought not to have been sold—loaded like that. I was just looking at it——'

"I stopped short and shammed exhaustion. Then I felt that I was not shamming exhaustion. I was exhausted. Gods ! but the stuffing was out of me ! I was sinking, sinking, out of the bedroom, out from among this group of people. They were getting little and faint and flimsy. Was there anything more to say? Too late if there was. I was falling asleep, falling into a sleep, so profound, so fathomless. . . .

" Far away now was the little roomful of people, and infinitely small.

" ' He's going ! ' somebody said in a minute voice.

" I seemed to come back for an instant.

" I heard the rustle of Milly's dress as she came across the room to me.' . . .

" And then, then I heard Hetty's voice again and opened my eyes and saw Hetty bending down over me—in that lovely place upon this mountain-side. Only Hetty had become my dear Sunray who is mistress of my life. And the sunshine was on us and on her face, and I stretched because my back was a little stiff and one of my knees was twisted."

" ' Wake up ! I said,' said Sunray. ' Wake up,' and I shook you."

" And then we came and laughed at you," said Radiant. " Firefly and I."

" And you said, ' then there *is* another life,' said Firefly. " And the tale is only a dream ! It has been a good tale, Sarnac, and somehow you have made me think it was true."

" As it is," said Sarnac. " For I am as certain I was Henry Mortimer Smith yesterday as I am that I am Sarnac here and now."

The Epilogue

§ 1

THE guest-master poked the sinking fire into a last effort. "So am I," he said, and then with profound conviction, "*That tale is true.*"

"But how could it be true?" asked Willow.

"I should be readier to believe it true if Sarnac had not brought in Sunray as Hetty," said Radiant. "It was very dreamlike, the way Hetty grew more and more like his dear lady and at last dissolved altogether into her."

"But if Smith was a sort of anticipation of Sarnac," said Starlight, "then it was natural for him to choose as his love a sort of anticipation of Sunray."

"But are there any other anticipations in the story?" asked Willow. "Did you recognise any other people who are intimate with you both. Is there a Fanny in this world? Is there a Matilda Good or a brother Ernest? Was Sarnac's mother like Martha Smith?"

"That tale," said the guest-master, stoutly, "was no dream. It was a memory floating up out of the deep darkness of forgotten things into a living brain—a kindred brain."

Sarnac thought. "What is a personality but a memory? If the memory of Harry Mortimer Smith is in my brain, then I am Smith. I feel as sure that I was Smith two thousand years ago as that I was Sarnac this morning. Sometimes before this in my dreams I have had a feeling that I lived again forgotten lives. Have none of you felt that?"

314

"I dreamt the other day," said Radiant, "that I was a panther that haunted a village of huts in which lived naked children and some very toothsome dogs. And how I was hunted for three years and shot at five times before I was killed. I can remember how I killed an old woman gathering sticks and hid part of her body under the roots of a tree to finish it on the morrow. It was a very vivid dream. And as I dreamt it by no means horrible. But it was not a clear and continuous dream like yours. A panther's mind is not clear and continuous, but passes from flashes of interest to interludes of apathy and utter forgetfulness.

"When children have dreams of terror, of being in the wild with prowling beasts, of long pursuits and hairbreadth escapes, perhaps it is the memory of some dead creature that lives again in them?" asked Starlight. "What do we know of the stuff of memory that lies on the other side of matter? What do we know of the relations of consciousness to matter and energy? For four thousand years men have speculated about these things, and we know no more to-day than they did in Athens when Plato taught and Aristotle studied. Science increases and the power of man grows but only inside the limits of life's conditions. We may conquer space and time, but we shall never conquer the mystery of what we are, and why we can be matter that feels and wills. My brother and I have much to do with animals and more and more do I perceive that what they are I am. They are instruments with twenty strings while we have ten thousand, but they are instruments like ourselves; what plays upon them plays upon us, and what kills them kills us. Life and death alike are within the crystal sphere that limits us for ever. Life cannot penetrate and death will not penetrate that limitation. What memories are we cannot tell. If I choose to believe that they float away like gossamer nets when we die, and that they float I know not where, and that they can come back presently into touch with other such gossamer nets, who can contradict me ? Maybe life from its very beginning has been spinning threads and webs of memories. Not a thing in the past, it may be, that has not left its memories about us. Some day we may learn to gather in that forgotten gossamer, we may learn to weave its strands together again, until the whole past is restored to us and life becomes one. Then perhaps the crystal sphere will break. And however that may be, and however these things may be explained, I can well believe without any miracles that Sarnac has touched down to the real memory of a human life that lived and suffered two thousand years ago. And I believe that, because of the reality of the story he told. I have felt all along that whatever interrupting question we chose to ask, had we asked what buttons he wore on his jacket or how deep the gutters were at the pavement edge or what was the price he had paid for his cigarettes, he would have been ready with an answer, more exact and sure than any historian could have given."

"And I too believe that," said Sunray. " I have no memory of being Hetty, but in everything he said and did, even in his harshest and hardest acts, Smith and Sarnac were one character. I do not question for a moment that Sarnac lived that life."

§ 2

"But the hardness of it!" cried Firefly; "the cruelty! The universal heartache!"

"It could have been only a dream," persisted Willow.

"It is not the barbarism I think of," said Firefly; "not the wars and diseases, the shortened, crippled lives, the ugly towns, the narrow countryside, but worse than that the sorrow of the heart, the universal unkindness, the universal failure to understand or care for the thwarted desires and needs of others. As I think of Sarnac's story I cannot think of any one creature in it who was happy—as we are happy. It is all a story of love crossed, imaginations like flies that have fallen into gum, things withheld and things forbidden. And all for nothing. All for pride and spite. Not all that world had a giver who gave with both hands. . . . Poor Milly! Do you think she did not know how coldly you loved her, Sarnac? Do you think her jealousy was not born of a certainty and a fear? . . . A lifetime, a whole young man's lifetime, a quarter of a century, and this poor Harry Smith never once met a happy soul and came only once within sight of happiness! And he was just one of scores and hundreds of millions! They went heavily and clumsily and painfully, oppressing and obstructing each other, from the cradle to the grave."

This was too much for the guest-master, who

almost wailed aloud. "But surely there was happiness! Surely there were moods at least of happiness!"

"In gleams and flashes," said Sarnac. "But I verily believe that what Firefly says is true. In all my world there were no happy lives."

"Not even children?"

"Lives, I said, not parts of lives. Children would laugh and dance for a while if they were born in Hell."

"And out of that darkness," said Radiant; "in twenty short centuries our race has come to the light and tolerance, the sweet freedoms and charities of our lives to-day."

"Which is no sort of comfort to me," said Firefly, "when I think of the lives that *have* been."

"Unless this is the solution," the guest-master cried, "that everyone is presently to dream back the lives that have gone. Unless the poor memory-ghosts of all those sad lives that have been are to be brought into the consolation of our happiness. Here, poor souls, for your comfort is the land of heart's desire and all your hopes come true. Here you live again in your ampler selves. Here lovers are not parted for loving and your loves are not your torment. . . . Now I see why men must be immortal, for otherwise the story of man's martyrdom is too pitiful to tell. Many good men there were like me, jolly men with a certain plumpness, men with an excellent taste for wine and cookery, who loved men almost as much as they loved the food and drink that made men, and they could not do the jolly work I do and make comfort and happiness every day for fresh couples of holiday friends. Surely presently I shall find the memories of the poor licensed innkeeper I was in those ancient days, the poor, overruled, ill-paid publican, handing out bad stuff in wrath and shame, I shall find all his troubles welling up again in me. Consoled in this good inn. If it was I who suffered in those days, I am content; but if it was some other good fellow who died and never came to this, then there is no justice in the heart of God. So I swear by immortality now and henceforth—not for greed of the future but in the name of the wasted dead.

"Look!" the guest-master continued. "Morning comes and the cracks at the edge of the door-curtain grow brighter than the light within. Go all of you and watch the mountain glow. I will mix you a warm bowl of drink and then we will sleep for an hour or so before you breakfast and go your way."

§ 3

"It was a life," said Sarnac, "and it was a dream, a dream within this life; and this life too is a dream. Dreams within dreams, dreams containing dreams, until we come at last, maybe, to the Dreamer of all dreams, the Being who is all beings. Nothing is too wonderful for life and nothing is too beautiful."

He got up and thrust back the great curtain of the guest-house room. "All night we have been talking and living in the dark Ages of Confusion and now the sunrise is close at hand."

He went out upon the portico of the guest-house and stood still, surveying the great mountains that rose out of cloud and haze, dark blue and mysterious in their recesses and soaring up at last into the flush of dawn.

He stood quite still and all the world seemed still, except that, far away and far below, a mist of sounds beneath the mountain mists, a confusion of birds was singing.

THE HOGARTH PRESS

This is a paperback list for today's readers – but it holds to a tradition of adventurous and original publishing set by Leonard and Virginia Woolf when they founded The Hogarth Press in 1917 and started their first paperback series in 1924.

Some of the books are light-hearted, some serious, and include Fiction, Lives and Letters, Travel, Critics, Poetry, History and Hogarth Crime and Gaslight Crime.

A list of our books already published, together with some of our forthcoming titles, follows. If you would like more information about Hogarth Press books, write to us for a catalogue:

30 Bedford Square, London WC1B 3RP

Please send a large stamped addressed envelope

HOGARTH FICTION

Death of a Hero by Richard Aldington
New Introduction by Christopher Ridgway

All in a Lifetime by Walter Allen
New Introduction by Alan Sillitoe

The Olive Field by Ralph Bates
New Introduction by Valentine Cunningham

Ballantyne's Folly by Claud Cockburn
New Introduction by Andrew Cockburn
Beat the Devil by Claud Cockburn
New Introduction by Alexander Cockburn

Born in Exile by George Gissing
New Introduction by Gillian Tindall
The Emancipated by George Gissing
In the Year of Jubilee by George Gissing
New Introductions by John Halperin

Twenty Thousand Streets Under the Sky by Patrick Hamilton
New Introduction by Michael Holroyd

Saturday Night at the Greyhound by John Hampson
New Introduction by Christopher Hawtree

Where the Apple Ripens by Jessie Kesson
The White Bird Passes by Jessie Kesson
New Introduction by Douglas Dunn

All Day Saturday by Colin MacInnes
June in Her Spring by Colin MacInnes
New Introductions by Tony Gould

Her Privates We by Frederic Manning
New Introduction by Lyn Macdonald

The Marionette by Edwin Muir
New Afterword by Paul Binding

H.G. Wells

In the Days of the Comet

New Introduction by Brian Aldiss

A new comet moves into earth's skies, filling the world with fear. In the midst of the rising panic, among the allotments and furnaces of a grim Black Country town, young Leadford sets out with murder in his heart to find the unfaithful Nettie and her wealthy lover. But then the comet strikes, the Great Change occurs, and anything, or almost anything, seems possible. A grand sweep of comic realism mixed with a fantasy of equality, pacifism and, of course, free love, *In the Days of the Comet* is a utopia such as only H.G. Wells could have imagined.

Norman and Jeanne MacKenzie

The Life of H.G. Wells: The Time Traveller

Revised, with a new Epilogue by the authors

H.G. Wells was a man revered from Washington to Moscow: founder of modern science fiction, master of realistic comedy, social prophet, influential educator, and incorrigible lover of women – Elizabeth von Arnim and Rebecca West among them. This celebrated biography, now updated, brings together his public achievements and private passions (some only recently revealed) to paint the man himself: brilliant, charming and self-destructive.

H.G. Wells

Marriage

New Introduction by Victoria Glendinning

A plane crashes into a peaceful rectory garden: its
dashing aviator hurtles into the life of the rector's
daughter – educated, socialist, a thoroughly modern
miss. While marriage may be the end of the comedy it
turns out to be only the beginning of the drama. Here
Wells attacks a perennial problem – how can marriage
survive when convention stifles passion, domesticity
dulls ambition? The couple set off to find the answer on a
bizarre adventure which takes them halfway across the
world.

One of Wells's engrossing novels about the interplay
between sex and society, *Marriage* drew an enraged
review from the young feminist Rebecca West, thus
starting a new chapter in the saga of his own life.

Mary Shelley
The Last Man

New Introduction by Brian Aldiss

The fame of *Frankenstein*, Mary Shelley's classic tale, has, over the years, eclipsed the splendour of her other novels. Perhaps the most unjustly neglected of these is *The Last Man*, an apocalyptic vision of love and loss set in a republican England of the twenty-first century and one of the most innovative novels of its time. Against ever-changing landscapes of fast-flowing torrents and vast starry skies, a tiny band of adventurers leave their pastoral idyll for the turmoil of national politics, Mediterranean wars and worldwide catastrophe. With its tender fictional portraits of Byron, Shelley and Claire Clairmont, *The Last Man* is a paean to a lost generation; it is also one of our great Romantic novels.

Patrick Hamilton
Twenty Thousand Streets Under the Sky

New Introduction by Michael Holroyd

This melancholy, comic city trilogy is Patrick Hamilton's masterpiece. The raucous life of London in the thirties swirls through the hypnotic stories of Bob, barman of the Midnight Bell, Jenny, the young prostitute who obsesses him, and Ella, the barmaid who loves him in silence – twenty thousand streets of cruelty and kindness, comedy and pathos, wasted dreams and lost desires.

David Garnett

Lady into Fox &
A Man in the Zoo

New Introduction by Neil Jordan

'The most amazingly good story . . . I think it is
perfectly done'

So wrote H.G. Wells when he reviewed *Lady into Fox* in
1922. This parable about a young Edwardian woman
who turns into a fox before her astonished husband's eyes
is published here with the equally delightful novella
which David Garnett wrote two years later about the first
man to be exhibited at London Zoo. Beautifully illustrated with Ray Garnett's original wood-engravings,
these are piquant love stories combined with exquisite
observations of our social behaviour. They have too
the timeless quality of the fable, revealing not only the
idiosyncrasies of the animal kingdom, but also the
vagaries of the human heart.

Frederic Manning
Her Privates We

New Introduction by Lyn Macdonald

'It is the finest and noblest book of men in war I have ever read' – *Ernest Hemingway*

On July 1st, 1916, the Somme offensive began. This is the battle from behind the lines, of those sardonic, humorous troops honoured from *Henry V* to *The Virgin Soldiers*. No grand heroics here, but as they try out their French on village beauties and wangle a cosy billet, dodging shells and sergeant-majors, Privates Bourne Shem and little Martlow build up a friendship which supports them through terror and pain to the edge of the grave.